BY THE AUTHOR

STARK SECURITY
Shattered With You
Broken With You
Ruined With You

THE STARK SAGA
novels
release me
claim me
complete me
anchor me
lost with me

novellas
take me
have me
play my game

seduce me

unwrap me

deepest kiss

entice me

hold me

please me

indulge me

For all of JK's Stark World and other titles,
please visit www.jkenner.com

Praise for J. Kenner's Novels

"PERFECT for fans of *Fifty Shades of Grey* and *Bared to You. Release Me* is a powerful and erotic romance novel that is sure to make adult romance readers sweat, sigh and swoon." *Reading, Eating & Dreaming Blog*

"I will admit, I am in the 'I loved *Fifty Shades*' camp, but after reading *Release Me*, Mr. Grey only scratches the surface compared to Damien Stark." *Cocktails and Books Blog*

"It is not often when a book is so amazingly well-written that I find it hard to even begin to accurately describe it . . . I recommend this book to everyone who is interested in a passionate love story." *Romancebookworm's Reviews*

"The story is one that will rank up with the *Fifty Shades* and Cross Fire trilogies." *Incubus Publishing Blog*

"The plot is complex, the characters engaging, and J. Kenner's passionate writing brings it all perfectly together." *Harlequin Junkie*

A sizzling, intoxicating, sexy read!!!! J. Kenner had

me devouring Wicked Dirty, the second installment of *Stark World Series* in one sitting. I loved
everything about this book from the opening pages
to the raw and vulnerable characters. With her
sophisticated prose, Kenner created a love story
that had the perfect blend of lust, passion, sexual
tension, raw emotions and love. - Michelle, Four
Chicks Flipping Pages

SHATTERED
WITH **YOU**
J. KENNER

M&O

Shattered With You Copyright © 2019 by Julie Kenner

Excerpt from *Release Me* © Copyright 2012 by Julie Kenner (used with permission from Penguin Random House/Bantam Books)

Cover design by Michele Catalano, Catalano Creative

Cover image by Annie Ray/Passion Pages

ISBN: 978-1-940673-89-9

Published by Martini & Olive Books

v. 2019-3-31P

M&O

I know I shouldn't want him.

I wish I didn't crave him.

With every day that passes, I pray that the sweet throb of yearning will dim. And yet it doesn't.

Awake, I can feed the pain. Can fall back into those memories that cut as deep as a knife. Passion erased. Love eradicated.

Before, there'd been a man who wanted me. After, only a scorch mark remained, like a shadow burned into the ground from a nuclear explosion.

Awake, I can hold onto my anger.

But in my dreams, I always surrender.

I tell myself I'm better off without him. But I need him. His skills. His help.

I have no options left. He is the place where desire and fear meet. And all I can do is pray that I don't shatter like glass under the weight of my regrets.

1

BUILT IN 1931, the historic Hollywood Terrace Hotel once reigned supreme as the place to see and be seen along the famous boulevard. But time wreaked its revenge, and like the fading beauty of Golden Age starlets, the Art Deco palace fell into disrepair as flappers gave way to hippies and Baby Boomers, all of whom were overrun by Millennials who watched as the twentieth century rolled inexorably into the twenty-first.

For the first decade of the new millennium, the once majestic icon stood faded and broken. The exterior stucco dulled to a lifeless gray. Windows soiled and cracked. The famous gardens overrun with vermin and weeds.

The interior fared no better. Mold grew around leaky pipes. Rats scurried the halls, surrendering only to the feral cats who claimed the dark spaces as their own. Carpets rotted. Wallpaper peeled. And a fine dust covered every surface like a blanket of neglect.

With the determination of a beleaguered prize-fighter, the building fought to stay upright despite the repeated blows of weather, earthquakes, and the monotonous parade of progress marked by shiny new storefronts. When yellow tape emblazoned with *Condemned* and *Do Not Cross* appeared across the etched glass doors, the locals were certain that the final blow had been landed.

Then Scott Lassiter rode to the rescue, and it turned out that the story of the Hollywood Terrace wasn't a boxing movie after all. It was a makeover. *My Fair Lady* for the bedraggled hotel.

The international real estate developer pulled out all the stops, remaking The Hollywood Terrace into the gem it had been almost a century before. He turned the mezzanine conference rooms into his private suite of offices, and claimed the entire top floor as his stunning penthouse residence, complete with an indoor pool and a formal ballroom.

Everyone who was anyone attended the grand re-opening five years ago, and Lassiter was feted by the town's movers and shakers as a hero. A miracle worker. A true citizen, devoted to preserving the history that had put this corner of Southern California on the map when those first pioneers with cameras had hustled to the land of manna and sunshine.

That party had made headlines across the globe, the Hollywood connection and the many stars on the guest list making the story too delicious to ignore.

Tonight's party was even more lush. Dozens upon dozens of guests filled the meticulously restored Art Deco ballroom with its bold colors and geometric designs. The combined incomes of the well-heeled, international guests made a Hollywood star's bankroll look like a teenager's allowance. Rare champagne vintages flowed in fountains of pure silver. The women glided over the marble floors in formal gowns designed to accentuate assets of the non-gemstone variety. And any man in a suit that cost less than twenty-five grand was obviously a poser.

And yet despite the beautiful people floating on clouds of money-soaked power, there was no press in the ballroom for this soirée. No photographers clicking away for sexy images to post on Page Six or Instagram. On the contrary, this party was an intimate affair conducted in Lassiter's own private fiefdom.

And only a *very* select and very exclusive clientele had been invited.

Stark Security operative Quincy Radcliffe was not on the guest list. Not officially, anyway. That, however, didn't stop him from signaling a passing waiter and snagging a scotch and soda.

He sipped it slowly, his dispassionate gaze studying the cadre of tailored men and coiffed women who moved in and out of Lassiter's orbit, as if they were coming to pay tribute to a god.

Blind fools.

All they saw was Lassiter's money and power. They had no idea that their host's hefty bank account had been generated less by his real estate portfolio and more by the percentage he took from money laundering and protection schemes.

Scott Lassiter was a manipulative prick whose sharp talons reached deep into the criminal underground. And someday it would be Quince's pleasure to pull the rug firmly out from under the feckless tosser, then ensure that Lassiter abandoned his plush penthouse for a different view. The kind with dozens of iron bars.

That, however, wasn't on tonight's agenda. For the time being, Lassiter was the lesser of two evils, and if everything went as planned, the pathetic wanker would be an unknowing conduit to the sex-trafficking, sub-human monster who was at the core of tonight's mission: *Corbu. Marius Corbu.*

"Incredible, isn't he?"

The breathy voice came from a brown-eyed blonde with long, straight hair that hung to the middle of her back and a soft fringe of bangs that brushed her perfectly arched brows. She wore a filmy gold dress and make-up so expertly applied it seemed invisible except for the dark liner that shaped her wide eyes and lipstick so red he couldn't help think of ripe cherries.

"You're referring to our host, Mr. Lassiter?"

She giggled and sloshed her champagne as she struggled to clap her hands. "O.M.G.,"—she actually said *O.M.G.*—"You're British."

"Bloody hell. Am I really?"

She laughed again. "And funny, too. No. What's that word? *Droll*. You're very droll." She cocked her head, studying him. He knew what she saw. Dark hair, a lean face, and deep-set gray eyes. He wore an Ermenegildo Zegna bespoke suit that cost more than his car, and according to his partner Denise, he looked "fabulously fuckable."

The blonde apparently agreed, because he saw the exact moment that her gaze shifted from amused to predatory. "I like a funny man." Her voice was low. Sultry. "A man who laughs probably does other interesting things with his mouth, too." She tilted her head provocatively. "I'm Desiree. What's your name?"

"Canton," he said, giving her his mission alias as a hedge fund manager based in Hong Kong. "Robert Canton."

She eased toward him, the dress shifting from opaque to sheer as she stepped into a puddle of light. She was entirely bare under the flimsy gown, and he felt his body tighten in reflex, but not desire. Slowly, she ran her fingers over the lapel of his jacket, then continued the downward motion until she was cupping his cock, hard now because, after all, he wasn't dead. Nor was he surprised. This party was about sex, after all. Paid, kinky, anonymous sex. And God knew he wasn't immune to the charms of a beautiful woman.

She pressed her free hand to his shoulder as she leaned in to whisper. "Well, I'm all yours, Mr. Canton. However you want me, all the way until the sun comes up." She nipped at his earlobe, and he thought how easy it would be. She'd be willing to do bloody well anything—that was the point of tonight's little meet-and-greet. And damned if he didn't need to take the edge off.

Some operations were harder than others, and this one was a right pisser. It had gotten into his head. Worse, it had gotten into his blood. And it burned there like a slow poison. Or more accurately like a fuse. Let it burn too long, and he'd explode. The dark memories would win out, the monster would grab control, and—

Bloody hell.

"Oooh, I think that's a yes." She started to slowly stroke him. "I've never fucked an English guy, and I promise you I'm worth it. Please tell me you haven't given some other girl your key."

He produced a thin smile, then slowly moved her hand off his crotch. "Sorry, love. I'm sure you'd give me a right proper ride, but my key's already spoken for."

"Maybe not," the female voice said into his ear. It was Denise, and she was currently on the roof across the street. And also in his ear. Listening to absolutely everything since their coms were on VOX. *"I can't get the transmitter arm to lock in place. I'm going to have to stay up here and position it manually."*

"Bloody hell."

"What?" Desiree asked.

"It's just a pisser that you won't be in my bed tonight. But rules are rules." And the rules of this party mirrored the old suburban key parties of the sixties and seventies. Bottom line—a man claimed a woman with a key, she went to his room, and he spent the night enjoying her, as Desiree had said, any way he wanted until the sun came up.

The beauty of the party from the perspective of the men was that every woman was a sure thing because each and every female was a high class call girl who was well-paid by Lassiter to attend. Denise included, although to be fair, it was her alias—Candy—who was getting that nice pay day.

As for the men, they each paid Lassiter a hefty sum, supposedly for a room at the hotel. In reality, the payment assured the privilege of finding a Miss

Right willing to satisfy any and all kinks, fetishes, and predilections. As a bonus, they each enjoyed the smug satisfaction of buying sex without actually paying for sex.

Quince didn't need a woman in his room. He needed a partner to act as a lookout and keep the small signal booster in perfect alignment with both the transmitter and Lassiter's computer. The transmitter that Denny was battling on the nearby roof wouldn't do a damn bit of good if the signal wasn't captured in his room on the fourth floor, then boosted down to where Quince would be hacking Lassiter's computer on the mezzanine level.

And while Desiree might be willing to fulfill his every kinky fantasy, he doubted that she would regard helping him hack into Lassiter's system as a genuine fetish. Besides, she'd already wandered off in search of another key master.

Easy come, easy go.

"You realize this is a problem," he murmured, lifting his glass to hide the slight movement of his lips, then taking a long swallow because he damn sure needed it.

"No, really? I'm so glad you're here to explain things to me."

He swallowed a laugh. "Temper, temper."

"You can't tell, but I'm flipping you off."

"I'd expect nothing less." He crossed to the window so that he could talk more easily, keeping an eye on the guests in the reflection as he pretended to study Hollywood below. Denny was out there, perched atop an old department store that had been converted to office space.

"Fuck it. I'm going to use a strip of duct tape to get as close to dead-on perfect as I can. I can get back pronto. You need me in that room."

He did, dammit. But they also needed certainty with regard to the transmission. This mission was the pivotal point in a joint EU and Spanish task force operation to take down Corbu and his international sex-trafficking operation. Stark Security had been hired to handle this one critical piece of the puzzle. A single, limited mission to get in, obtain and decrypt Lassiter's contact files, then pass along the contact protocol for Corbu to the task force.

Fail and Stark Security would lose its growing reputation in the international intelligence community. More important, thousands of innocent lives were at stake, and the window of opportunity was tight. As they said at America's NASA, failure was not an option.

"I'm coming to you." He knew damn well she was more than competent, but he had to try. "Maybe I can secure the arm."

"There's not enough time. I have to capture the signal in fifteen minutes and you need to be in position in twenty. Blow the window and we're fucked."

He pulled out the antique Patek Philippe pocket watch that had once belonged to the father he'd barely known. Exceptionally crafted, it still kept perfect time, though its accuracy had little to do with why Quince wore it religiously. Almost superstitiously.

The Patek Philippe was a reminder of the past, a warning against the future.

It would never lead him astray, and right then it told him that Denny was right.

Bollocks.

"All right," he said. "Get over here." It was a huge risk, but the powerful transmitter was designed to allow for the transmission and reception of the massive data packets necessary for the cutting edge decryption software hosted back at the SSA. With luck, Denny's rigged up anchor would allow the transmitter to capture and relay enough of the signal to the booster in Quincy's hotel room. That device worked much like a WiFi router, and it would send the signal out into the interior of the hotel, where it would hit the tech that Quince would be using to hack into Lassiter's system.

For that to work, however, the transmitter's signal had to hit the booster with dead-on accuracy. Anything less, and the booster would be relaying garbage to Quince, not the high-end hacking software created by Stark Applied Technology. Not an ideal situation, but they had no choice.

He turned back to face the room. He needed to know where Lassiter was so that he could slip down to his assigned room on the fourth floor without being noticed. *There.*

Lassiter was standing in a group of five men and two women, his hand low on a slim brunette's back. Reddish-brown hair fell down to her shoulders, her smooth skin revealed in the low-cut dress that came close to revealing the crack of her perfect, heart-shaped ass. There was something so familiar about her...

He brushed the thought away as irrelevant. "All right. I've spotted Lassiter. I'm heading—"

Then she turned, and he saw her face.

He froze. He absolutely fucking froze.

Eliza? Surely it couldn't be Eliza.

"*Quince?*" Denny's voice was tight. "*Is it Lassiter? Is he suspicious?*"

"Not Lassiter. A ghost."

"*What?*"

Because she had to be a ghost. The woman with mahogany hair and sky-blue eyes. The woman whose dimple had once made his heart flip.

The woman he'd cherished. Whose scent still lingered in his dreams.

The woman he'd loved more passionately than he'd believed possible. And who now surely hated him more than he could imagine.

There was no way that woman could be at a party like this. No way at all.

Could she?

Dear God, what had she gotten herself wrapped up in?

Without conscious decision, he moved toward her, his long strides eating up the distance as Denny chattered in his ear. *"What's going on? Dammit, I'm on my way. Rendezvous at the room in four minutes."*

He knew he should turn around. There was too damn much riding on this mission. The lives and freedom of so many innocents who'd become ensnared in the Romanian kingpin's sex trafficking confederation. Thousands upon thousands of tormented victims, including one innocent, terrified thirteen-year-old girl.

Her abduction was the trigger that had pushed the EU task force into immediate action. The daughter of the Prince Regent of one of Europe's smaller monarchy's, the princess had been abducted during a school trip. Her father had gone to the task force's leader, a classmate from Eaton, and essentially opened up the monarchy's massive coffers to fund whatever it took to get the girl back and shut down Corbu's operation.

Quince shuddered as the image of another teen girl flashed in his head. *Shelley.* Her trusting eyes. Her choking sobs. And his own screams of terror and helplessness as fiery pain ripped through him and the world collapsed around him.

And in that moment, he knew what he had to do.

"Stay on the roof," he ordered Denny.

"What? But—"

"Trust me. I've got it covered."

He'd been too damn weak to save Shelley.

He'd failed her. Hell, he'd failed himself.

He damn well wasn't going to fail again.

Even if that meant pulling Eliza Tucker into this buggered-up scheme.

2

HE'S TOUCHING ME. This too-polished, too-twisted, smarmy son-of-a-bitch actually has his hand on the small of my back, his thumb rubbing the bare skin at the base of my spine. It's intimate. It's possessive. It's revolting.

It's my own damn fault.

I'm the one who shoved my tits into this too-tight dress. I'm the one who caught Scott Lassiter's eye. And now it looks like I'm the one who's going to have to endure a night in bed with him if I don't want to risk blowing my cover.

My cover.

The irony isn't lost on me. For my entire life, my sister Emma has been my protector. A brilliant, strong, vengeful angel standing between me and the dangers of the world. Didn't matter if it was mean teachers, street thugs, or our own monstrous prick of a father, she was always right there, doing whatever she had to in order to keep me safe.

And now here I am, stuck in the middle of a situation I don't fully understand as I pretend to be my sister. Or, more accurately, as I pretend to be my sister pretending to be a call girl.

Thank goodness I've spent over a decade working as a semi-struggling actress. Sliding in and out of roles. Commercials, community theater, the occasional bit on a soap opera, and a few small parts in films shot in New York.

I've never tried to land a recurring television role or a long-contract run on or off Broadway. It just doesn't appeal. I want success, sure. It's just that there's something compelling about variety. After all, the more I can get lost in someone else's life, the less I have to examine my own.

All of which makes me an excellent chameleon. Which is probably the only reason that no one is pointing a finger at me à la *Invasion of the Body Snatchers* and screaming that I'm a fraud who doesn't belong here.

Because I don't. I really don't.

And when Emma finds out that I'm not only impersonating her but that I'm putting myself in danger, she's going to be royally pissed. But that's okay. Pissed means she's alive. And all things

considered, I want her ranting and raving and furious. Because the alternative is too horrible to even
contemplate.

I draw a deep breath. My worries about Emma
have been a constant for a full twenty-four hours,
ever since I realized she was missing. But I need to
push them down, because I have more immediate
problems. Like how I'm going to extricate myself
from this perv who's decided that I belong to him
tonight. Because every minute I'm trapped with
Scott Lassiter is another minute I don't have
answers.

I shift slightly and glance around the room,
wondering who my contact is supposed to be.
According to Emma's partner, a few days before
she disappeared, an anonymous source had reached
out to Emma. He called himself Mr. X and
promised her information about a case she was
working. All she had to do was meet him at this
party.

"They couldn't grab a booth at McDonalds?"
I'd asked.

A wide grin had split Lorenzo's ruddy face.
He'd run a hand over his head, pushing a tuft of
hair to one side to reveal his growing bald spot.
"Pretty sure that wasn't on the table, baby girl."

I crossed my arms and cocked my head in
response to the endearment, but he brushed me off.

I've known Lorenzo since I was nine and he was a beat cop in Venice Beach who'd looked the other way when he caught Emma and me sleeping in an abandoned car.

All Lorenzo knew was that Emma had been working on one of her pro bono cases. After over a decade working for the government, she'd gone out as a full-time private investigator a few years ago. Her passion is helping runaways and other endangered kids, and Lorenzo told me that she'd stumbled across some sort of exploitation conspiracy that was organized in forums hosted on the dark web.

"I'm guessing Mr. X is in deep, but wants out," Lorenzo had said.

"So he contacted Emma and set a meet," I guessed. "But before it could happen, the real baddies also realized she was poking around in the forum. Somehow they figured out her identity and grabbed her."

"That's what it looks like to me."

My chest tightened as I forced out the next words. "Did they—do you think they killed her?"

"I hope not," he'd said, his basset hound eyes profoundly sad.

"I have to go to the police."

"And what would they do? For starters, they'd tell you to wait. Her apartment is relatively neat—"

"Someone was in it." I was sure about that.

"*You* say. But it's not ransacked. You say things are out of place, but that doesn't necessarily mean foul play. All you know is that she's gone and you don't know where. But she's a grown woman. She could have left on a whim. Gone off with a man. Decided to take up fly-fishing."

"She always tells me where she's going. We don't keep secrets." I think of the things she's told me that she should have held close. Dangerous things if anyone found out.

No. She wouldn't keep something important from me.

"Last I heard, you were supposed to be on some cruise ship," Lorenzo says when I point that out. "She said you'd told her not to bother calling, but that you'd check in from various ports."

I grimaced. All true. Except that I never even had the chance to set sail.

I'd landed a role in a shipboard musical. Three full months at sea visiting a variety of ports. Three months of one and two week excursions, a different set of passengers on every journey. Ninety full days with no one from my past, and no one who would be part of my future. The job had sounded like heaven, and I'd jumped all over it.

But then the cruise line cancelled the show entirely, replacing the large-cast musical with a single stand-up comedian. Budget cuts. Which left me not only out of work, but at loose ends.

Which was why I'd decided to fly to LA to visit my sister.

Emma, however, was gone.

"She would have sent an email if she decided to take a last minute vacation," I told Lorenzo. "You know she would." Emma and I are more than just sisters. She practically raised me. And it had been the two of us against the world ever since that horrible day when she'd pulled me from the house that was never, *ever* a home.

Lorenzo had nodded sagely. "I know it. You know it. The cops don't. You need more if you want help. *We* need more. You think I'm not worried? This is Emma we're talking about. She's like a daughter to me. You both are."

"You really think this Mr. X knows something?"

"I think he's the only lead we have. I'd go if I could, but I don't think I can pull off a low-cut evening gown."

He was right. I knew it. And not just about how he'd look in drag.

I either went to the meeting or I let time slip away until the cops might legitimately get interested.

Put it that way, and there was no question.

Emma was in trouble, and that was all that mattered to me. Because at the end of the day, *she's* all that matters to me. Well, her and Lorenzo. They're all I have. All I've ever had.

Once upon a time, I thought there might be someone else. Dark and edgy, sweet and sensual, Quincy Radcliffe had an intensity that had drawn me to him and a strength that had held me close. In his arms, I'd felt safer than I had since I'd left Emma and Los Angeles. I'd opened the steel cage around my heart and invited him inside.

We were together for almost three months, and in that time I let my guard down completely. I let myself love him, and I thought he loved me, too.

I'll never make that mistake again.

He ripped me apart. Shattered my soul from the inside out.

He'd made me love him. And I can't forgive him for that.

But I have to thank him, too. Because I learned my lesson that spring in London. I'd thought that maybe I could change. That perhaps the wall I'd built and the masks I put on didn't have to be permanent. That I could chip away at those barriers and try to let someone else inside.

Quince made me want to try. He made me hope.

And when he betrayed me ... well, he taught

me that I needed those walls. They were what kept me safe.

Now Emma lives inside the walls. Lorenzo, too.

Just them. Only them.

They're all I have, and that's why I'm here in the Art Deco elegance of the Hollywood Terrace penthouse ballroom.

It's why I followed Mr. X's detailed instructions for the meet. Why I'm pretending to be one of the many call girls hired for the evening. And why in addition to my slinky black dress, I'm wearing a red ribbon as a bracelet, just as instructed. The point is to signal to Mr. X that I'm the anonymous BAB, the alias Emma was using in the forum.

It stands for Bad Ass Bitch, though I'm probably the only one in the world who knows that. Right now, I don't feel particularly bad ass. I wish I did. Because a bad ass bitch could probably figure out a way to disengage herself from the man who seems determined to keep me at his side.

Then again, I'm supposed to be in character. A call girl named Bunny. And girls like Bunny aren't bad asses. On the contrary, girls like Bunny drop to their knees or spread their legs on command. I understand Bunnies, so I'm not exactly stretching my acting chops tonight.

Maybe if my name for the night was Amber or Domino or Serena. If I had a riding crop instead of a red ribbon. Maybe then I could put on a show.

Really step out of myself and pull on the BAB persona.

But I don't. I can't.

Just as well, I think. Because from what I can tell, this is a party full of Bunnies. Not Serenas.

In other words, I've stepped into a world that is run entirely and completely by men. Rich, powerful, controlling men. With dark and dangerous appetites.

Oh, Emma. What did you stumble into?

I've been asking myself that question ever since Lassiter zeroed in on me, which happened the moment I'd entered the penthouse. At first, I'd thought it was because he saw through my cover. Later, when he commented on my unusual bracelet, I breathed a sigh of relief, assuming that he was Mr. X. Soon enough, though, I realized that he just wanted me naked.

Now, I'm stuck with him when I need to be mingling. I need to be reaching for drinks on waiters' trays, making sure I flash the red ribbon enough that Mr. X can't miss it. At the same time, it's very clear that female autonomy is not the buzzword for the day, and that if Lassiter wants me at his side, then I'm stuck there until he deigns to set me free.

Fuck.

"Actually, I'm already in progress on similar remodels in Chicago, Houston, and Manhattan," Lassiter is saying to some billionaire mucky-muck with a thick Italian accent who'd asked if Lassiter was planning to expand his "business model." Since I'm disgusted by the whole scenario, I tune him out, only to jump when I hear my name. Or, rather, when I hear my hooker name.

"—like Bunny here."

"I'm sorry, what?"

Lassiter smiles indulgently, then squeezes my ass. I refrain from slapping him, since that would definitely be out of character. "I was telling Mr. Scutari that all of the women at my soirées are delightful, but there are a few who have a rare quality. A stunning allure." He brushes my hair behind my ear, and I have to force myself to smile instead of flinch. Not that I'm a shiny, pure little angel. Far, far from it. But there are men who can have me in their bed and men who can't.

Lassiter lives deep in *can't* territory. And right now I'm praying that Mr. X finds me soon. I'd even be okay with a massive earthquake hitting LA. Anything to keep Lassiter from presenting me with his key and aiming me toward his room. Because I'm pretty sure that the only reason he hasn't keyed me yet is that he's the host, and he has to wait until all his guests have selected their girls.

I expect him to continue waxing poetic about the quality of the merchandise, but instead the conversation shifts to international finance. As if this is an average cocktail party and I'm his dutiful, doting girlfriend.

The whole thing is very surreal, and with every moment that passes, I'm afraid that coming here was a mistake. I'm not any closer to finding Emma, and as the night drags on the chances of ending up in Lassiter's bed are increasing. I'd known that was a risk, of course. But I'd assumed that Mr. X would find me, then we'd go to his room, purportedly for sexy shenanigans, but really for an intensive, clandestine discussion of what happened to my sister and how we can help her.

So where the hell is he?

I punctuate the thought by twisting around to survey the room. Lassiter's hand stays possessively on my back, and I force myself not to grimace. I'm so focused on not jerking my body out from under his touch that I can barely take in the room around me.

Which explains why I don't immediately register the man stalking toward us, his long stride eating up the ground as he crosses the length of the ballroom.

Quincy Radcliffe.

The man who left me. Who broke my heart.

My mouth goes dry, my blood running hot through my body.

My palm tingles with the desire to slap him. And when I see those deep gray eyes lock onto mine, I silently scream out a warning begging him not to say my name.

That's when it hits me.

That's when the pieces fall together.

Quincy Radcliffe is the reason I'm here. My Quincy is Mr. X.

So what the hell am I going to do now?

3

I watch his face as he approaches, searching for some hint of pain. Some shadow of regret.

There's nothing, though. His face might as well be carved out of stone, his gray eyes forged in steel. He doesn't waver. His expression is carefully blank. If I didn't know better, I'd think he didn't recognize me at all.

But he does, of course.

For three glorious months, Quincy Radcliffe had been my everything. My champion. My knight. He'd stood at my side and battled my demons, and I'd surrendered to him completely, shedding my fears and, yes, even nurturing my hopes.

He was my love. My heart.

The man whose smile had teased me and whose body aroused me. The man with whom I'd shared my secrets and my tears.

He knew me better than any man ever had, and he cut me more deeply than any man ever could.

I want to rip my arm away from Lassiter. I want to sprint out of this room on these nail-point heels. I want to forget everything—Quincy, Emma, Mr. X.

Most of all, I want to escape myself and my memories.

But I can't. And as I stand there gawping at the gorgeous bastard who is advancing toward me, the floor opens up, and suddenly I'm hurtling more than four years into the past ... and into the memories of the man who destroyed me.

———

It was my last full day in the UK, and despite the September chill and the light drizzle, I walked the short distance from my tiny, eclectic flat in Soho to the Waterstones bookstore at Picadilly Circus. I wanted to buy a novel. Something uniquely British that wouldn't be published in the States for at least a few more months. And I wanted to go upstairs and enjoy afternoon tea by the window while I savored the first chapter. Then I'd silently close the book and tuck it away to finish on my flight back to Manhattan.

To be honest, I couldn't wait to get on that plane and escape this cramped island, so small that my memories had no place to go, and so they clung to me. Weighing me down.

Back home, I'd be able to shake them off. Banish them. *Go west, damn memories!* But here...

Here in this ancient city, it felt like he was everywhere. And all I wanted to do was escape the foolish, horrible pull that Quincy Radcliffe still had over me.

How quickly things change, right? Because when I'd arrived six months prior, I'd been giddy at the thought of living in the UK for half a year. I'd come to London to join the cast of a unique improv company that performed modern riffs on favorite Shakespeare plays. The thought of playing a different role each night had made my heart soar and my creativity sing. The run was supposed to be five months, and afterwards, I'd spend a month sightseeing before heading back to Manhattan where I'd already lined up a small role as a murder victim in the upcoming season of a popular television show.

But that's not how things panned out. The show closed after one week, which meant I was in a foreign country with no income. I considered going home—I didn't have immediate work lined up there, either, but auditioning in New York was at least a familiar process. Plus, I knew all the best temp agencies.

Emma had come to my rescue, as usual. She

reminded me that I'd flat-swapped. Which meant that I didn't have a home to return to, since a British author was currently in my apartment, using the time to finish his latest project. "You've already got the flat in London," she'd said. "All you need is spending money."

Since she knew I wouldn't take her cash as sisterly charity, she offered me the long-distance job of organizing her and Lorenzo's online files. It was a little bit of a gimme, but not entirely. Both Emma and Lorenzo lacked the organizational gene. They could scan, download, or type information into a computer, but then it just stayed there like a dead fish stinking up their hard drive. My job was to shove all those rotten fish heads into tidy little digital folders. Hard for them, easy for me.

Which meant that I was gainfully employed in London with a job that took very little effort and left me with all the time in the world to explore the city, pretending I was a Londoner. Or maybe a runaway heiress. Or a travel photographer. God knew I took enough shots with my ancient Canon.

And, in fact, it was the camera that introduced me to Quincy.

It was an unusually warm day in March, my tenth day in London, and my twenty-fourth birthday. Since I had no one in town to celebrate with, I spent the day wandering London with my camera. Around lunchtime, I was taking photos of the ducks in Hyde Park—because you can't have too many cute duck photos—and I'd been backing up slowly as I tried to adjust the composition. At the same time, Quincy had been walking down the path toward me, sipping a coffee and talking into his phone. He looked down as I stepped back, and *boom*, his white-starched shirt was drenched in black coffee.

"Bloody buggering hell," he snapped, then went immediately contrite as I turned around, completely and totally mortified. "Oh, bloody fuck, I'm sorry."

"No, no. It was my fault. I was ... well, actually, I blame the ducks."

"Ah, I thought they might be up to something. They look a bit shady around the eyes."

I nodded sagely, ridiculously pleased that such a ruggedly handsome man shared my sense of humor. "And you see how they're just meandering around now, pretending to be all innocent? But we know. We can see their devious little duck natures hiding right beneath the soft, feathery surface."

I was kidding, of course. Except maybe I wasn't. There's far too much darkness buried just below eye level. I should know. I've watched the shadows rise up more times than I like to think about.

I started to brush away my words, to add something light to the conversation so he would only see the joke and not get an inadvertent peek into something deeper. But then I saw his eyes, and I stumbled. And that's when I knew he understood. This was a man who'd stood at the threshold and looked into the abyss, too.

I shook myself—it was a ridiculous thought. "Anyway, right. I should let you get going. You probably want to change that shirt. Actually, I should have it cleaned for you."

"Shall I take it off, then? Hand it over to you, and we can meet here again tomorrow?"

"I—" He was teasing; I was certain of it. And yet my senses kicked into overdrive as I imagined him unbuttoning his shirt, stepping closer to give it to me. The scent of him. The frisson of awareness as our hands brushed. And then the anticipation as he leaned closer and—

I took a firm step backward. "Maybe I should just write down my number and you can call me with the bill?"

"Why don't you let me buy you lunch and we'll call it even."

"Oh. Well—wait. I think you've got that backward."

His smile shot straight through me, warming me from the inside. "No," he said. "I didn't."

"Oh." I rarely date. I'd had my share of one-night stands, though. Bar pickups. Friend fix-ups.

Most of the time, those encounters were just

fine. Nothing special, but more entertaining than an evening with a battery-operated boyfriend.

It was the next morning that was always the kicker. Because no matter how energetic that romp in the sheets might have been, it was never quite right. Never quite what I needed. What I craved.

And what I knew I shouldn't want.

The next morning was always an awkward, silent, stumbling hell. Stilted conversation and that too-familiar tightening in my chest, because the bottom line was that I didn't know how to tell Mr. Last Night that he really hadn't gotten it done.

Not that this coffee-soaked stranger was inviting me into his bed. At least not overtly. But there was an electricity between us that was already snapping and crackling. Go with him, and I was certain that the afternoon would lead into evening, and the evening would lead to sexy hijinks.

Did I want that? Another attempt to find a guy who filled that hole inside me? Another futile fuck and then the disappointment of slinking away unsatisfied? Because I was *always* unsatisfied.

Part of me liked it that way, because if I ever did find a guy who touched those secret, hidden desires, I'd have to finally acknowledge those dark needs that had teased me since puberty. But that wasn't a place I wanted to go. Because that was the place that reminded me of *him*. That reminded me that his blood flowed in my veins, and that at my core lay something very, very bad.

I stifled a shiver, hugging myself as I looked up at this smiling stranger with the stormy eyes. Better to just push him away now and be done with it. At least then I could go home and enjoy the delicious fantasy of the man and avoid altogether the disappointing reality.

That was the plan, anyway. The execution turned out to be a lot harder.

His gaze bore down on me. "I'm not quite certain if I should take your silence as a yes or a no."

"Sorry." I stifled a wince. "I appreciate the offer. Really. But I probably shouldn't."

He said nothing for a moment, just looked at me with those dark, penetrating eyes. Then he took a single step toward me so that he was close enough that I could reach out and touch him. Close enough that I caught the scent of musk and male hidden under the overpowering aroma of coffee.

A charged silence hung between us, broken only by the low quacking of the ducks. My breath came shallow, and I could feel my pulse beating in my throat. And the longer his eyes stayed on me, the more an unexpected heat built between my thighs.

Really shouldn't, indeed.

When he finally spoke, there was no disap-

pointment in his voice. Just a low, even tone that
suggested that nothing ever ruffled him. And that
he was used to getting what he wanted.

"Are you saying no because you're afraid of
what will happen between us? Or are you more
afraid that nothing will happen at all?"

"I—"

That's all I managed before the words caught in
my throat and my mind turned to mush. My senses
were on overdrive, and every warning bell in my
head was going off. This was the kind of guy who
could get under my skin. This was the kind of guy I
should run from.

Finally, I gathered my wits enough to answer.
"Those are my only two choices?" I lifted my brow
in what I hoped was a haughty gesture. "I think
you're being awfully presumptuous."

"I'm not. But I also have rules, and one is that I
never argue if a woman says no. So tell me, Eliza.
Are you declining my invitation to lunch?"

"I—wait. How do you know my name?"

His eyes dipped toward the ground where I'd
dropped my camera bag. *Eliza T.* Right there on the
top, along with an email address to help the bag
find its way home to me in case it got lost.

"Right." I shoved my hands in my pockets, not
entirely sure why I was still here. Hadn't I already
assessed this guy? Didn't I already know he was
dangerous?

But maybe a little danger was exactly what I needed.

No. Don't go there, Eliza. Do not go there.

"What's your name?" I asked, taking that first tiny mental step in the absolute wrong direction.

"If we're parting ways, I hardly think that matters." He reached out, and I was surprised to find my hand rising to meet his. "Will you tell me something?"

"Maybe."

His thumb lightly stroked my skin, sending shockwaves of pleasure coursing through me, teasing that already growing ache at my core. "Why are you hesitating when you clearly want me—"

I sucked in air, irritated by his presumption. And by the truth of it.

"—to take you to lunch."

"Oh."

He cocked his head, the corner of his mouth twitching. I felt my cheeks burn. Obviously, he knew exactly what I'd been thinking. "Don't shy away from what you want," he said, his voice soft but commanding, full of a quality I couldn't define but that I knew I craved, even as it scared me.

"Say yes," he continued. "I promise, you won't regret it."

"I don't usually go out with strangers I meet in the park." My suddenly dry mouth made my voice rough.

"I like being an exception."

I looked him up and down, and I had to grin. "Yeah. I bet you do. Fair enough, Mr. Mystery. But I'm buying lunch."

"Not a problem," he said with the kind of sexy grin designed to make a woman melt. "I'll buy breakfast."

I tilted my head, making a show of looking him up and down. "In that case, I think you better tell me your name."

4

IT WAS QUINCY. Quincy Radcliffe, which seemed so very British to me. But not in a clichéd stuffy way. Quincy had more of a sexy, James Bond vibe.

"I like it," I announced. "It suits you."

"Most of my friends call me Quince," he said.

"Really? You seem like a two syllable kind of guy."

He eyed me sideways as we continued walking through the park toward the street, though I wasn't sure which street. Hyde Park is huge, and I'd managed to get completely turned around.

When we finally escaped paradise for the hustle and bustle of cars and cabs and buses, I turned in a circle, trying to get my bearings. No luck. "In case you hadn't guessed, I'm not from around here. Any suggestions on where to feed you? And don't even try to talk me out of paying."

"What makes you think I'd do that?"

"There's a chivalrous look about you."

"You have something against chivalry?"

"Let's just say I like a little bad in my boy." *Oh my God, where had that come from?* It wasn't true at all. I was fishing in the nice guy pool, and I was certain that eventually I'd catch one who wasn't lacking. Who'd satisfy me in a way that didn't touch the scary shadows in my soul.

Bottom line? I needed a guy who was way the hell and gone from my father. Which meant I *definitely* didn't need a bad boy.

He paused on the sidewalk, and I turned back to see what had caught his eye, only to realize that it was me.

"What?" I asked, suddenly antsy under his attention, like I'd walked through a charged electrical field.

His smile was slow and easy, the kind that reached his eyes and suggested that he knew a secret.

"Quincy," I demanded. "What?"

"Nothing," he said in voice that telegraphed the opposite. "I just think that you're a woman with a lot of layers, Eliza T. And I'm going to enjoy peeling away each and every one of them."

"Presumptuous, much?" I spoke archly, but it was just for show. That electrical sizzle had ramped up, making the tiny hairs on my arms stand up and the back of my neck prickle. Right then, a little peeling sounded just fine by me.

For a moment we simply looked at each other until, finally, I cleared my throat and looked away.

"No," he said.

I turned back. "No?"

He reached out, and my breath caught as he gently ran the pad of his thumb along my jaw. "No, I'm not being presumptuous."

"Oh." My cheeks burned, and not from the bright spring day. "I—um, I still have absolutely no idea where to eat around here."

His hand left my jaw, leaving a warm spot on my skin that suddenly consumed every ounce of my attention. Or it did until I felt that same hand at my lower back, the pressure just enough to guide me down the sidewalk. I realized I was grinning like a fool, and I looked down at the ground to hide my goofy expression. I wasn't entirely sure what was going on here, but I couldn't deny that I liked it.

As I'd insisted, I did buy him lunch, and although I hadn't planned on a full-on formal dining experience, the cute little pub in Mayfair he guided us to was significantly less posh than I'd intended, especially considering we ended up at the take-out window.

"Was your shirt so cheap that you think it would be unfair for me to shell out for a full meal?"

I knew it wasn't cheap, of course. When you grow up watching your sister pull off complicated cons just to score a room for the night, you learn a bit about the wardrobe habits of the rich and successful. From what I could tell, Mr. Quincy Radcliffe was either a very experienced con, or he came from money.

Note the *came from*. Not *new money*. And yeah, there's a difference. A newly monied man might have been polite about the soiled shirt, but he would have still been irritated. And he certainly wouldn't still be wearing it, the brown stain across his chest like a beacon declaring his—or my —clumsiness.

"First of all," Quincy said, "some of London's best food comes from pubs. And second, I'm going to guess that you've never had a Scotch egg."

I wrinkled my nose. "I'm more of a wine girl."

He just chuckled, then held up two fingers to the man at the window. "Trust me," he said, as I shelled out very few pounds in exchange for two little paper boats. In each sat what appeared to be a giant hush puppy surrounded by sweet potato fries.

I looked at the meal dubiously, then followed him to one of the outdoor tables. "Do I get a hint?"

"A hard boiled egg, sausage, bread crumbs. And it's deep-fried. Need I say more?"

"Not to me." I wouldn't call myself a foodie, but I'm definitely a girl who likes to eat. Which explains why I also like to work out. Although *like* might be a slight exaggeration.

I used a little plastic knife to cut through the breading to reveal exactly what he'd described. An egg nestled in a delicious layer of sausage-y goodness. I cut a piece off, used the toss-away fork to spear it, and then bit into what had to be a tiny niblet from heaven.

"Holy wow." I covered my mouth with my napkin—my best first date manners—and looked up at him. "You are an amazing human being for turning me on to these."

"I'm very glad to hear it." His mouth twitched.

"Don't even say it." I could hear the laughter in my voice, because I knew *exactly* where he was going.

"Say what? That I'm very happy to have turned you on? I wouldn't dream of being so forward."

"Mmm." I took another bite, and wisely decided to stay silent. An easy plan to stick to since the food was delicious and my mouth was fully occupied.

Despite his earlier tease that he'd buy breakfast, I'd expected him to make his escape. Probably he'd tell me he needed to get home and change before an evening meeting. Because clearly this was a guy who worked in the private sector. But he never even hinted that he wanted to get away from me. On the contrary, when I told him that I'd only been in London for a little over a week, he suggested one of the hop-on/hop-off double-decker tour buses. And because I'm a total geek about that kind of thing, I accepted immediately.

It was only when we were settled next to each other on a small bench seat at the top of the bus that the import of his offer hit me. Somehow, our chance encounter in the park had morphed into an actual date.

I really needed to remember to thank those ducks.

Despite a decent guide who spoke to us from the front of the bus, I learned nothing about the city. Instead, I spent the next hour flirting with the man beside me. Sharing details about our lives and cracking the occasional stupid joke.

"Actress," he said, when I refused to tell him what I did and ordered him to guess.

"You're good. Most people I've chatted up over here think I'm a grad student."

"I spend a lot of time watching people."

"Is that part of the job description for an international financial consultant?" I'd gone first in the guess-my-job game. I'd guessed that he was in the corporate world, but he'd narrowed down the specifics for me.

He shook his head. "No. Let's just say it's one of my special skills."

"So lay it out. What marks me as a woman of stage and screen?"

"For one thing, the prop." He glanced down at my camera bag, then back up at me, the certainty reflected in his face both impressing and scaring me. No one but Emma had ever seen me quite so clearly.

"Prop?" I tried to keep my voice nonchalant, but I don't think I succeeded. "I like to take pictures, that's all."

He nodded, as if encouraging me to talk, and despite telling myself that I was going to shift the conversation around to him, I heard myself saying, "I'm lousy at it. Snapshots, sure. But anything that resembles actual art? Or skilled photography? Really *not* me."

"But you enjoy it."

I shook my head slowly, trying to find the right words. "I enjoy the idea of it. The camera gives me an excuse to go places. To just walk and look."

"Why do you need an excuse?"

I shifted on the warm leather seat. "I don't, I guess. But I like being someone."

The corners of his mouth turned down, and I could see that he was thinking about my words. Analyzing them. Probably seeing more than I'd intended him to. That seemed to be Quincy's special skill.

I expected him to eventually offer a platitude.

Something along the lines of, "Everybody's some-body," or some equally facile bullshit.

But what he said was, "Is it really that much better to have a role than to be yourself?"

"I—" I sat back in the seat, my focus on our guide and not on the man beside me.

"Eliza?"

I told myself I didn't want to answer. That he was digging too deep for someone I barely knew. But that mental lecture was for nothing, because it *felt* like I knew him, and before I even realized I was speaking, I heard myself saying, "I guess I've never been very good at being me."

Considering how ridiculously cryptic that was, I expected a moment of silence preceding a snappy change of subject. Instead, he said, "What are you hiding from?"

The question surprised me so much, it stole my words, so that all I could do was sit there and wonder about this enigmatic man who saw so much. More, in fact, than I wanted him to see.

An awkward silence hung between us. I considered not answering at all, but I was enjoying our time together and didn't want to put him off. At the same time, I didn't want to tell him the truth. Or maybe I didn't really know the truth.

Finally, I lifted a shoulder and simply said, "Isn't everyone hiding from something?"

He pursed his lips, as if he was truly consid-

ering the question. Then he nodded. "In my experience, yes. I'd have to say that's true."

I leaned sideways, butting my shoulder against
his. "Lots of clients hiding their funds? The deep,
dirty, and mysterious world of high finance?"

"Something like that," he said, in the kind of
voice that made me think that my joke had more
truth in it than I'd intended.

I wanted to ask him more, but I wasn't sure if I
should. I felt a connection to this guy, yes, but I
didn't trust it. Not yet. What if it was just the
euphoria of meeting a nice, good-looking guy on a
lovely spring day? What if he wasn't feeling the
connection, too?

I thought he was, but—

Screeeeeeech!

My thoughts were rudely cut off by a burst of
feedback from the guide's microphone. "Sorry," the
guide said. "But at least it woke you all up, because
we're about to enter one of London's poshest neighborhoods. Even if you don't recognize the politi-
cians' and executives' names, I'm sure you've heard
of Madonna, one of the most famous former resi-
dents in this ritzy part of London. Can you guess
some others?"

As other guests in the group started to shout out
the names of celebrities, I turned my attention back
to Quincy. "So how often do you do this?"

"This?"

"Invite tourists you've stumbled upon to ride the double decker bus."

"Would you believe me if I said this was my first time?"

I started to laugh, but something about his tone stopped me. "Actually, yeah." I flashed a shy smile, and I'm really not that shy a person. "Yeah, I think I would."

Our eyes met, and if we'd been in a movie, that was where the couple's theme would have started, low at first and then building to a dramatic kiss, probably with Big Ben in the background and the sun setting so that the sky was ablaze in orange.

I was so lost in the fantasy that I was surprised when he broke the mood and said softly, "This is where I grew up."

"London? I assumed as much, though I guess anywhere in the UK would—oh, wait." I cocked my head, then looked around at the stunning homes, like something out of an incredible movie. Or at least a fun one. Like the über-posh townhome where the British version of Lindsey Lohan lived in *The Parent Trap*. "You mean *here* here?"

"Just down this road, actually."

"Wow." I grinned. Apparently I'd been right about that whole *came from money thing*. "Which house?"

He hesitated, then started to point in the direction of a stately white home when the guide, who'd paused to field celebrity guesses, began to speak again. "But it's not all celebrities and high-flying business moguls. This neighborhood has a dark side, too."

"Oooh," I said, in the same voice I'd used for a campy horror movie. "Now we're getting to the real gossip." I expected Quincy to crack a smile, and when he didn't, I sat back, a little embarrassed by his less than enthusiastic reception to my sometimes warped sense of humor.

"Take the house to my left—number 806. It looks like your typical high-end home. A lovely place, you'd think, to raise a family. To be a child, carefree and young."

I frowned, because number 806 was the mansion that I thought Quincy had indicated.

"But this home—which became famous as the site of the murder of heiress Emily Radcliffe—hosts a dark history with a sad cast of characters. A terrified little boy. A mother, killed in her effort to protect him. A father who disappeared into the wind, only to be found assassinated within the year, and revealed as a traitor to both Britain *and* to the foreign power he'd so blithely and secretly served."

Beside me, Quincy stiffened, his shoulders back and his face unreadable. I didn't know if I should, but I couldn't stop myself. I reached over, and I twined my fingers with his. At first, his hand was a dead weight. Then his fingers gently curled around mine.

"It's a hop-on/hop-off bus," I said quietly. "Why didn't we get off before we turned in here? Surely you knew they'd mention it."

"Everyone has a story, Eliza. As an actress, you must know that."

"Maybe," I agreed. "But not everyone shares their stories so easily."

"You're the first person who's learned that about me in a long, long time. Not since Dallas. My friend," he clarified. "Not the city. And I told him a lifetime ago."

"Oh." Part of me wanted to ask why he let me learn this dark fact about him. Sure, the guide mentioned the name Radcliffe, but that's hardly an unusual name. If he hadn't started to point to the house—if he hadn't reacted when the guide told the story—I doubt I would have guessed.

I didn't ask why, though. Instead, I heard myself saying, "I'm sorry about your dad. My father—well, he wasn't a good man either." And wasn't that the understatement of the year?

"I'm sorry."

"I don't want to say it was the same—it wasn't. It was bad." I licked my lips, forcing myself to just talk and not to remember. "But it was different. He—well, it doesn't matter. I just ... I guess I just wanted you to know that I understand at least a little."

The bus had maneuvered to a stop, and several of our co-riders were getting off. Quince glanced at me, and though he didn't say a word, we rose together and headed for the stairs in the front. When we reached the sidewalk, we didn't talk about either of our fathers again, but that didn't matter. Something fundamental had changed. At first, the connection between us had been like lighting. Fast and surprising and a little bit dangerous. Now, it felt warm and steady, like a softly glowing ember that had the power to ignite into flame.

He took my hand silently, and I fell in step beside him. We walked out of the neighborhood, twisting and turning on small residential streets, narrow lanes lined with shops, and around a few fenced neighborhood gardens. The sun was beginning to creep lower, and we walked through more shadows cast by the many trees that lined the neighborhoods, their leaves dappling the late afternoon light.

We walked for over an hour, talking about everything and nothing. The kind of conversation that flows easily among old friends. And it really did feel as if I'd known him forever, as if the pain in both of our pasts had forged a bond between us. As if I hadn't come to London for a job at all, but to see this man.

After a while, we realized that it had been hours since we'd had lunch, if a single Scotch egg and fries could be considered lunch. I had no idea where we were, but Quincy quickly surveyed the area, announced that we were at Marble Arch, and that we'd managed to return very near to where we left the park. "If you don't mind a walk, I know a great little Indian food place just over that way."

"I'd do pretty much anything for great Indian food," I told him.

"I'll keep that in mind," he countered, and there was no mistaking the suggestive tease in his voice.

"Good," I said boldly. Because, yeah, this whole day had been good. *He* was good. For that matter, *we* were pretty damn good.

Dinner was good, too. We ordered almost every curry on the menu and shared them all. We also shared a bottle of wine. Okay, two bottles of wine. And it's fair to say that I drank most of it. Because I knew what would come next. I knew he'd come to my apartment. I knew we'd get naked. I knew it would be fabulous.

And I also knew that by morning this would all be over. Because it always was.

"You're frowning. Tired of me already?"

I had to laugh. Only a confident man would ask a question like that, and I already knew that Quincy was a confident man. I liked that. It attracted me. Hell, it aroused me.

But I knew damn well it wouldn't be enough to satisfy me, even though I wished otherwise with all my heart and soul. I wanted him. Right at that moment I craved him. Just watching him eat—the smooth motions as he lifted a fork. The small sounds of pleasure when he tasted a particularly satisfying dish. The heat in his eyes when he offered me a fork full of something delicious, as if it wasn't the fork I was closing my lips around, but something so much more intimate.

Oh, yeah...

I wanted him.

At the same time, I didn't want it to end. And wouldn't that be an awkward conversation? *So, listen, Quincy. I'm pretty much so desperate for you that I'd do anything you asked, but the thing is that I know as soon as we do it'll all be over, so I think I'd rather skip all that. Maybe we can just play chess?*

Yeah, not so much.

He chuckled, and I realized that I'd just allowed a crazy gap of silence after he suggested I was tired of him. Definitely not earning stellar date points tonight.

"Sorry. I think I'm getting tired. Or tipsy. Or both. This is a lot of wine on top of a lot of walking."

He reached across the table and took my hand, and wild bolts of anticipation shot through me. In that moment, I knew I had to be the mega slut of the year to want him so much even though I knew that would be the end of it. But I couldn't help it. I wanted him. I wanted to feel his lips on me, his cock inside me. I wanted to be surrounded by his scent and lose myself to the sweet surrender of the wine as he whispered naughty things to me and then did every one of those things to my body. I wanted to fall asleep in his arms, and wake up with him beside me. I wanted a night of bliss. A night of passion.

A night so incredibly transcendent that even though it would be the last time, I could hold onto it forever, a delicious memory to spice up my fantasies and keep me warm at night.

He lifted a hand to signal for the check. "I think it's time we get you home."

"Yes, please." My pulse pounded in my throat. Hell, it pounded between my thighs. With each moment that passed, I was more and more turned on. I blamed the wine—it's definitely my aphrodisiac of choice—but those lovely grapes weren't entirely responsible for this sweet longing. On the contrary, that was all the man.

A man who took my hand and very gingerly helped me down the narrow stairs to the street, where he hailed a cab. "I'll have to remember you're a cheap drunk," he said, his hand sliding down to cup my bottom. I bit my lower lip and leaned into it, then moaned with satisfaction as he nuzzled my neck. "That's valuable information to store away."

"If that's the kind of information you want, I'll tell you anything. Just don't stop doing that."

"Ah, but I have to. Your chariot awaits."

He stepped around me, leaving me bereft from the sudden lack of contact. He opened the door like a perfect gentleman, then stepped back, as if to close it, rather than sliding in beside me.

"Are you getting in on the other side? I can slide over."

"You're going home alone," he said, and my entire body went cold from the giant bucket of rejection he'd just dumped all over me.

"I—what? Why?" I frowned. "I thought you were buying me breakfast. I thought we were going to—" I closed my mouth because under the circumstances I really wasn't going there.

"You thought I was going home with you. That I was going to kiss you. That I was going to pull you so close your breasts were crushed against me, and your ass was tight in my hands."

"I—Quincy..." I shot a mortified look at the driver, who was sitting like stone, his hands glued to the steering wheel as he looked straight ahead.

"Hmm," Quincy said, then leaned over and handed the driver a ten-pound note. "Sorry to keep you waiting. This should cover the inconvenience."

And then, as if the delay was the only thing odd about this situation, he turned back to me and said, "That would be my very great pleasure, Eliza."

"But. Wait. What?" I wasn't sure if it was the wine or the shock, but he was making no sense.

He put a hand on the roof and leaned in. "You're dangerous, Eliza. You and me, we're a lot alike."

"That's bad?"

"I told you. It's dangerous."

"Oh. I see." I swallowed. And told myself not to cry. I didn't know him well enough to cry. Which begged the question of why tears were pooling in my eyes. "Well, it was—I mean, I had a nice day. Thank you. It, ah, it was really nice to meet you." *Bastard.*

His mouth twitched, and for a moment I feared I'd said that out loud. "Is that a brush off?"

"What, no. Wait—I thought *you* were brushing *me* off."

"Do you want me to?" Again with that tiny smile.

"No, and you're teasing me. What the hell, Quince?" At that, he laughed outright.

"Now I know."

"What?"

"If you and I spend much time together—and I certainly hope that we will—when you call me Quince it's because I'm in trouble."

I tilted my head and crossed my arms in a display of irritation. And I *was* irritated. But I was also hopelessly, giddily relieved. "Fine. You're in trouble. Don't scare me like that. You acted like you just wanted to send me on my way."

"I'll tell you what I want," he said, bending lower and speaking softer. But not so soft the driver couldn't hear.

"I don't just want to go home with you. I don't simply want to fuck you. I want to claim you, Eliza. I want you to surrender completely. To give me your trust entirely."

"I don't understand. I don't know what that means."

"I think you do. I want control." He brushed my lips with the pad of his free hand. "To take you how I want you. In the back of a cab like this. In your bed. Tied down. On your knees. I'll give you pleasure, Eliza. More than you can imagine or have experienced."

"You can't know that."

"I can, and I do." He hesitated a moment, his eyes burning into me. "I can't promise to save you from whatever darkness is inside you—only you can do that. But there are shadows in your eyes, and I want to be the one to bring back some light."

I tried to speak, but I couldn't. His words... His promises...

Was this really happening?

"I don't understand."

"Then let me make it perfectly clear. I want you. All of you. Not just a body in my bed. I want your trust, but not blindly. I will earn it. I can promise you that. And in exchange, the power over your pleasure belongs to me. It's a responsibility I will cherish. And that you will enjoy. Surrender, Eliza, and let the layers fall away."

My mouth had gone entirely dry, and though I knew I shouldn't look, I could see the driver's wide-eyed, open-mouthed reflection in the rearview mirror. I told myself to get out of the cab. To put a stop to this unexpected and entirely inappropriate proclamation.

But I didn't.

Instead, I asked, "Why?"

He smiled. That's when he knew he had me. And I couldn't even rally against his smugness because, dammit, he was right.

"Why?" I repeated, because right then, that was the only control I had.

"Because that's what I want. And I think we both know that it's what you need. Isn't it, love?"

"I—I barely know you."

"We both know that's not really true."

I opened my mouth to respond, but he pressed a finger over my lips and continued.

"I want every thing I said. I do. But not now. Not tonight when you're drunk and aroused and flattered and vulnerable. All I want from you tonight is to think about it."

"To think about it?" I sounded like a parrot and hated myself for it.

"Tomorrow," he said. "The offer for breakfast still stands." He nodded toward a small cafe at the end of the block. "If you want what I'm proposing, then meet me there at ten. I'll buy you that breakfast, and then we'll go from there."

"And if I don't?"

"I'll be disappointed, but I'll respect your decision." He leaned forward and kissed me on the cheek. "Good night, Eliza. I hope to see you tomorrow."

His words tormented me through the night. Making me ache with need. And also making me tremble with fear at the thought of being at his mercy. Not fear of him. Not fear that he would hurt me. But at the realization that what he was describing was the very thing that I'd been craving.

I went to him, of course. How could I not? He'd said I had the power to walk away, that the decision was mine. But it wasn't. Not really. He'd claimed me with his words. His touch. His promises. And so we had breakfast. And then, dear God, we had so much more.

———

Those sweet and bitter memories wash over me as I stand in The Hollywood Terrace's ornate ballroom and watch as Quincy Radcliffe walks toward me. The man to whom I once gave my heart and my soul, my submission and my trust. The man who, for three months in London, was my entire world.

I'd revealed so much to him. Secrets. Hopes. My deepest fears, my most horrible memories.

I'd told him things that only Emma knew, shared all the shadows of my past.

I'd opened my heart, and he'd challenged me. Pushed me. Protected me.

He'd taken me in hand, and he'd peeled away the layers, just as he promised he would. He'd revealed desires and needs I'd kept buried, and in his arms I felt more like myself than I ever thought possible.

He'd loved me. He'd cherished me.

At least that's what I thought.

Because once he'd truly captured me—once I was so in love with him that it felt like I'd been filled with light—he shattered me completely.

He left.

Just up and walked away, taking my heart and my soul with him.

And the son-of-a-bitch never once looked back.

So what the hell can he possibly know about Emma's disappearance?

5

"*TRUST YOU?*" Denny's words rattled in Quince's brain as he closed the distance between him and Eliza. "*Hell, yeah, I trust you. But I still want to know what you're up to.*"

"So demanding," he murmured.

"*Dammit, Quince. I'm your partner, not some nosy neighbor.*"

He put a hand over his mouth as if stifling a yawn. "I've located an ally."

That wasn't exactly true. Once upon a time, Eliza Tucker would have done anything for him. But things had changed. Hell, he'd been the one who changed them.

He knew he'd hurt her, and God knew it had ripped him up inside. Everything he'd suffered—every horror that he'd endured during those ten torturous weeks had felt like nothing compared to the pain in his heart when he realized that he couldn't go back to her. Couldn't even say goodbye for fear he'd—

No.

Now wasn't the time, not when he was working to a tight window. Not when Denny and the task force were waiting. And certainly not when the life of a thirteen-year-old girl hung in the balance.

Eliza might hate him—most of the time, he hated himself—but she *would* help him. He'd make sure of it.

He drew a breath, forcing his mind back to the present as he closed off those dark memories, locking them up tight inside the hidden corners of his mind. Over the years, he'd become an expert at pushing away the hell he'd endured. Or, at least, he told himself that he had. Considering how often the past seemed to haunt him lately, he couldn't help but wonder if those walls were starting to crack.

"An ally? Who the hell—"

"Not now." The words were terse, his lips barely moving. He was closer now, and Eliza had noticed him. From the Arctic ice in those deep blue eyes, he knew he'd been right; this wasn't going to be a warm and welcoming reunion.

Then again, under the circumstances, any greeting milder than castration counted as a win. God knew he deserved a hell of a lot worse.

"Mr. Canton!" Lassiter unpeeled his right hand from Eliza's back, then held it out to Quince for a firm handshake. "You have the look of a man who's enjoying himself."

Quince flashed his most charming smile. "You assured me that this would be a spectacular party. My compliments. For the event, for this stunning renovation, and," he added as he deliberately turned toward Eliza, "for the spectacular ornamentation."

"You have good taste," Lassiter said. "I'd say she's among the loveliest of the flowers decorating the room."

Quince knew the role he was supposed to play. With deliberate slowness, he let his eyes roam over her, as if inspecting the merchandise. When he reached her face, he allowed himself a hint of a smile, like a satisfied customer.

She didn't smile back, and he was surprised at the wave of loss that crested over him. During their time in London, he'd come to rely on that cockeyed smile, as dependable as the rising sun. She'd see him across a room, and her lips would curve in greeting, her dimple flashing and her eyes sparkling with an invitation that was impossible to ignore.

Considering the situation, he shouldn't have expected to see any sort of light in her eyes. But while reason knew that, his heart was less astute.

He willed his features to stay bland, fearing

that his disappointment would show on his face. Damn, but he wished he didn't still want her so much. Didn't still crave those wonderfully sweet days they spent exploring London—and the wickedly sensual nights they passed exploring each other.

He wanted to hold onto those memories. Wanted to wrap himself in them when the nightmares came. But how could he when they were so inextricably intertwined with pain? The bloody, brutal, fucking pain that he battled down every goddamn day. It had changed him. Tainted him.

He'd walked away so that he wouldn't soil her, too, and he'd sworn to himself it would be a clean break for both of them.

And yet here he was, standing in front of her, about to demand help from the one woman in the world who truly—and deservedly—hated him.

Beside him, Lassiter cleared his throat, and Quince realized that he was still staring at Eliza.

He turned to his host, his demeanor casual. As if he couldn't be bothered about anyone else's comfort or expectations. "Since she's with you, I assume she has yet to be keyed by one of the guests?"

He spoke matter-of-factly, and only to Lassiter. Eliza was chattel tonight, and although that simple reality burned a hole in his gut, there wasn't a damn thing he could do about it right then.

"Ah, I'm afraid I've been keeping Bunny occupied," Lassiter said, which Quincy understood as his claim on Eliza. Lassiter couldn't key her outright—he was the host, after all. But he could subtly suggest that if Quince disrupted his plans for the girl, then Lassiter would ensure that Robert Canton's name was conveniently dropped from future guest lists.

As far as Quince could tell, it was working. In just the time it had taken to cross the room, he'd noticed at least three of the guests stealing hungry glances her way. And one, a broad-shouldered man with a goatee and short ginger curls, hadn't taken his eyes off Eliza.

Fortunately for Quince, this was a one-time gig. He stepped toward her, then took her wrist, using the tip of his forefinger to trace the red ribbon she'd tied there. *Why had she worn it? Coincidence? Probably. But maybe there was a tiny bit of affection still lingering beneath the hatred? A sign that while she hadn't forgiven him, there might be a few lingering memories that she cherished?*

After a moment, she tugged her hand away. She met his eyes, silently daring him to call out her bad behavior.

"She and I have met before," he said, speaking again to Lassiter and not Eliza. "London, perhaps. No, it was Paris. Tell me, Scott. Do you know Sir Jonathan Semple?"

Lassiter's face showed that he did, and Quince wasn't surprised. Semple was an entitled British prick who had spent his life bouncing from party to party, spending his massive inheritance on drink and women. And he had a tendency to buy his friends' loyalty by buying them women.

Quince had infiltrated one of Semple's parties during his time at MI6, but that was long before he'd met Eliza. The mention of Semple's name to Lassiter was nothing more than camouflage.

He and Eliza had gone to Paris, though. One Friday on a lark they'd popped over to St. Pancras station, bought two same-day tickets, and taken the Chunnel to Paris. They'd found a small hotel on *la Rive Gauche*, and had wiled away a weekend both in bed and wandering the streets and shops of the City of Lights.

Because she said it was the memories that mattered, she'd turned down all the gifts he'd offered her except for a bundle of roses and a hard-bound copy of *Le Petit Prince*. "Emma used to read it to me," she'd told him. "I've always wanted to learn enough French to read it in the original language."

As for the roses, they'd stayed in the hotel room until they returned to London, when they'd left the still-lovely blooms for the maid. But he'd taken the ribbon that had bound the stems and tied it around her wrist. He hadn't known why at the time, other than some primal need to mark her as his own. She'd declined his offer of a Cartier diamond and sapphire bracelet, and he assumed she'd laugh at the ribbon, then take it off once they left for the train station.

But she kept it. For that matter, she wore it continuously.

She'd even been wearing it on that day he'd gone to see her. The day she didn't know about.

He'd watched her from across the street, and his heart had wrenched at the sight of her. He'd almost approached her. But how could he? He'd never again be the man in Paris who gave red ribbons. That man might have been a bit damaged and rough around the edges, but at his core, he was whole.

The man who'd watched her in silence was broken. Inside and out. And the shards of his soul would cut her to pieces.

He'd watched, hidden in the shadows. He'd mourned what might have been.

Then he'd left.

And when he finally reached the tiny, anti-septic government dorm that had become his temporary home, he'd wept.

Today, he didn't have the luxury of turning away. Didn't matter if it would hurt either one of them, he and Denny needed help. The princess needed help. Every one of Corbu's tormented victims needed help.

And Eliza was the only one he could turn to.

"You and Bunny crossed paths at one of Semple's parties?" Lassiter said. "What a stunning coincidence."

"Small world." Quince put on his most charming smile. "At the time I believe she was hopping all over the continent. If I recall, she was well worth the, ah, time I spent spent with her." He rubbed his fingers together to suggest her very steep price. But of course neither Robert Canton nor Lassiter would be so uncouth as to talk about a call girl's price out loud.

As Lassiter watched with a frown, Quince took Eliza's hand, forcing himself not to react to the visceral memory that washed over him merely from the feel of her warm, smooth skin. "It's a pleasure to see you again, Bunny."

Eliza's expression never changed, but she turned her hand over and opened it, so that Lassiter could see the ornate brass key now resting on her palm. "I'm a creature of habit," Quince said. "Once I find something I enjoy, I claim it for my own."

"A very wise policy, Mr. Canton." Lassiter seemed to be talking through his teeth, his desire for Eliza warring with his duties as a host.

Eventually, duty won out. "Go with Mr. Canton, Bunny." He gave her a pat on the rump, and Quince fought the urge to land a right hook on his jaw. "Make sure he enjoys himself this evening."

"Of course, Mr. Lassiter." Her voice was as smooth as he remembered, strong and musical. A good voice for the stage, and he wondered what had happened to her acting career. He'd checked on her over the years, and he knew she worked steadily. So why was she now performing sex acts for strange men instead of Shakespeare? The question sat heavy in his gut, especially considering everything he knew about her. Was she here merely as a practical solution to some unmanageable debt? Or was there a darker need lingering under the surface? Some void she was desperately, foolishly trying to fill?

He wanted to know. Hell, he wanted to help.

But now wasn't the time. "With me," he said, relieved when she came easily, almost eagerly.

"So what do you have to tell me," she whispered, as soon as they were out of earshot.

Tell her? Tell her what?

What he was doing there? Why he'd left her?

A thousand possible questions burned in his brain, but he didn't have time to examine any of them. Right then, all that mattered was getting her to his room and getting her hands in position on that relay.

"Sounds like you're on the move," Denny whispered in his ear. *"Cough to confirm."*

He coughed.

"I'll expect to hear from you in three. Get to the room."

He didn't bother acknowledging again. But he did pick up his speed. Eliza's heels clicked beside him. "Qui—I mean, *Robert*."

"We'll talk in my room." They'd reached the elevator where several groping couples waited for the car to arrive. He slid an arm around her waist and for a moment he was lost in the memory of her soft curves. Of the way they'd once fit together so perfectly, as if they were two halves of a whole.

Then she stiffened and the illusion shattered. Now, he was all ragged edges and missing pieces. Maybe they'd fit once, but they could never again.

The doors opened and they followed the other couples into the mirrored interior of the elevator car. He saw them reflected back at him. Men falling into lust. Women dialing up the heat. For these ladies, he knew, it was all about the payday. But you couldn't tell from the images in the mirror. Each and every one was putting on an award winning performance—and not a single person in the car was paying any attention at all to him and Eliza.

And thank God for that.

The car descended to the fourth floor, and they

got off, along with two other couples who turned in the opposite direction. Quince kept a firm hand at Eliza's waist, afraid she'd say or do something to attract attention, but she moved in step with him, cooperating fully. By all appearances she was just as keen to get to the room as he was. She wanted an explanation, of course. And he'd give her one—he owed her that.

But it would come after they'd completed the mission. Call it incentive. Hell, call it payment.

Whatever it took, he'd promise it. Because one quick glance at the analog face of the Patek Philippe confirmed what he already knew—they were running out of time.

The lights from the city illuminated the hall-way, streaming in through a floor-to-ceiling window framed by an ornate, geometric carving. A similar window stood in his room opposite the king sized bed. And that window was handy for two reasons. One, it had provided Denny with access to the fire escape that led to street level, allowing her to slink across Hollywood Boulevard to the opposite office building. The original plan had been that she'd set up the transmitter, then return to this room and operate the relay, adjusting for any variation in the alignment so that the signal coming through the window was fully captured, then relayed into the building's interior. And Lassiter's office.

Now, of course, she had to keep the transmitter

steady. Eliza would have to take over the role of middleman, making sure the relay's indicator stayed in the green zone so that he could do his job downstairs.

Hell of a risk, but he had no choice.

At the room, he pulled out the flat, hotel-style card key. The brass key Quince had given Eliza was only for show—he'd tried it out of curiosity and learned that not only did it not unlock the door, but that the door couldn't be unlocked from the inside without the card key. Apparently the men who'd come expecting companionship for the night required assurance that their companion wouldn't be taking her leave before they were done with her.

Quince used the card key and opened the door, ushering Eliza in before him.

The second the door closed behind them, she whipped around. "Why did you insist on the red ribbon? You couldn't have possibly known it was me. Did you know it was Emma?"

He stared at her, trying—and failing—to make sense of her words. All he understood was *Emma.* But he didn't know what tonight's party or the ribbon had to do with her sister. And right then, he didn't have time to find out.

"Eliza, I don't—"

"*No.*" She thrust her hands up and out, landing them hard on his chest. The move was so completely unexpected that he didn't have time to compensate, and he stumbled back, then landed against the door with a *thud*.

"What the bloody hell do—"

"Goddammit, Quincy! Don't you dare play games with me."

"She's Eliza?" The shock in Denny's voice reverberated through his head. Of all of his friends, Denny was the only one in whom he'd confided about his past. About Eliza. And about what had happened. Not everything—God, he barely let himself remember everything—but he'd told her enough. And he knew her well enough to know she had to be both curious and sympathetic.

Mostly, though, she'd be worried about the mission.

A thought that was borne out by her next comment. *"Put it away for later, Q. The clock's ticking."*

"I know," he snarled.

"Then talk to me," Eliza pressed, talking over his thoughts and Denny's curse in his ear. "You're the one who contacted me, dammit."

"Fuck." He ground out the word at the same time he grabbed Eliza's wrist. In one swift motion, he whipped her around, so that they'd completely changed positions. Now she was against the door and he was the one blocking her.

He had one hand on her wrist, pressed tight above her head. The other he had cupped over her elbow, which was also firm against the door. In that position, there were only inches between them. They were intimately close, and he could feel her heat—her fury—burning through him.

He was a full head taller than her, and he looked down into her fiery upturned face. Her eyes burned like a blue flame, and he could practically see the wheels in her mind turning.

"Let. Me. Go."

He ignored her. "I don't know why you're here. I don't know why you think I know something about your sister. I do know that you hate me, and I can't say that I blame you." He saw the flicker in her eyes and the shadow on her face. He ignored it. "We can talk. I'll help you if I can. But right now you're going to help me. It's not a question. It's not a request. I'm running out of time, and I need you."

She spat in his face.

She actually, truly, spat in his face.

"Six minutes. You have six minutes to get into the office and online."

Shit. Two floors below and he had to break into the office and then boot up the computer.

"I'm really sorry about this, Eliza."

Her eyes widened as her mouth parted, either to spit again or to ask what he meant.

He didn't take the time to find out which. "But I need your help."

"What—" she began, but her question was cut

off as he tugged her away from the door, and in one smooth motion spun her around and tossed her onto the bed. She yelped and started to rise, but he didn't give her the chance.

He moved fast, getting onto the bed and straddling her waist before she even had time to react. Then he leaned forward, drew a pair of fluffy pink handcuffs out of the bedside table, and said very simply, "Trust me."

6

"WHAT THE HELL, QUINCY!" He's holding fuzzy pink handcuffs in one hand and reaching for my arm with the other. With one quick, efficient movement, he snaps the cuff around my left wrist. "Trust you?" I kick, trying to dislodge him, but his knees are tight at my waist, like I'm a bucking bronco and he's a rodeo star. "I tried that, remember? And it didn't work out too well for me."

He's holding onto the free end of the cuff as he leans toward one of the metal bars that make up this party theme-compatible headboard. His hips rise a bit as he stretches, and I take advantage by bouncing my ass on the bed, then thrusting up, trying to dislodge him.

It doesn't work. All it does is upset his balance so that he falls on top of me, crushing my breasts as he knocks the wind out of me.

For one moment, he hovers over me, his lips slightly parted as his breath comes hard and fast. His eyes are locked on mine, his pupils dilated. I can see his pulse beating at his temple, and I can smell his cologne. That's what does it. That's what finally makes my muscles go slack in surrender— that familiar scent that I'd once associated with feeling safe and warm and loved.

"Quincy," I whisper, at the same time I hear a sharp, distinctive, *click,* and he sits back, once against straddling my hips in a position that would be intimate if it weren't so damned infuriating.

Dammit, dammit, *dammit.*

I yank my arm, wincing when I can't pull it down from over my head. "I swear to God, Quincy, I'm going to—"

"—do exactly what I say," he finishes. "Because I don't have time to argue or explain."

He reaches for my other hand, and I completely lose my shit. I kick and scream and writhe and practically growl at him. I'm not *scared* so much as confused and pissed and frustrated. I came to find a clue about Emma's disappearance. I didn't bargain on Quincy, and seeing him has thrown me completely off balance.

Despite my contortions, he grabs hold of my wrist. I wasn't a match for him when I was completely free, and since I'm now attached to the bed, my resistance is both lame and futile. I'm quite certain there's another set of cuffs in that drawer, and that pretty soon I'll be spread-eagled across this damn bed.

The thought sends a shiver of anticipation running through me, and that—more than anything Quincy has done tonight—is what really pisses me off.

"I swear to God, if you cuff my right hand to the bed you better intend to leave me here forever, because I will rip your balls off with my teeth."

"How remarkably innovative," he says mildly. "And I'm not cuffing you."

That surprising statement is punctuated by him taking something about the size of a cell phone out of his pocket and thrusting it into my right hand. He curls my fingers around it, then holds them in place. My thumb's on a toggle button, and I'm staring at a small screen with a single vibrating needle. The needle's intersecting a line that's red on both sides and green in the middle. Right now, it's moving toward the red.

"Push down," he says. "Keep the needle in the green."

"Why should I do anything you say?"

"Eliza, please." He presses a gentle kiss to my forehead, the gesture so surprising that my control slips, and I feel tears prick my eyes. "If our time in London meant anything, then do this one thing for me."

I want to ask why. I want to ask what the hell this is about. I want to ask—oh, hell. The whole thing is so damn strange I don't even know what I want to ask. All I know for sure is that I don't know anything at all. Except that I'm pretty sure he doesn't know a thing about Emma.

He's off the bed and practically sprinting toward the door.

"You're *leaving* me?"

He brushes a hand over his ear, then mutters a curse. "I'm out of time. Remember, keep it in the green. There's a little girl's life at stake, El. And she doesn't have an Emma watching over her like you did. Just do this."

Before I can catch my breath, he's gone, and I'm left tied to a bed and holding the freaky gizmo as the needle wavers toward the red.

For a fraction of a second I allow myself the fantasy of hurling the device across the room.

I don't do it.

I have no idea what Quincy's in the middle of, and I damn sure don't trust him. But as I lie there cuffed to the bed, I realize one vital thing—I believe him.

I know one more thing, too. I never really knew Quincy Radcliffe. Because the man who cuffed me to this bed and bolted out of this room isn't a financial consultant. Not now. Probably not ever.

I spent three glorious months in a foreign

country falling in love with a man who was a ghost. Who didn't really exist. And for the life of me, I can't decide if that makes me feel better or worse.

———

I'm not wearing a watch, and there's no clock in the room, so I don't know how much time passes as I toggle and adjust, toggle and adjust. It's hardly a difficult chore, but I give it my all, not only because Quincy said it was important, but also because the minute adjustments occupy my mind, leaving only a tiny bit of mental background space in which to wonder about what he's doing and who he really is.

I've zeroed in on the big picture, of course. He's either law enforcement or intelligence, that much would probably be obvious to anyone, but to me it's like a big, red beacon of *duh*. After all, my sister was scary-deep in the intelligence world for over a decade, and a PI for even longer. First as her government cover, and then as a legit, full-time job after she left the agency.

I've even worked part time in her office, running skip-traces on her computer, filing documents, and typing client reports for both her and Lorenzo.

So, yeah. I know the signs. And they're flashing neon where Quincy is concerned.

Then again, maybe he's a master thief who

tossed in the bit about the teenager because he has a talent for the con.

If that's the case, I can go back to hating him.

If he's a spook ... well, then I have to wonder if that's what he was doing back in London. And if so, is that why he disappeared? Some botched up mission?

It makes sense, and I like it better than the alternative theory that he simply tired of me and walked away.

But that begs the question of why he didn't come back to me when he came back to London.

Because I know he returned. I saw him. The day before I returned to Manhattan I'd been at loose ends. Part of me was desperate to get home and away from the memories that lurked around every corner. Another part wanted to hold on tight to my time with Quincy. I still couldn't quite believe that he'd really just up and disappeared. One day, he'd been touching me intimately and telling me that he loved me. The next, he was gone.

It didn't make sense. The man I knew—the man in whom I'd confided my deepest secrets and most intimate desires—couldn't be the kind of man who could cut me so deeply. On the contrary, my months with Quincy had been like a balm to my soul. He'd not only healed me, he'd helped me discover parts of myself that I'd kept buried since childhood, and I couldn't wrap my head around his betrayal. Because if he'd truly left me—if he'd actually, purposefully walked away with no contact and no explanation—then that's exactly what it was. A betrayal of the most brutal kind.

He'd left on a Friday for what was supposed to be a quick weekend trip. "I have to play nice with the client. Handhold a bit and play the social game." I'd nodded my understanding. Networking is a huge part of acting; I assumed it was the same in the corporate world, too. I'd expected him back on Monday, but didn't start getting worried until Tuesday. He hadn't called or texted while he was away, but that was easy to justify. He was busy. International rates were expensive. They'd gone into rural China where cell service is spotty.

Those were all the justifications that ran through my head on Tuesday and Wednesday. By Thursday I was dialing Emma for reassurance, then hanging up before it rang and telling myself I was being a baby. By Friday, I was officially nervous, and I let the call to my sister ring through. She told me not to worry. It was probably nothing and he'd come home with apologies and presents. That soothed me over the weekend, but by Monday I was a wreck.

I tried to hold off calling. I told myself he'd gotten sick. He was catching up at work. He was in Switzerland counting the money in a private numbered account. Probably not accurate, but since I had no idea what his job actually entailed it was the best I could come up with. But it wasn't good enough, and I called his office at eight o'clock sharp.

He'd given me his card after our first actual date—the one that had started with breakfast and lasted a full thirty-six hours. "In case you ever need someone experienced in financing multinational corporations."

"Oh, I'll definitely keep it handy then," I'd said, then tucked it neatly into my back pocket. I hadn't needed it since then. Why would I when we'd been together almost constantly from that moment on?

I'd so thoroughly convinced myself that he must still be out of the country—*had I gotten the dates wrong?*—that I actually apologized when the receptionist answered the phone.

"I hate to bother you—and I know he's probably still in China—but I'm trying to reach Quincy Radcliffe. Is he—"

"One moment please." The crisp, efficient female voice was followed in short order by soothing classical hold music. Which was good. Because her reaction had surprised me. And, yeah, I needed to be soothed.

What did it mean? That he was right there at his desk? That he'd flirted with her that morning? That we only dated for three months and even though that time had been magical, I needed to get over myself?

"This is Andrew Donovan. How can I help you? Hello?"

"I—what? Oh." I blinked, only then realizing that I'd lowered the phone. I pushed the button to switch to the speaker. "I'm here. Sorry. I'm trying to reach Quincy Radcliffe."

"Who's calling, please?"

"My name's Eliza Tucker. I'm his—I mean, we were sort of dating, and then he went on a business trip and—" I broke off, feeling suddenly foolish, then cleared my throat. "I just haven't heard from him, and I'm a little worried."

"I see. Yes, well I'm sorry to tell you that Mr. Radcliffe decided to transfer to our Taipei office."

My knees turned to liquid and I slid down the wall. "I see." I didn't see. I couldn't see a single freaking thing. "Um, can you give me his new work number? I've tried his cell, but—"

"I'm sorry, but all client calls are being routed through our switchboard."

"Oh, well, that's fine. You can just route me that way. What time is it in Taipei?"

"I'm afraid we can only forward client calls."

"But I—"

"I'm sorry we couldn't be of more help."

"But—"

"Have a good day, Ms. Tucker."

And then he hung up, which is when I threw my phone across the room, shattering the damn thing.

I didn't care. I was too numb to care.

And for three days, all I did was sleep.

On the fourth day I told myself that something really massive must have gone down at work. He was battling for his career, and of course calling me got pushed to the back burner. But we were pushing on two weeks, and surely he'd left a voice mail by now.

Which, of course, I couldn't check because of my phone.

Getting a replacement was a bit of a production because I wasn't in the good old U.S. of A., but Emma and DHL helped, and soon a replacement phone fully loaded with my account info arrived at my London flat. By that time, I'd learned how to check voicemail remotely—there was nothing—but I was holding out hope that a half dozen text messages would pop up the moment I had a signal.

Nada.

I wasn't really surprised. My computer receives messages, too. And Quincy knew my email address.

That's when I went back to bed. A nest lined with pillows, quilts, five remotes, and a variety of crisps and biscuits, even though I was craving chips and cookies.

For the record, I was done with London. Done with Quince. Done with men.

And I would have gotten my ass right back to Manhattan if I'd had a place to go. Since I didn't, I wallowed, alternating between sleep, action movies —*no* romances—and junk food.

Three days later, I woke up to Emma stroking my hair. "You need a shower," she'd said.

"Great to see you, too." I shoved myself up on my elbows and blinked. She'd turned on the lights, and I grimaced as a million tiny pins started poking at my eyeballs. "How'd you get in?"

Her brows rose, and I waved the question away. "Forget I asked that." Emma started working on her B&E skills when I was four and she was eleven. That was the year our father started locking us in the utility room. To say she has mad skills now is an understatement. Emma has lots of skills. Most of which I'm not supposed to know about. She swore me to secrecy the day everything changed for us. The day her murder arrest went *poof* and she got a scholarship to Pepperdine.

My sister's life is like something out of an action movie, but to me, she's always just been Emma. Sister, mom, friend. There's nothing we won't do for each other, and tops of that list is that we don't spill secrets.

"You didn't have to come," I said.

"Don't be stupid." And then my sister did

exactly what she'd done for my entire life. She pulled me out of hell. She protected me. And she made me strong again.

So strong, that for my remaining months in London, I convinced myself that Quincy hadn't destroyed me. That our time together had been a fun dalliance, but that's all. Sexual exploration, a few hundred mind-blowing orgasms, and a new level of self-awareness for yours truly.

It wasn't a travesty that he'd disappeared. Soon enough I would have zipped off back to the States anyway. On the contrary, it was convenient. No unpleasant goodbyes. No trying to squeeze a square vacation romance into a round life hole.

That, at least, was the mantra I repeated daily, and as my time in London drew to a close, I even started to believe it.

At least until that last day when I got it into my head to walk by his office.

I remember sighing as I went into the lobby with no real purpose other than to rest my feet. I sat there, scrolling through my phone, and when I'd looked up, there he was.

Not that he'd seen me. No, he was in the lobby coffee shop, undoubtedly ordering a double espresso, something he did every day and which I told him was completely un-British. Weren't Brits supposed to be all about the tea?

I started to push off the bench—*he was here. He was back.*

But then the real truth of the matter hit me. *He was here—but he hadn't called me. Hadn't left a message. Hadn't done a single, goddamn thing.*

Maybe he had a family tucked away and maybe he didn't. Maybe he was based in Taipei now and maybe he wasn't.

I didn't know. I told myself I didn't care.

Because the bottom line was that Quincy Radcliffe had walked away. And when he'd come back, he hadn't returned to me.

———

The click of the lock yanks me from my memories, and my eyes cut to the door as I exhale with relief. I want to pass off the responsibility for this gadget, and then I want to get out of here, away from Quincy and the brutal memories that keep assaulting me.

Most important, I need to get back to square one. Because if Quincy isn't Mr. X, then that means that Mr. X never showed up at the party, and I'm no closer to finding my sister.

"Finally," I say as the door begins to move. "Take your gizmo and—"

He steps inside, and I snap my mouth closed.

It's not Quincy.

This man has short, curly red hair. His face is too large and his eyes too small. He wears glasses that sit on a bulbous nose, and his lips are unnaturally pale, so when he speaks, it's almost as if a hole is opening up in his face.

He speaks now, and I instinctively scoot backward until my back is pressed against the headboard, my cuffed arm twisting awkwardly as my free hand clutches the gadget for dear life.

"You're a hard woman to find."

He's such an unattractive man, that his pleasant, almost gentle voice surprises me into speech. "I —I didn't know you were looking for me."

Even as I say the words, I realize my mistake. I'd noticed him watching me at the party, but paid him little mind. After all, he never approached me and never commented on the ribbon tied to my wrist. I assumed he was just a guest sussing out the possibilities.

"You," I say, sparing a look at the gizmo and toggling the switch down to edge the needle further into the green. "You're Mr. X." I relax a little. After all, this is the man I'd come to meet. "Why didn't you come to me? We could have—"

My words are cut off by my scream as he leaps onto the bed, yanks my hair back, and presses the blade of a knife against my throat. I go completely still, completely cold. His face is right in front of mine, and I don't see anything human in his eyes.

I hear a small mewling noise and realize it's coming from me.

"Where is she?"

I open my mouth, but it's too dry to speak. I don't know what I'd say anyway. He can't be talking about Emma. He thinks *I'm* Emma. Doesn't he?

His thumb presses tight against my jugular. "I could just as easily push down with this blade. Do you understand?"

I'm too afraid that a nod will slice my throat, and I can't find my voice. I manage a strangled sound that he takes as an affirmative.

"I'm glad we understand each other. The girl, you fucking bitch. Where did you hide the girl?"

That's when it clicks. *Quincy's thirteen-year-old.* That's who he's looking for.

And not only do I have no clue where she is, I'm terribly afraid that I've just destroyed Quincy's chance to protect her. Because in my terror at being attacked at knifepoint, I'd managed to lose the gadget.

I squeeze my right hand as if it will magically appear, but there's only air. I whimper, terrified for me and also horribly guilty about that girl. I know what it's like to be young and afraid. Emma had been there to protect me, just as Quincy's trying to protect this girl. And I went and screwed it up for him.

"Where?"

I start to speak, but I can't tell him that I don't know, and I'm too scared to concoct a lie. All I can manage to do is gape at him and whimper an incomprehensible medley of "I, uh, I—"

"Stupid cunt," Mr. X snarls as he takes the knife from my neck and, before I can even breathe a sigh of relief, drags it from my neck to the slit at my thigh, slicing my dress in one easy motion, then pulling it wide, so that I'm naked except for my tiny thong panties.

The tip of the knife must have grazed my skin, because I see small dots of blood gathering in a line from my cleavage all the way down to my belly button. I hadn't felt pain in the moment, but now the wound begins to sting and tears prick my eyes. I'm terrified and lost and entirely at this bastard's mercy. I want to scream for Quincy—for anybody— but I know that if I do, it will be the last sound I make.

Futilely, I tug on my cuffed arm as I throw my free arm over my breasts to shield myself. I try to pull up my legs so that I can curl up into a ball, but he's sitting just above my knees as he moves the knife slowly back and forth above the band of my thong.

"Please." My voice is shaking. "Please don't."

"Don't?" He lifts the blade. "But why not? It's a party, isn't it? And you're all soft and pretty." As he talks, he's creeping up my body until his face is over my breasts. I could thrust my hand up and punch him—I'm certain of it. I was even in a movie once where I did that very thing. In the movie I knocked out the bad guy and got away.

I'm thinking that won't happen here.

"Move your arm, bitch."

I shake my head and keep my arm protectively over my breasts.

"Have it your way," he says. "You want to stay that way, then fine by me. But remember it was your choice." His eyes meet mine, and all I see is a man who's dead inside. "You move and you'll regret it."

And then, as I fight to stay absolutely still, he zips the razor sharp edge of the blade along the underside of my breast.

I whimper, more in fear than the pain, because it's happened so fast I haven't even registered the pain yet.

"Shut your mouth, you cunt. I barely nicked you. But next time, I'll slice the whole titty off."

"No. Please, no." My eyes and throat are full of tears, my body sharp with pain and fear. "Please, please no."

"Then talk you useless whore. Where'd you stash the little bitch?"

"She's in ... she's in..." I don't have to work to make my voice tremble; I'm already terrified. Especially since I don't know what to tell him, and all I can do is buy time and hope that if he believes I know where the girl is, that he won't kill me right this very second.

"*Now.*"

I yelp as he rests the knife blade against my nipple, then I scrunch my eyes closed and cry out inside my head to my sister. *I'm sorry, I'm sorry. I'm so, so sorry.*

I failed her. I failed me. And I'm all out of options.

The mattress shifts, and I gasp as the knife clips the underside of my chin. "Talk. Now. Or else I skewer you."

I'm dead, and I know it.

I never expected the end to come like this.

Except it didn't. It hasn't.

With a jolt, I realize that the pressure against my chin is gone, as is Mr. X's weight on top of me.

More than that, I feel the lingering sting of the slice under my breasts, the pain ratcheting up with each breath and beat of my heart. Not something I'd usually celebrate, but surely if I were dead there'd be no pain at all.

I giggle, and a voice in my head tells me I'm in shock. The voice is probably right. This really isn't a giggling kind of scenario. And, in fact, I swallow the next bubble of laughter when I open my eyes and see Quincy beside the bed, his arm around Mr.

X's throat in what looks to be the kind of hold that could easily snap a neck.

And you know what? I'm perfectly okay with that.

But instead of falling down dead, Mr. X thrusts his body backward so that Quincy is shoved against the dresser near the now-closed door. The impact makes Quincy loosen his grip, and Mr. X breaks free. Immediately, he lunges, leading with the knife. Even I can tell that was a mistake. Quincy knocks it free with a sideways swipe of his arm, and at the same time his leg lashes out to slam into Mr. X's kneecap.

Mr. X lets out a wild howl, then stumbles toward the door. He yanks it open, then slams past a wide-eyed blonde in a sheer black dress over what looks like a black unitard.

"Fuck!" She bends over and pulls off a black-heeled sandal, then hurls it down the hall in the direction Mr. X disappeared. At the same time, Quincy races out the door and disappears from view, his cry of, *Check her!* lingering in the air.

Immediately, the blonde is in the doorway. Her eyes skim over the room and over me. She's clearly a professional, because her only reaction is a pair of slightly widened eyes. Outside the room, I hear glass shatter. She must hear it, too, but she doesn't react. Her attention is entirely on me, and she rushes to my side, then sits carefully beside me on the bed.

"I'm Denise," she says, pressing her hand gently to my forehead. "I'm going to help you."

I nod, in shock. I'm lying on top of the spread, and I'm grateful when she reaches over me and tugs the free half over my exposed body. She's searching the drawer for the handcuff key when Quincy enters. He takes one look at me, and I watch the emotions play over his face. Fear, then fury, then something soft and tender.

Then absolutely nothing at all.

"He went through the window."

Denise looks up at him. "What? He jumped?"

"Not exactly."

I see that register on her face, and she nods. "Any activity from the other rooms on the floor?"

"Not so far. Party's shut down and everyone's snug in their rooms."

Denise nods. "At least in that regard we seem to have caught a break."

"Did you," I begin, but my throat is so dry, I have to clear it. They both look at me when I begin again. "I dropped the thing. When he came in."

The damn tears start up again, and Quincy comes to sit by my side, then gently takes my hand.

"I didn't mean to," I say. "Did I—I mean, is it okay? Will the girl be okay?"

His expression never changes, but nods. "You did good. We got what we came for thanks to you."

I nod, relieved. My eyes are so heavy. Intellectually, I know it's the shock. I need to sleep. But I don't want to stay here. "I want to go home," I murmur.

"I'm all for getting out of here, too," Quincy says.

"No argument from me." Denise crosses to the window, then grimaces. "I need to go down. See if he survived."

She starts to lift the sash, then looks from me to Quincy, then back to me again. "On second thought, maybe you should go." She's clearly speaking to Quincy—I'm hardly in a position to go anywhere—but she's looking at me. And right away I understand that she knows at least some of our story. For all I know, she knows more of the real story of Quincy and Eliza than I do.

"I'm not leaving her."

"Quince." Her voice is as firm as his, and I decide in that second that I like this woman. She reminds me of Emma.

"It's okay."

They both turn to look at me, and I realize that my voice is so low and so raw that they probably couldn't even make out my words. I lick my lips and try again. "Quincy can stay."

She nods and raises the windowpane, and for

the first time I realize she's planning to leave that way. I must look confused, because she says, "Fire escape."

"Send me a status on our red-haired friend when you hit ground level. I'll get her out of here and signal you when we're clear."

"Will do." She starts to pull the shift-style dress over her head, leaving her clad in skintight black.

"What the hell, Denny?"

She tosses it to him. "She'll need it."

She's right. It's thin and black and won't cover anything, but technically I'll be dressed. And at a party like this, no one will think twice if I walk down to the lobby in it.

By the time Quincy brings the dress to me, she's gone.

He sits on the edge of the bed, then takes my free hand. His grip is firm but gentle. As soothing as his proximity. I don't know what's going on here tonight, not really, but in this tiny bubble of time, I'm grateful that he's with me.

He gently pushes my hair back off my face. "How badly are you hurt?" His voice is even. No nonsense. Like a doctor. And for some reason, that soothes me even more.

As he speaks, he pulls the cuff key out of his pocket and leans over me, reaching for my right wrist. The position puts his face in front of mine, his chest brushing against the spread that now covers my bare breasts. It's oddly intimate, the memories of him mixing with my lingering fear and the way that he is now so sweetly tending to me.

"Eliza?"

I have to rewind the conversation to remember his question. "Oh. Um, I don't think I need stitches. He—ah, he cut my dress off. And he—" I turn my face away.

"He cut you?" He sits up quickly, his voice sharp. My wrist is free now, and I use my right hand to massage it. For a moment, I don't even notice that his abrupt motion caused the spread to shift off me, exposing my bare hip and the side of my breast.

I start to tug it back, but he stills my hand, and as he does the side of his hand brushes my bare hip and I tremble in response to the sweet, horrible, visceral memory that washes over me, culminating in a wave of regret and longing so powerful I almost curl up into myself.

If he notices, he doesn't react. "Let me see what he did to you."

I shake my head and hold the spread in place.

"Eliza. I need to see. I need to know if you need stitches."

"I'm fine."

"No, love, you're not."

I close my eyes. "Don't call me that." I hear the break in my voice and hate myself. "Please."

When I open my eyes, he's looking at me, his gray eyes stormy. "I'm so damn sorry."

"Now isn't the time."

He stands, then shoves his hands into his pockets. "I suppose it isn't. But dammit, Eliza, it's my fault this happened to you. Please. I need to be sure you're okay."

For a moment, he just looks at me. I want to ask him about our past. I want to ask what the hell he's doing here. I want to ask about Emma, even though I'm pretty sure he knows nothing about her, and about the little girl. I need to tell him why I came here tonight. That Emma is missing, and that the man who attacked me had set up a meeting through a message board. I need to tell him that Mr. X asked about the little girl, and I don't understand why.

Somehow, Quincy is tied into the same thing that Emma was investigating. Which means he can help me find her. Which means I need him.

But I don't tell him any of that. Instead, I say, "It's not your fault, and I don't think I need stitches. But I definitely need some Band-Aids."

And then, because I really do understand that he needs to see for himself, I bite my lower lip, then carefully readjust the bedspread to reveal the incision at the lower part of my breast as well as the long, thin trail of blood from my breastbone to my bellybutton.

"Eliza. Oh, Christ, baby, no." He drops to the

edge of the bed, and in that moment he looks as exhausted as I feel.

"Is it that bad?"

He shakes his head. "Yes. No. You don't need stitches." Slowly, his finger traces the curve of my breast, not touching the cut, but near it. His finger is warm, and I bite my lower lip, but I don't tell him to stop. Right or wrong, I want his touch. Not intimately. Not sexually. But so help me, I want to be tended to. I want to be taken care of. I want answers and my sister and peace. I've fallen down the rabbit hole of a nightmare, and I don't have the slightest idea how to claw my way out again.

And right now, the only thing that's keeping me anchored is the touch and attention of this man who once destroyed me.

7

RAGE BURNED THROUGH HIM. A cold, hard fury at himself for pulling her into this, and at the red-haired man for torturing her for something that she wasn't even part of.

He'd walked away from her in order to keep her safe and whole. And now, because of him, she'd been scared, tortured, and mutilated.

He clenched a fist at his side, fighting against the monster now rising in his chest. A beast that fed on his anger, his helplessness. That he had to battle back if he was going to be any help to her at all.

Slowly, he unfurled his hand, letting himself feel every motion, assuring himself that he was in control. That it was *him* in this room with her. Quincy James Radcliffe. That he was here. That he was present. And that no one—not him, not the red-haired man, not anyone—would hurt her.

"Quincy?"

He drew in a breath, then gently cupped her cheek. Her blue eyes locked on his, and he saw the trust reflected back at him. Despite every way he'd hurt her, she wasn't running.

Maybe she should...

He pushed the thought away as foolish. As dangerous as they might be together, until he got her the hell away from The Terrace, he was keeping her close.

"I'm on the ground," Denny said. *"Subject terminated. Witness called it in, so we'll have company soon. I'll catch you at HQ."*

"Roger that."

Eliza lifted a brow, and he just shrugged. He'd fill her in later. Right now, he was more concerned with her wounds. Gently, he ran his finger over the long scrape marks on her belly. Lines and dots, like Morse code.

She bit her lower lip, wincing slightly, but she didn't flinch. "I'm so sorry," he said, even though the words were nothing but hollow platitudes.

"It's not that bad. At least the bleeding's stopped. And considering I was expecting to be dead, I'm perfectly fine with the pain." She grimaced as she pushed herself up onto her elbows, sucking in air. "Okay, maybe *fine* isn't entirely accurate."

"We'll find you some pain killers. First, we

need to get out of here." He'd always intended to exit the building after downloading Lassiter's files, but now it was even more of a necessity. Once the police or a witness identified the window from which Red fell, they'd surely come inside and start knocking on doors.

He studied Eliza with a frown. "Do they know your real name?"

She shook her head.

"Good." He nodded, indicating Denny's dress. "Do you need help putting it on?"

Her cheeks flushed, and she dropped her gaze. "I—no. I can manage it. Can you, um..."

He stood and turned away from her, facing the window. As he did, he realized that he could see a partial reflection in the raised pane. A gentleman would divert his eyes. He watched. Once upon a time, he'd believed he could be a gentleman. Now, he knew better.

She stood gingerly, as if it hurt to move, which he knew it did. He thought of the shallow cuts that had once covered his chest and abdomen, along with his inner thighs. The wounds were no longer open; instead he was marked by a web of thin, white scars. The skin had long ago knitted, the pain only a brutal memory. But that didn't mean he was healed. Far from it.

He pressed his fingers to his temples, and forced the memories back, focusing instead on the reflection of the woman who had once belonged to him.

She moved slowly, and the motion of raising the dress over her head accentuated her small waist and perfect breasts. She had an athletic frame. Long and lean and lovely. Some men might consider her breasts too small, but they'd be wrong. He'd tasted those breasts, held their weight in his hands. He recalled one time in particular when he'd dragged his teeth over her erect nipple. It was as if he'd lit a firecracker inside her. Her ankles and wrists had been bound to the bed, and she'd arched up, her body practically vibrating with pleasure as she moaned his name and begged him for more. For everything.

He'd slid his hand under her skirt, his fingers teasing their way inside her soaked panties. She'd bucked against him, fucking his hand like a wild thing, and then begged for his cock. He'd denied her, of course. Made her wait until she was so hungry for him she could barely breathe. Then he'd buried himself in her, his fingers squeezing her nipples as he watched passion and euphoria rise on her face as he took her to the limit and she exploded in his arms, her loud cries pushing him over the edge along with her.

That same memory had threatened to burst free earlier, when he'd pulled out the cuff and attached her to the bed. He'd pushed it brutally away, both because he needed to focus on the job and because he had no business remembering. Not when he could no longer have her. There was no point to self-flagellation, after all. It didn't even faze his demons.

Now, though...

Now he realized that he was either a shamefully weak man or a fucking masochist, because even though he knew that he couldn't ever have Eliza in his bed again, he'd still opened the floodgates to his memories, and now his cock was straining against his trousers, on high alert from the enticing, delicious, erotic images flooding his brain.

"Okay," she said as he heard the first wail of sirens approaching the building. "I'm dressed. Not that it makes much difference in this outfit..."

He focused on the carpet, drawing deep breaths before he turned around. It wouldn't do for her to see just how much her presence—and his memories—had affected him. But as soon as he saw her standing there in the sheer black shift, her nipples hard against the thin material and her tiny, flesh-colored thong barely covering her sweet pussy, his cock sprang to attention all over again.

She met his eyes, then crossed her arms over her chest.

Damn. "Sorry, love. The dress suits you."

She rolled her eyes, but at the same time, some

of the tension dropped away. "Are we ready?" She took a step toward the door.

"Not that way."

She turned, her brow furrowed. "Teleportation?"

"Funny. The fire escape."

He expected her to protest, and he had all the reasons why they couldn't go out the front lined up and ready to go. Most important, avoiding the authorities.

As for reason number two, that stemmed from the fact that he'd just hacked Lassiter's computer system and now held in his pocket a flash drive with stolen information that he was quite certain Lassiter would kill for. Probably Lassiter had yet to discover the breach. But that wasn't a gamble Quince was willing to make, especially not with Eliza in his care. So any exit that reduced the chance of stumbling over Lassiter, the better.

Eliza didn't argue. She just nodded and stepped toward the window, then hitched the dress up to mid-thigh, giving him an enticing view as she hooked her leg over the sash.

He frowned at her bare feet. "Shoes?"

She glanced down at the impractical heels she'd left on the floor. "I can't climb in them."

True enough; the fire escape was constructed with a metal grating, and the heels would sink right through. Still, they needed to look like a couple out

for the evening once they hit street level. He took
one more look at her, the dress even more sheer
now that it was backlit by the city's ambient light.

"Here," he said, shrugging out of his suit jacket
and handing it to her. Then he bent and picked up
the shoes. "I'll carry them. We'll need to blend."

She drew in a breath, squared her shoulders,
and didn't protest.

Considering the nightmare he'd dragged her
into, she was being quite compliant. He had no idea
how she'd ended up at this party, but he could
assume. Her acting career had stalled. She needed
cash. One of her friends moonlighted as an escort
and told her about these parties where a girl could
earn enough in a night to last her six months. It had
been too tempting to pass up, and Eliza had turned
into the real-life version of Denny's alias—a struggling actress resorting to selling herself to make
ends meet.

And didn't that just break his heart?

As far as Quincy was concerned, a woman
could make a living however she wanted. In theory,
he had no problems with sex as a commercial trans-
action. So long as the person getting paid was
entering into the arrangement fully of his or her
own free will, then the details of what went on in
the bedroom—including activities or payments—
were nobody else's business.

But Eliza wasn't just anybody. She was *his*, dammit.

The thought hit him like a sledgehammer, and he shook himself as he mentally backtracked. Because she wasn't his. Not anymore. She hadn't been for a long, long time.

But just because he no longer had a claim on her, didn't mean he no longer understood her or cared about her. He *knew* her, dammit. Her heart and soul; her fears and doubts.

She'd told him how she'd grown up. The abusive father. The protective big sister. The months living the streets. She'd witnessed the kind of perversions that no little girl should ever have to deal with, and yes, her past had scarred her.

But it hadn't destroyed her.

He knew that; he'd seen it. Hell, he'd helped her discover what she needed to feel whole. For Eliza, sex had always been about the connection. The surrender.

The trust.

The Eliza he knew would have to be truly desperate to sell herself to a stranger.

And yes, he'd taken her places she'd never gone. Pushed her limits. Claimed her submission. And together they'd lost themselves in shared ecstasy. But the road they'd traveled had been paved with trust. With passion. And, yes, with love.

A love that he'd betrayed, goddammit, but that was hardly the point now.

No, the real bottom line was that she had no business being at a party like this, and the thought of her naked and bound in another man's bed made him want to punch something.

It didn't matter if he'd walked away—didn't matter if he could never claim her again—didn't matter that he had no right to judge her or to help her. All he knew was that she didn't belong in a place like this. Didn't deserve to be touched by a man who only wanted to get off. Who saw her only as a tool for the satisfaction of his cock. Who only wanted—

"—now?"

He snapped to attention. "What?"

"I said, are we going now?"

"Sorry." He tapped his ear, feeling only slightly guilty about the suggestion of a lie. "I was listening."

"Did she say if it's clear?"

He made a non-committal noise, then pointed up. "We're going over. Up to the roof, down to the back alley. Everyone will be in front with Red, so we're going the other way."

She didn't argue or complain. Instead, she just slipped out the window in her bare feet, her small body lost inside his jacket.

He followed her up the ladder to the roof,

staying a few steps below in case she stumbled, a position that gave him an enticing view of her ass peeking out from under the hem of his jacket. He swallowed, told himself he'd be better off looking at the small of her back, and soldiered on.

Once they reached the flat, gravel-topped roof, he took her hand and they hunched down as they crossed, staying mostly in the shadows thrown by the smattering of utility boxes and access sheds that dotted the roof.

When they reached the far side, he peered down, making sure no one was on the ground looking back up at them. Then he helped her over the edge and onto the ladder that led down to the highest platform of the fire escape. Thank goodness Lassiter had kept the building's original features. So many remodels did away with the external fire escapes.

Within five minutes, they'd reached the alley, and he held her steady as she slipped on her shoes. Another five minutes and they'd reached Hawthorne, the street that ran parallel to Holly-wood Boulevard.

"Do you have a cell phone?"

She shook her head. "A friend dropped me at the hotel. I thought it was better not to bring anything personal." She met his eyes. "I wanted to be anonymous."

He nodded, assuming that *friend* was code for

Madam. He considered asking her if it was money or something else that had brought her tonight, then told himself it was no longer his business. Instead, he pulled out his own phone, intending to summon an Uber once they'd reached the intersection of Hawthorne and La Brea. "I'll get you home. I'm sorry to have dragged you into this mess. I don't know how Red got wind of what Denny and I were doing, but—"

"Quincy—"

"No, wait. There's more I need to say. I know tonight was a freak occurrence. But even so, this kind of thing isn't safe. Some of the men who come to parties like this ... Eliza, they aren't—"

"Like you?" Her brows rose as she stopped at an intersection. "Are you telling me that the kind of men who come to parties stocked with call girls might actually hurt me?" Her voice rose as if in indignation.

He allowed himself a mental sigh of relief, pleased that she understood. "That's exactly what I'm saying."

She crossed her arms over her chest, her eyes practically burning through him. "But you'd never hurt me, would you, Quincy? You'd never dream of ripping my heart out or tearing my soul to shreds."

His gut twisted, both from the truth of her words and the fact that he'd walked right into that. "Eliza, that's not what I—"

"Fuck. You." She started walking, her heels clicking on the pavement.

He caught up with her, then took her elbow and tugged her to a stop. "If you need money, I'll help you. But this kind of party—come on, love, you know it's a bloody awful mistake."

She nodded slowly, and he hoped she was considering her words. He assumed she'd either tell him to go to hell or she'd agree to his offer. But he definitely wasn't expecting her question. "Tell me about the girl."

"The girl? Denny?"

She rolled her eyes. "No. I think I've got that. You work with her. You might be sleeping with her —that part I'm not sure of."

"No, I—"

"I'm talking about the thirteen-year-old. The girl you said needed my help, remember? The reason I had to hold that receiver thingie."

"Do you think I made that up?"

"I think she's missing."

He stopped, shocked by her words.

A moment later, she stopped, too, then turned back to look at him. "So I guess I'm right."

"Walk me through it, Eliza. Every little thing you think you know."

She bit her lower lip, clearly considering her words. "Red wasn't in that room because of whatever you and Denny were doing."

"What are you—"

"He was there because of me."

He took a step back, her words hitting him with the force of a slap. "You? Why on earth do you think that?"

She flashed a wry smile as she held up her wrist, still decorated with a simple red ribbon. "Freaky coincidence, huh? But he's the one who picked the ribbon as the way to identify me. Or, Emma, really. I kind of showed up in her place."

"Emma was supposed to be at the party?"

"Not like that. She was coming in undercover. For a meeting."

He nodded, remembering that Emma had worked as a PI. "She was on a case? And you're telling me that ribbon was a signal?"

"Exactly."

"Then why were you there instead of Emma? And what does any of this have to do with Ariana's disappearance?"

"That's the teenager? I don't know how any of it ties together. All I know is that I snuck in because Emma's gone missing, and the message about the meet and the ribbon was the only clue I had."

She blinked, and for the first time since she'd climbed through the fire escape, he saw her control start to slip. "I don't understand what's going on— really I don't. But that red-haired bastard thought I was Emma. And he asked me where the girl was. That's all he wanted to know."

She met his eyes, hers scared but defiant. "Which means I need your help. Because your missing girl must somehow be connected to my missing sister, and—"

"—that means I'm not sending you home after all. Instead, you're coming with me."

8

"*YOU'RE COMING WITH ME.*"

Those delicious, familiar words rumble through me as I climb into the backseat of the Uber that's pulled up beside us, then slide over to make room for Quincy. I hug myself as I watch him get in next to me, but I'm not seeing the man as he is now, in his fine tailored suit. Instead, I see his hard, lean body in jeans that hug his perfect ass and tight thighs. I see a pale gray Henley under a black leather jacket instead of a starched white shirt. I see a man whose hard eyes appraise me and whose appreciative smile warms me.

I see the Quincy of that first morning when I'd made up my mind to meet him, and as this Los Angeles ride share pulls away from the curb and the man from tonight sits silently beside me, I let myself drift back to London and into those memories of the man from before...

————

I'd spent most of the night after he'd put me in the London cab telling myself that I wasn't going to meet him that next morning. Our time exploring the city together had been incredible, sure, but the man was too arrogant. Too unpredictable. I'd expected to spend the night with him, and he'd turned that expectation on its ear. Teasing me instead of satisfying me, and making arrogant assumptions about what I wanted. And how could he possibly know what I craved when I hadn't even figured it out for myself?

Better to chalk it up as one of those incredible tourist experiences. Something a brochure would headline *An Encounter With a Native*. But definitely not something that needed to go any further.

Those were the things I'd told myself, anyway. I even used my stern and reasonable voice. And yet when morning rolled around, I found myself showering and dressing, and then taking the tube back to Marble Arch and winding my way down the London streets to the little cafe that he'd pointed out.

With every step I told myself that I would leave *if*.

If he wasn't there, I'd turn around and go shopping.

If he said that he knew I would come, I'd tell him I only came to let him know that I wasn't giving him the satisfaction.

If he even hinted that I'd come only because his raw sensual promises had enticed and aroused me, then I would turn on my heel and go. I was intrigued, true. But no way was I going to trust my body to a man who would so cavalierly toss my curiosity and desire back in my face.

The first *if* was negated when I walked through the door. Even though I arrived a full ten minutes early, he was already sitting in the third booth, positioned so that he faced the door. And the moment I stepped over the threshold, I saw the smile light his eyes. He stood, then lifted a hand to signal me over, making no attempt to hide his pleasure.

"I was hoping you'd come. I was afraid I'd scared you off."

Poof. There went the second *if*, evaporating into a cloud of smoke.

"You might have made me a little nervous," I admitted, sliding into the booth. "But not scared."

"I'm sorry about the nerves, but I'm very glad you came. I had a good time yesterday. I hope you did, too."

"Very much," I said, realizing that he'd thoroughly annihilated all of my excuses. I was stuck there by my own rules, and perfectly happy about that.

The cafe served American-style pancakes, and I ordered a stack of chocolate chip, black coffee, and a side of bacon. I was starving and ate the entire thing, which is not something I'd normally do on a date, as I don't want to come off as a human vacuum. But the taste of home was too good to pass up, and honestly I was so lost in the conversation I didn't even realize how much I'd eaten until the waitress took away my empty plate.

"How much have you played tourist during your time in the city?"

"Not much," I told him. I'd already explained yesterday about the show closing and my unexpected freedom.

"That's what I thought." He tilted his head. "I hope you're free all day. There are so many things I want to show you."

If I wasn't already prepared to spend a full day with him, the heat in his voice would have prompted me to clear my day completely. He took me all around London on the back of his Ducati, which was, frankly, the perfect way to see the town.

"Do you mind?" he'd asked, passing me a spare helmet. "I can hire a car if you'd rather."

"Are you kidding? This is fine." I meant it, too. I've known how to drive a motorcycle since I was twelve, though Emma almost always took the controls. It was our primary mode of transportation until she was old enough to get a license. Nobody bothered us on the bike, even when she was too young. It was as if we were invisible. Which was probably why she continued to ride it for so long, only really using the car when she had something to carry or a passenger. Or when she was on a stake-out. It's hard to hunker down for the long haul on a bike.

All of which meant that I was more than happy to slide onto the bike behind him. And, frankly, the feel of my inner thighs against his hips wasn't a bad way to spend the day at all. In fact, as the day went on and my body rubbed against his and the motor-cycle revved beneath me, my thoughts drifted more and more to the naughty promises he'd made last night. His promise to claim me. Pleasure me. To make me surrender.

I wanted that. And the more I thought about it the more my body thrummed with anticipation.

And yet the hours kept ticking by, without even a passionate kiss to suggest that there was anything more on the agenda.

We rode all over town, with Quincy showing me his favorite open air markets, then taking me to some stables near Hyde Park where we saddled two horses and went exploring. Or, rather, I explored. He knew exactly where he was going, as it turned out that he owned the horses.

"I love riding out here, but I rarely take the time," he told me as we took a break to sit by a pond and have some wine and cheese that he'd asked one of the stablehands to prepare. He took my hand, his thumb lightly stroking my skin in a way that shot fire through my entire body. "I'm very glad we came today."

When he spoke, he looked straight at me, as if I was the only thing that mattered in the entire world. It was a nice feeling, and a rare one. And the truth was that Quincy had a way of always making me feel like that.

He somehow arranged a private tour of the Tower of London, including the Crown Jewels —"connections," he told me, making me suitably impressed—and it wasn't until the evening approached that he took me to his place. That same house that we'd seen on the bus tour. Only Quincy, it turned out, had converted the backyard servant's cottage into his private residence.

"I thought we'd order a light supper for delivery," he said, as he helped me off the bike.

"Um, sure," I said, as I followed him inside the charming residence. In truth, I'd thoroughly enjoyed spending the day with him, but it hadn't panned out the way I'd been expecting. From what he'd said the previous night, I'd anticipated some sort of fantasy encounter like a scene from a sexy late-night cable show.

As if he could read my mind, he bent to my ear and whispered, "Foreplay. The motorcycle especially, don't you think? All that power vibrating between your legs?"

My mouth went completely dry, and he flashed a mischievous grin, took my hand, and led me to the living room. "Wine?" he asked as I settled onto the sofa. His voice and attitude were perfectly casual, as if he hadn't just made perfectly clear that he knew exactly where my thoughts had been all afternoon.

I nodded, and he brought me a glass of red. I drank it, welcoming the buzz and barely even tasting the grape. All I wanted was for him to kiss me.

And finally, thank God, he did.

He didn't ask. He simply set his glass down, then took mine from my fingers and set it on the table, too. Then he leaned in and closed his mouth over mine, and I just about melted from the pleasure of his lips on mine, his tongue teasing and demanding entrance. He buried his fingers in my hair and pulled me closer, taking the kiss deeper and wilder, as if he'd been thinking about nothing else all day, and now he couldn't get his fill. God knew I couldn't either.

Then his hands were at my waist and he was pulling me onto his lap. I was wearing thin black leggings, and I could easily feel his erection through his jeans, and the knowledge that he was as turned on as I was only made me more excited. I ground against him, letting the sweet sensations build as he deepened the kiss, one hand still holding my head steady and the other cupping my breast.

I lost myself in that kiss, in the feel of him. In the tremors of pleasure that coursed through me, more intense than anything I'd ever felt before.

"Take off your clothes and get on the bed," he said, and I froze, my hips going still in the midst of grinding myself to my own climax.

"What?"

He leaned back, putting space between us as he cupped both my breasts, his thumb and forefingers teasing the nipples that were straining against my lacy bra.

"I—"

"Do you trust me?"

I licked my lips, but I nodded. I *did* trust him.

"Then go. Naked," he said, as if I'd forgotten. "On your back. Your legs spread." He looked me up and down, and the heat in his eyes almost made me come right then. "And I want to see you touching yourself when I walk into that room."

I swallowed, not at all sure I liked this. Being on display. It was too much. And I didn't want those harsh memories rising.

"I don't think I—"

He brushed his thumb over my lower lip. "You can say no, Eliza. You can always say no."

"I can?" For some insane reason, that simple statement was a revelation to me. I'd never been able to say no with *him*. And Emma sure as hell hadn't been able to either. Did he mean it? My gaze dipped down to the very obvious bulge in his jeans. As if reading my mind, Quincy chuckled. "I promise, I'll survive. There are plenty of other options. Or we can just watch television."

He pulled me close, then kissed me sweetly. "I want to touch you," he whispered. "I want to take you places you've never gone, and I want to make you explode as you scream my name. But I don't want any of that unless you do. Whatever you want, Eliza. All you have to do is decide."

I drew a breath, then nodded. "Okay," I said, then started to turn toward the bedroom.

"Wait."

For a moment, fear bubbled inside me, and I was afraid that I'd hesitated too long and he'd changed his mind.

"Do you know what a safe word is?"

"I—kind of."

"It's another way of saying no. A better way, with no confusion. What's your safe word, Eliza? Something you wouldn't normally say in bed. Something you can remember."

"Ducks," I said, thinking of the first moment I'd met him. "Ducklings."

It was silly, but from his smile and nod, I could tell that he approved.

"Go on," he said, and with those two words, his entire demeanor changed. Where only moments before he'd been warm and careful and instructive, now he seemed dark and sensual and a little dangerous. But not scary. My fear had entirely disappeared.

I did as he asked and got undressed.

Naked and with my heart pounding, I climbed onto the bed. And though I started out wildly embarrassed, once I closed my eyes and imagined Quincy watching me, I actually got into touching myself. So much that by the time I heard his footsteps and his soft command to keep my eyes shut, my body was already sparking with the precursor to an amazing orgasm.

"Beautiful," he murmured, and I felt the bed shift under his weight as he sat on the edge of the mattress. Then he gently lifted my hands and I gasped in surprise, almost opening my eyes when I felt him put velcro padded cuffs around my wrists.

"Quincy..."

I heard the tension in my voice, and he must have as well, because he whispered, "Shhh. It's okay. Keep your eyes closed." And then, as if to ensure that I did, he slipped a blindfold over my eyes.

Without conscious thought, I pulled my legs together, as if my body was trying to claim some amount of modesty in response to the fact that I couldn't move my legs. "Oh, no, love. None of that."

I whimpered, then bit my lower lip, but he showed no pity. Instead, he moved down to my ankles, binding me fully to the bed, my body forming an X. Honestly, I was glad for the blindfold. I don't know that I could have stood the embarrassment of seeing the way he looked at me, even though the tone of his voice and the words he spoke told me that he both liked the way I looked and that he was very turned on.

I'd never done anything like this before, and I got lost in the slow, delicious sensuality of his touch. First teasing me with a feather, then tormenting me with an ice cube. But those touches were nothing compared to an actual vibrator that created such a riot of sensations that I writhed and strained against my bonds, trying desperately to close my legs as my body both rebelled and rejoiced from a harsh pleasure so intense it bordered on pain.

With expert skill, he teased me, taking me close to orgasm and then pulling back until I was teetering on the edge and begging for release. Only then did he continue his erotic assault with his own fingers and mouth, as I shamelessly bucked against him, craving a control that he'd forbidden and begging for the feel of him inside me.

When I finally came—when he finally *let* me—the force of the orgasm was overwhelming, more than I'd ever experienced as every cell in my body seemed to turn inside out until I was nothing more than a limp, satisfied shell of a woman.

"You're amazing," he whispered, his hands stroking me as he moved along my body and down to my ankles and wrists. Gently, he released me so that I could curl up beside him. "Do you have any idea how incredible it is to watch you? To see you writhe in pleasure from my touch?"

I couldn't answer; I was too spent. But I molded my body to his, my face tucked in against his neck, and murmured something about being lost in heaven.

His low laughter rumbled through me, and he pulled me close, then stroked my hair as I floated somewhere above the earth until finally—*finally*—I came enough back to myself to form coherent sentences.

"I thought I would hate it," I murmured, then gathered enough strength to prop myself up so that I could see his face. "I thought I'd cry out the safe word in the first few minutes."

His forehead creased, and I knew that I'd

worried him. That he understood that I wasn't talking like a woman who simply hadn't ever played these kinds of sex games before. But instead like a woman with secrets.

Gently, he brushed my cheek. "Eliza, love. What is it you haven't told me?"

I knew I should have said something before, but even as nervous as I was, I'd wanted to be with him. To experience everything he had to give. And I hadn't wanted him to back away, believing that I was too fragile.

But when we were all relaxed after, I did tell him. Even more, I wanted to.

I wanted him to understand my hesitations. And—God help me—I wanted to share that deepest, darkest piece of me.

So I told him. I told him about my father.

About the horrible things he did to Emma. The things he did to me.

True, we weren't tied up. No wrist cuffs or ankle restraints. But we still couldn't get away. Our father had all the power.

It was horrible, and I told Quincy all of it.

And then, as he brushed away my tears, I confessed that I thought it would be like that with him. "I thought I'd feel trapped. Used." I ducked my head, embarrassed. "But it wasn't like that at all."

For a moment, he simply looked at me, and I

thought that I'd blown it. That I should have just kept my mouth shut. "You thought you'd be helpless," he said. "The way you were with him?"

I nodded as he hooked his arm under my shoulders and propped me up while he used his free hand to point out the window. "I know a bit about that," he said. "Do you see that window?"

I nodded.

"That was my parents' bedroom. The night those men came in—the ones who had the vendetta against my father—I was seven years old. I'd been playing on the foot of the bed while my mother read a book. She shoved me under the bed and told me not to come out for anything. I was flat on my belly and shaking with terror and there wasn't a bloody thing I could do."

He turned to face me. "So I understand helpless. It's when you have no control. When it's ripped from you. Like me with those men when I had no chance in hell of protecting my mother. And you with your father, when you were powerless to do a goddamn thing."

I blinked away the tears that had pooled in my eyes.

"With your father, you had control ripped away from you. With me, you have all the control."

"I don't understand."

"You gave control to me, El. *You* did that. You had the power to stop at any moment. You gave me your trust. And that was your gift to me. You surrendered control. I didn't steal it. Do you get it?"

"Yeah." I thought about it, then grinned as I rolled on top of him. "Want to try it again?"

He laughed, but he didn't turn me down. And, honestly, I could have spent the rest of my months in London in bed with him. At that point, I was addicted.

As it turned out, we explored the city as much as we explored each other. Quincy made me feel free. Confident. Most of all, he made me feel loved, and every day we grew closer, as we learned each other's boundaries. We pushed each other's limits sexually, and I discovered things about myself that I'd never known. We played and experimented and laughed, and through him I learned that I truly enjoyed sex. That it wasn't something to be endured, but something to be shared.

Maybe I would have eventually discovered that on my own, but that wasn't the point. Because with Quincy, I'd fallen in love.

I would have stayed forever if he'd let me, and for those three months, I truly believed that he would.

I never expected that his love for me was an illusion. That our days together were nothing more than a fantasy, something ephemeral that could be swept away on a whim, or flicked out of existence like a rabbit on the wrong end of a magician's wand.

But that's what happened. And soon enough our storybook romance ended, and I was thrust rudely out into the cold, bitter embrace of reality.

And now here I am, tossed into the backseat of a car zipping through Los Angeles with the man who threw me away.

And all I can think is that this time I will not trust him.

This time, I know that he lies.

9

"ANYTHING?" Quincy asks, as he paces along a row of computers. They're all dormant, a 3D rendition of the SSA logo tumbling across the otherwise quiet screens. All except for the one where Denny sits, now wearing black track pants and a white tank top—both also with the SSA logo.

"Yes, I've cracked the case," she says, without looking up. An incomprehensible string of numbers and letters pour across the screen like a reverse waterfall, moving so quickly it almost makes me dizzy.

Denny looks back over her shoulder at Quincy. "The butler did it."

I laugh, and Quincy turns the scowl he'd aimed at her in my direction.

"Seriously, Q. It's encrypted, remember? And

you only walked through the door ten minutes ago. I'm good, but give a girl some space."

Quincy catches my eye, clearly frustrated. As for me, I have a total girl crush on his partner.

I've pulled my hair back into a ponytail and am dressed similarly to Denny, the outfit provided by the fitness room of the Stark Security Agency. According to Quincy, it's a relatively new venture, part of the broad universe of billionaire Damien Stark.

The same Damien Stark who—even though it's three in the morning—is in the glass-enclosed conference room on a speaker call with another man who, unlike Stark, I've never seen in the tabloids. He has hair the color of mine, and a no-nonsense smile. Quincy identified him as Ryan Hunter, the head of the SSA, and promised he'd introduce me to both men when they were off the call.

There'd been another man in the office when we arrived, too. Liam Foster. A tall black man with military bearing, a rock-solid build, and kind eyes that looked like they'd kept a lot of secrets. He'd taken my key and gone off to Emma's condo. Not only to retrieve the phone that I'm desperate to check, but also because I'd told Quincy that Lorenzo and I disagreed about whether someone had poked around in Emma's things. Quincy assured me that if anyone could clock the signs of an intruder, it would be Liam.

I glance at the digital clock on the far wall and consider calling Lorenzo again. But I've already called twice. Once in the Uber using Quincy's phone, and once from a landline in the fitness center. Both times had rolled to voicemail.

I'm frustrated, but not too concerned. True, Lorenzo knew that I was going undercover to the party, but he also knew that I might have to play the role of party girl all night in order to maintain my cover. I'd seen the disapproval in his eyes when he'd hit that realization, but to his credit, he didn't try to talk me out of it. Other than Emma, no one knows me better than Lorenzo, and he knows that there are no limits to what I'll do for my sister.

So while he knew I might not check in until morning, I also expected him to be glued to his phone. But considering it's almost four in the morning, I should probably cut him some slack. He probably fell asleep. And despite all the stereotypes about law enforcement types being constantly aware, Lorenzo sleeps like the dead.

He wakes at six every morning, so I'll call him then. In the meantime, I watch Denny's fingers fly across the keyboard as I try to figure out what she's doing. Since I haven't got a clue, I quickly tire of that activity. I find Quince at a nearby workstation. He's wearing half-frame reading glasses that make him look both intellectual and ridiculously sexy, and he's scowling at something on the screen.

I consider going and peering over his shoulder, but decide against it. My relief and gratitude at being saved from Red's knife has already started to melt away, once again exposing all my raw edges where Quincy Radcliffe is concerned. And here—in this fancy office in front of these strangers—is really not where I want to get into it.

Instead, I cross the giant room to the western-facing wall of windows. This building is located at the center of a new Santa Monica office park called The Domino. According to Quincy, the SSA takes up four floors, with this first floor serving as home base for analysts and the IT staff, which explains the rows and rows of computer-topped work-stations.

This wall is made entirely of one-way glass, and I stand there now and look out at a tranquil garden area, obviously designed as a respite from all the craziness going on around it.

Because of the lighting, I can see Quincy's reflection as he approaches me. He slides his hands into the pockets of his trousers. He hasn't changed clothes, and while I look like a sloppy student who rolled out of bed for class, he looks like a master of the universe.

The disparity pisses me off, which isn't fair, but I'm bone-tired and no closer to finding my sister than I was before. Only now instead of being on my own and befuddled I'm surrounded by gazillions of dollars in tech and befuddled.

That doesn't make me feel better.

As if that weren't enough to be going on with, I've spent the last few hours with a man I once loved who it turns out I never really knew. And I'm not sure if that's his fault for keeping secrets or mine for being so ridiculously naive.

His eyes meet mine in the glass. "How are you hanging in there?"

"Fine. Who doesn't like to be tossed down the rabbit hole?"

A single brow arches, and my heart twists painfully. It's a trademark Quincy affectation, and one that used to make me melt. Now, I just want to slap him. "What?" I demand.

"Seems to me you walked into the warren of your own free will."

"The party, you mean?"

He nods, and on that point I have to agree. Possibly not the smartest of decisions, especially when I factor Red into the equation and the fact that he seemed to want me—or at least Emma— dead. But I wasn't thinking about that. "I meant you," I tell him. "The rabbit hole of you."

I turn so that I'm looking at him rather than his reflection. "The slippery slope of realizing that the man I spent three months with—the man who I confessed my love to—the man who fucking walked out on me—was never the man I thought he was. Sucks for me, right?"

He doesn't react. Of course he doesn't. Quincy always did have one hell of a poker face.

I yank the ponytail holder off my hair, just for something to do with my hands, and my hair spills over my shoulders. "This isn't a new venture, is it? You didn't suddenly get tired of the world of high finance and decide to leap into the wide and exciting world of private intelligence. Did you?"

"No," he says. "I didn't."

"No," I repeat. "Score one for me. Let's see how I do on the bonus round, because I'm thinking that the closest you ever got to high finance was your family's net worth. I'm thinking that before you worked here, you worked for the government. British, obviously, so I bet you were with MI6. Or, I don't know, whatever private paramilitary organizations hang out around London."

"Hang out?"

I cock my head and cross my arms. "I lay all that on you, and the only response you have is to criticize my word choice?"

"Go on."

I make a show of raising my brows. "What? There's more? Or are you talking about the fact that you were in intelligence even back when we were together? Because I'd bet money that you were. And I'll even double down and say that it was some mission that called you away. What I don't get is why the hell you stayed away. Because honestly, Quince, I really don't know how I surv —*shit*."

He says nothing, just watches my face. And there is no way I am confessing the depths of my pain. No way at all.

Instead, I roll my shoulders back and focus on his face. "I was in love with you."

He swallows, but his expression doesn't change. For a moment, he is silent, then he says simply, "And now?"

I consider lying, but what would be the point. "Now? Now I kind of hate you."

I exhale, feeling a little better since that is off my chest. I don't look at his face. Instead, I turn and walk toward Denny, then slide into the chair next to her.

She glances sideways at me, and I have the feeling that she understands more than she's letting on. For the first time, I wonder about her relation-ship with Quincy. Are they work partners? Or is there more going on between them?

Considering I just told Quince that I hate him, I probably shouldn't care one way or the other. But, of course, I do.

I clear my throat and nod at the computer screen. "I'm confused," I confess. "I thought I had to hold that gadget so that some sort of decryption software could get beamed down to Quincy. But if that's the case, then what are you decrypting now?"

She glances toward Quincy, who's watching us from the window, and I see him nod, giving permission to bring me into the loop.

"That software got us past the system security and also instituted a high speed cloning program."

"So you stole his database, but it's still encrypted?"

"Pretty much."

I frown. "But you can decrypt it, right?"

"Me personally? No. But fortunately I work with some of the best geniuses Mr. Stark's money can buy."

"So why did you steal it? What's on there, and who hired you?"

She runs her fingers through her fine, blond hair. "I'm pretty sure that's above your pay-grade."

I let out a frustrated sigh. "Fine. How long is it going to take? I'm only here because our problems overlap, and I want to know if that thing's holding information about my sister."

"Well, that's the million dollar question. And the reason we took the clone with us instead of hanging around. Could be five more minutes. Could be five months."

"It won't be five months," Quincy says, joining us. "My friend Noah ran the team who developed that fine piece of software. It'll work fast. You can count on it." He cocked his head toward the conference room. "Come on. They're off the call. I'll introduce you."

I've met a lot of celebrities over the years. It comes with the territory when you do as many random roles as I have. But I've never met someone like Damien Stark. He's tall and lean, and I remember that he used to be a professional tennis player before reinventing himself as one of the wealthiest men in the world. He has dark hair and fascinating dual colored eyes—one black and the other amber. He projects a commanding manner that should be intimidating but isn't.

"Ms. Tucker," Stark says, extending his hand. "I apologize for keeping you waiting. Quincy, nice work in the field."

"Except that database still isn't decrypted," I say, because I'm so used to speaking my mind with Lorenzo and Emma that I forgot to turn on my filter.

"Denny will have that remedied by the time we're finished here," Ryan Hunter says. "I think Damien was talking about you. Didn't our redheaded friend come close to gutting you?"

"Oh." I realize that Quincy must have tapped out an update to the team during our ride from Hollywood to Santa Monica. Frankly, I'm flattered that Stark and Hunter think of me as anything other than someone who could have potentially gunked up their mission. But I do take his point, and I turn to Quincy with an apologetic smile. "Did I say thanks?"

Amusement lights his eyes. "You're welcome."

Ryan nods, then indicates the nearby chairs. I sit, grateful to be moving past the introductions. On the whole, Hunter seems more approachable than Stark, but at the same time, I think that's a facade. According to Quincy, Ryan's the big cheese at the SSA, which means part of his job is to get close. To watch. Right now, he's watching me, and I wonder what those blue eyes see in me.

I have a feeling both of these men make friends slowly, but when they do, they're loyal to a fault. It's a quality I admire, and which reminds me of Emma.

Looking at these three men now seated around the table, it's like I'm an extra in a movie featuring three A-list guys. They're that gorgeous. At the same time, all three seem like real people, with rough edges and a core of steel inside. Nothing airbrushed about them at all.

Between the three of them, Quincy is the most real to me. But even he seems a little rough around the edges. As if he isn't quite tame. I'd seen hints of that in London, but now it's more obvious. A dark watchfulness. The sense that he's on the hunt.

Whatever it is, there's even more of an edge to

him now, and I think that's partly why I've felt safe, even on what has been one of the most horrible nights of my life.

But safety with Quincy is dangerous, too. Because while I'm happy to not be dead from Red's blade, I'm terrified of knocking down the wall I built around my heart to keep Quincy Radcliffe out.

"—and then maybe a quick rundown? Eliza?"

I jump, embarrassed to realize that Ryan Hunter is talking to me and I've completely zoned out. "I'm sorry. It's been a really long day." True, but that's not the reason my mind was elsewhere. "What did you say?"

"Sorry. I know you're exhausted, but obviously our interests overlap. Quince gave us the short version of why you were at The Terrace. Could you fill in the gaps?"

I lean back in my chair. "Well, that depends." I look between him and Damien Stark, wondering at the extent of my moxie. "Are you going to tell me why you were hacking Scott Lassiter's system? Because, color me naive, but I'm pretty sure that's not legal."

"Bloody hell, Eliza." Quincy's voice is sharp. Frustrated.

I glare at him. "Excuse me for wanting to understand the level of shit I've stepped in the middle of."

"Ryan just wants to know—"

"No," Ryan says. "It's okay." He looks to Stark, who slides seamlessly into the conversation.

"Are you familiar with the name Marius Corbu?"

I frown, then shake my head. "Should I be?"

"Probably not. He's the leader of a Romania-based sex trafficking ring."

"Oh." I sit back in my chair. I'm not shocked. On the contrary, the pieces are starting to fall into place. "Go on."

"The ring's been in operation for over a decade, sometimes taking hits from law enforcement, but mostly flying under the radar. Or over it, depending on your perspective."

"Like the mafia."

He nods.

"Most of the victims are from underdeveloped countries. People trying to make a better life."

"I know. Lots of Nigerian refugees get sucked in." I know more than I want about sex trafficking since Emma spent so much of her time in intelligence fighting an essentially unwinnable fight.

"There's a European Union task force that's zeroing in on some of the key players, and so far it's done a good job. But Corbu is the holy grail, and he's a tough man to find. So Stark Security was commissioned to aid the task force by recovering a contact protocol for Corbu."

"At the party? But that doesn't—*oh.*"

Quincy nods, obviously realizing I've caught up. "Apparently Corbu is among Lassiter's clients. Whether Lassiter knows about Corbu's role in the operation is anyone's guess. From what we know, he's just your average scumbag with extortion, prostitution, and drug trafficking lining his bag of tricks. Worth going after, but right now he can lead us to bigger fish."

"Like Corbu," I say. "Because if Corbu's a client, then Lassiter must have some way to contact him."

"Exactly," Ryan says. "And our intel suggests that Lassiter keeps all client contact information on his highly encrypted hard drive."

"Which we now have," Stark adds.

"So this is all part of a sting," I say. "You get the protocol, then you contact Corbu, then—"

"Not us," Ryan says. "But presumably that's what the task force agents intend. As soon as Denny pulls the protocol off that disk and we transmit to the EU, the SSA's role in this operation is officially over."

"Okay," I say. "But what does that have to do with the thirteen year old girl that Quincy mentioned? She's got to be the same girl that Red mentioned, right?"

"We think so," Ryan says.

"Who is she?"

"Princess Ariana of Eustancia. And she was recently taken."

I feel my eyes go wide. "A princess? Seriously? Of what country?"

"Eustancia," Stark says.

"It's a small but incredibly wealthy monarchy tucked in near Switzerland and Italy," Quincy adds. I've never heard of it, but I believe him. "The task force isn't sure why Corbu would risk exposure by snatching someone so high profile," he continues, "but the sources are confident."

"And Stark Security is working the kidnapping, too?" I can hear the incredulity in my voice and hope that they're not offended. "But seriously, doesn't Europe have, oh, law enforcement?"

"Actually, we have nothing to do with the princess," Ryan says, sliding into the conversation. "Or we didn't until we got your intel."

"My intel," I repeat, looking at Quince. "You mean the fact that Red asked me about the girl?"

"So far, it's the only real lead."

"But he may not have even been talking about this princess."

"True," Stark says, "but the Regent is willing to take the gamble. He wants us to pursue the lead. And since I'm acquainted with him and his brother, we're taking the assignment."

"Oh." The closest I've ever come to royalty is meeting Queen Latifah when I had two lines in one of her movies. That and watching the changing of the guard outside of Buckingham Palace with Quincy. So right then, I'm a little in awe.

A hint of a smile touches Stark's lips, and I'm certain he's read my reaction perfectly. "Obviously, we need your help."

"I hate to be the bearer of bad news, but I've told you everything I know. I'm not sure how much more help I can be."

Ryan leans back in his chair. "Why were you at The Terrace?"

"You know why. I'm trying to figure out what happened to my sister." He already knows that, of course. I'd told Quincy everything in the Uber, and he already relayed it all to Ryan and Stark.

"The same sister that Red thinks knows about the girl?"

I nod.

"And we all assume that this girl is Princess Ariana?"

Again, I nod.

Ryan spreads his hands in a *there you have it* gesture. "Seems to me that we need to find your sister. And to do that, we need your help."

"And Eliza," Quincy adds gently, "I think you need our help, too."

I'm surprised by the amount of relief that courses through me. Lorenzo's smart, and I know he's just as worried as I am, but his resources are nothing compared to what's in this room. "Yeah," I whisper as Denny taps on the glass door. "I really think I do."

Ryan signals her to enter and she practically bounces into the room. "Got it," she says. "Am I amazing or what?"

"Your skills never fail to awe and inspire," Quincy says dryly. In reply she grins and buffs her nails on her chest.

"He's just jealous of my awesomeness," she tells me conspiratorially. I nod and force a smile as I realize that right then, I'm a little jealous, too.

The teasing doesn't faze Quincy, who steers me out of the conference room so that Stark, Ryan, and Denny can call the task force commander with Corbu's contact protocol.

As we exit the conference room, I see Liam coming in through the main door. He raises a hand in greeting, and we meet him halfway, the three of us grabbing chairs from the nearby computer stations. "Well, you were right," he tells me. "Somebody was in her place."

"I knew it," I say. "Lorenzo said I was just being paranoid, but I know Emma." I tilt my head, studying him. "You are as good as advertised. But how can you be sure?"

He holds out his phone. It's open to his photos, and I gasp when I see the first one. It's Emma's apartment, but it looks like a tornado has ripped through the place. "I'm thinking they came back after Red took a tumble," he says, as I nod numbly. "Also, your phone is missing. They may think it's Emma's."

"*Shit.*" The curse slips out, but it's heartfelt. My life is on that phone which, fortunately, is backed up to the cloud. It's locked, but if we're really dealing with international organized crime, I'm betting they can hack it. Which means that if they didn't already have Emma's email address and phone number, they do now. And if she sent me any messages, they have that as well.

"What if she messaged me?" I ask Quincy. "They'll know where she is. Hell, they can pretend to be me. And, oh, *fuck.* I have that location app that lets you find your friends. If she has her phone, they'll know exactly where she is."

Quincy takes my hand, and that tiny show of support strengthens me. "She's smart," he reminds me. "You've told me so a hundred times. Right now, you just need to take care of your phone."

He's right. I don't think there's anything on there that would cause me trouble—I don't have banking apps and I don't use my phone to pay for things—but even so, I swivel toward a computer. I need to log on and wipe the thing remotely, and I need to do it right now.

Quincy's way ahead of me, and he's already logging in and navigating to the iCloud site. I look around to figure out how to wipe my phone, then realize I can track Emma's phone from here. I click, the screen changes to a map, and I wait for the little dot that represents my sister to pop up.

Nothing.

"She wiped her phone, too," Quincy says. "Either that or she turned it off."

"Which means that she probably didn't contact you. At least not from her phone," Liam adds. "Probably not from her regular email address, either. Assuming she's as smart as you both say."

I nod slowly, relieved. Then I lean over and wipe my phone as well. It takes some time—the computer is determined to make sure I *really* want to remotely delete all my information—but soon enough, it's all gone.

I lean back, suddenly overwhelmed by the impact of what I've just done. Because for the first time in my entire life, I'm completely disconnected from my sister.

Beside me, Quincy takes my hand. "It will be okay," he says gently.

Once upon a time, I would have believed him, taking comfort in his words.

Now, though?

Now, I'm just scared. And even with Quincy beside me, I feel very, very alone.

10

QUINCY'S SANTA MONICA condo is smaller than I expected, and at the same time it suits him perfectly. There's a small entrance hall with a coat closet on the right and a galley-style kitchen on the left. The kitchen boasts a pass-through bar that opens into the living area, the far side of which is made up of a sliding glass patio door which can be closed even more thoroughly by a garage-style metal door that's currently in the up position. A dim porch light illuminates the patio, allowing me to see the cushioned metal chair and lounger that take up the small space.

Impeccably tidy, the condo is sparsely furnished with contemporary furniture in various shades of gray and black. A wall unit dominates one wall, the cubbies filled with an impressive stereo system, dozens upon dozens of vinyl albums and CDs, and what must be hundreds of hardback books ranging from well-known classics to historical nonfiction to loads of modern spy thrillers.

I don't see a television, and I'm not surprised. The Quincy I knew only watched television for the news, and then on a small set that he kept in his massive bathroom and turned on while he shaved. I wonder if that's still his routine, or if he's switched to getting all of his news from some app on his phone.

What does surprise me is the punching bag by the patio door. Not one of those little speed bags, but the kind that is huge and probably weighs more than I do.

It's not that Quincy doesn't keep in shape—unless things have changed, he's solid muscle under that suit, with a broad repertoire of martial arts skills. Before, I'd believed his interest in taekwondo, karate, and all the other disciplines stemmed from his childhood and his mother's murder. Now, I think it's bigger than that, and his array of skills is tied to his intelligence work. More, I have a feeling that despite being British, his skill set is way more Liam Neeson than James Bond.

Still, London Quincy wouldn't have had exercise equipment in his living space, and I wonder what it means that the bag takes up such a prominent corner. It's as if I'm getting a peek into the current life of this man I once knew so well, but I don't have the benefit of explanatory footnotes.

There are other hints as to the man he's become. Like, the cluster of framed photographs on the display table behind his couch. I recognize one as his mother; it's a photo that used to be in his London home. Another shows him and a pseudo-celebrity, Dallas Sykes, a well-known New York playboy dubbed "The King of Fuck," who'd been even more in the public eye after his affair with his adopted sister went viral.

I glance sideways at Quincy, but he offers no explanation, and I don't ask. I would never have guessed that Quincy would be friends with a guy like Sykes, but then again, there are all sorts of things I don't know about Quincy Radcliffe.

That simple reality makes me sad, and I push the thought out of my mind and start to turn away from the table. I stop, though, when a small photo on the end catches my eye. A smiling woman holding up a stuffed bear, a carnival shooting booth in blurry focus behind her.

Denny.

Immediately, I feel hot. No, cold. I'm honestly not sure, other than I don't like my reaction. Hell, I don't like that I'm reacting at all, because what do I care anymore what Quincy does in his personal life or who he does it with?

I tell myself to just walk away. Instead, I glance

up and find Quincy looking back at me. "I didn't realize you and Denny were together." I keep my voice bright. Chipper.

I feel like a fucking hypocrite, but no way am I letting him see that this peek into his life hurts me. Because it shouldn't hurt me; I shouldn't care at all.

"You didn't?" His brow furrows, and I suppose for good reason. I mean, they definitely had a rhythm going at the party. He must think I'm blind. "For about eight months now."

"Oh. She's great. I like her a lot."

"As do I. And now that she's getting back in the field more—"

He cuts himself off sharply, his head cocked as he studies me. Slowly, the corner of his mouth curls up, and I see his eyes sparkle with amusement.

"What?" I hear the wariness in my voice and wonder what I'm missing.

"She's my partner, El. That's all she's ever been. And even if she were single, that's all she'd ever be."

"Oh." And then the import of his words hit me. *Oh.*

He takes a step toward me, so that he's close enough now that he could reach out and touch me.

He doesn't.

I don't move either. I just stand there like a fool, looking up at him and kicking myself for revealing way, way more than I'd intended.

"I haven't been involved with anyone since you." His voice is soft. Soothing.

"Oh." I'm having a hard time breathing, and the air between us crackles. He takes another step, and now he's close enough that I can smell the scent of his cologne, still lingering despite being up all night. His eyes are locked on mine, but I don't have a clue what he's thinking. My breath stutters, and in that moment, I am certain that he will kiss me. But whether I'll melt against him or slap his face, I have no idea.

I don't have the chance to find out. Because in the end he does neither. Instead, he points behind me. "The bedroom is in there."

"I can't take your room. I'll sleep on the couch."

"No," he says. "My house. My rules. And that means that tonight, you're in my bed."

"Oh. Right." My cheeks burn even though I have nothing to be embarrassed about.

I pause in the doorway, then turn to face him. "I should have taken Mr. Stark up on his offer of a room at the Stark Century Hotel."

"I'd still be sleeping on sofa. If you think I'd leave you alone tonight, you're crazy."

"Technically, it's morning. And Denny would have stayed with me."

He looks me straight in the eye. "Probably. But I want you here with me."

My heart does a little flip-flop number, the

reaction pissing me off, because he has no right to make me feel this way. No right at all.

I backtrack my way into the kitchen, then help myself to a bottle of sparkling water from the fridge. "Why," I say with my back to him.

He doesn't answer, and I turn to find him standing just a few feet away, only the breakfast bar separating us.

"Quincy, why?"

"Because you've gotten caught up in something bigger than you anticipated. Because you don't understand all of what's going on, and no—do not even argue with me. You don't, and the reason I know you don't is because neither do I. You're in deep now, Eliza. And until I know you're safe, I'm not letting you out of my sight."

"Because that's your job," I say, unable to keep the tinge of dark sarcasm out of my voice.

His expression doesn't change at all, and throughout his silence, he keeps his eyes locked on mine. I see no reaction. None at all.

"Yes," he finally says. "It's my job."

Bastard.

I take a long swallow of water to camouflage my roiling emotions, then leave the small kitchen. I give him a wide berth as I return to the open bedroom door. "When you said I could stay here, I assumed there'd be two bedrooms. It seems small for you."

He glances around the tiny condo. "It's big enough for me. And it's only a rental. A friend owns it, and it suits my needs. And it's not that much smaller than my place in Manhattan."

"New York? You live in New York?"

"I did. Before I accepted Ryan and Damien's offer to join the SSA full time, I worked for a small organization based in the Hamptons. Moonlighted, actually. Most of the time I was with Deliverance I was still on the MI6 payroll." He casually lifts a shoulder. "When Deliverance disbanded. I considered retiring altogether, but decided to come here instead. Liam made the same decision."

"I see," I say, though I have a feeling he's only hitting the surface details. Not that I care much. I've locked onto the bigger picture. "Did you know I was still living in New York, too?"

He nods, and I swallow the hard knot that suddenly fills my throat. Not that his admission changes anything. But somehow the thought of him ignoring me from all the way across the Atlantic was easier to handle than the knowledge that he ignored me from only a few cross-town blocks.

I lift my chin as I return to the bedroom. "Good night, Quincy." I pause on the threshold, then look back over my shoulder. "Do you have any idea how long it took me to get over you?"

It's a lie, of course. I'm not over him at all, no matter how many lies I tell myself.

"I'm sorry."

"I'm sure you are. So what?"

He doesn't answer; what could he say?

I head into the bedroom and sit on the edge of the bed as he moves closer, hovering at the threshold, as if he's waiting for me to dismiss him.

I don't.

"Someday, you have to tell me why," I say. "I deserve to know."

I think I see a spark of emotion fire in those stormy gray eyes. "Maybe you do," he says evenly. "But I think we both know that in this life, you don't always get the things that you deserve."

Then he reaches for the switch and turns out the light before gently pulling the door closed, leaving me alone in the dark with my memories. And my regrets.

11

"HERE," Emma whispers, shoving Mister Wellington into my arms. "No matter what, you pretend to be asleep, okay? And you keep your back to the room and your face up against Mister Wellington's fur. You don't roll over, and you don't look. Promise?"

I nod, pulling the stuffed bear close.

"Say it," she orders. "It's only a real promise if you say it out loud."

I take my thumb out of my mouth and whisper, "I p-omise." I've just lost my first tooth, and I'm having trouble pronouncing my R's.

Emma—a grown-up with all her teeth to prove it—frowns as she looks at me. I can tell she's not satisfied, but she doesn't say anything else. She just nods, then climbs into bed with me.

There are two twin-size beds in our dank,

windowless room, but we never sleep apart. We're only apart when he comes in, and that's never a time for sleeping. That's only a time for pretending to sleep. For me, anyway. Emma has to be awake. He says he wants her eyes open. He says he wants her to watch while he touches himself that way.

I never look. I don't want to, but even if I did, I wouldn't. I trust Emma, and if she tells me to keep my eyes closed, I do. Because I know that she'll always take care of me. I know because she tells me so every day. And because she tells me she loves me, too. She's the only one who does. And she's the only one I love.

Certainly not him. I hate him. If I knew how to hurt him, I would, but I know I'm too little. Even Emma's too little, and she's fourteen.

Sometimes I wish our mother was here, but most of the time I don't. I know better than to believe in wishes, because they never come true.

I don't remember her, anyway, but Emma says she loved us. She says that our mother hated him, too, but that she wouldn't have left us alone with him on purpose. Not ever. She says it's his fault that she died, but nobody knows that. And she says that it will be okay. That she'll take care of both of us. That even though we miss our mommy, we don't need one. That she can be our mommy. And that some-day, we'll get away from him.

She just doesn't know when.

"Go on now," she urges, then shoves a lock of red hair out of her face. It's thick and wavy and I think she looks like a movie star. He likes it, too, and she says that she'd cut it off if she could, but it would make him angry. But she doesn't because it's not good when he's angry. Besides, she said our mommy loved her hair. She'd sit with Emma for hours and brush it. Emma tells me that's what she thinks about whenever he runs his fingers through her hair. She imagines our mommy and tries to block him out.

I know there's something different about tonight, but I don't know what. I already know that I'm supposed to always keep my eyes closed and never, ever look when he's in the room. So I don't know why Emma keeps reminding me today. She's acting weird, and I'm scared, but I don't want to tell her, cuz then she'll feel bad. So I just keep my face pressed up against Mister Wellington and my thumb in my mouth. Emma climbs in behind me and hugs me close, and I try really, really hard to go to sleep.

I can't, though.

I just lie there, breathing dusty bear fur and listening to the wind outside, making the limbs on the big tree rattle and scrape against the side of the house. It's spooky, but Emma's with me, holding me while I hold Mister Wellington, so I'm not too scared. Not of the house or the tree.

I'll be scared later, because I know he's coming.

And then he does. The heavy footsteps. That rough, wet cough.

I hear the jangle of the key in the lock, and then the creak of the door as it opens. I screw my eyes shut tighter and I fist my hands in Mister Welling-ton's fur. Emma's arms tighten around me, and I can hear her breathing. Then I feel his hand on my hip, and I smell his sour breath near my ear.

"Your turn, girlie-girl."

I freeze, then I remember Emma making me promise to pretend to be asleep no matter what. I tell myself I'm as still as a rock, I'm dreaming, I'm not moving at all.

"Is that so, you little bitch? Faking it, are you? We'll see about that."

Huge hands grab me around the waist, and I scream and scream and scream until the hands are gone and Emma is on top of me yelling and yelling, and I can't understand what she's saying until suddenly she's gone, and I look up to see her skinny body flying through the air to land on the other bed.

He reaches for me again, but she hollers, "No! Me! Leave Eliza alone. I'll do anything. I swear."

Slowly, I feel him move away, until I can finally breathe the air again.

"Anything?" he says, in a voice from my night-mares. "Well, I think we can make that work out just fine."

A tight arm hauls me up by the waist and plops me

back down. "Open your eyes, girlie. Or it won't be good for you and it'll be even worse for your slut of a sister."

I make whimpering sounds, and I hear Emma's wet, raw whisper saying, "It's okay, Eliza. I think you have to. I think we both do."

He makes me watch. Every night he makes me sit up in bed and hug Mister Wellington tight and watch the nasty things he does to my sister. One hundred and fifty-seven times. I count them, then mark them in pencil on the wall after he leaves and while Emma washes off in the little bathtub in the corner of our closet of a room.

One hundred and fifty-seven times before Emma figures out what to do. Before she saves us.

Or at least, before she tries.

She picks the lock of that tiny room, and she leads the way down the stairs. We move slowly, careful not to let the floorboards creak.

And I can see the front door ahead of us. It's open, and outside there's sun and clouds and a perfect day. Right there.

We're close. So very, very close.

That's when Emma's scream rips the air. When I see her fly past me down the stairs, tumbling into a broken pile of limbs and flesh and blood on the tiles below.

I turn away, horrified, and see him behind me. His bloodshot eyes. His crusty skin.

His lips curve into a hideous smile, and as I try to run, he grabs my arm and yanks me to him, then puts his mouth next to my ear as his hand slides down between my legs.

"You're next," he says, and I scream and I scream and I scream.

————

I wake in terror, my father's arms tight around me.

I can't get loose. I shake and I kick and I scream, but I—

"Eliza. Eliza, hush. It's okay. He's not here. You're safe. I've got you."

Quincy.

I relax, and the strong arms surrounding me loosen a bit.

"It's okay." His voice is gentle. Soothing, and I press my face against his chest and breathe deep, my hands clutching tight to his shirt. One breath in, one breath out as Quincy gently strokes my hair, his touch as calming as his familiar scent.

"I'm sorry." My words are muffled, but I don't want to move. My heartbeat has slowed, and I feel safe now in his arms. "I'm sorry," I repeat, my chest aching from the terror that had so recently pounded through me.

"Oh, love, no. There's nothing to be sorry

about." There's sympathy in his voice and understanding, and I melt just a little more.

"Do you want to tell me? Was it your father?"

Until Quincy, I'd never told anyone about my
father. And I've never told anyone since.

Neither has Emma. Not even Lorenzo, who we
both love and trust. Some things you have to hold
painfully close, because they're too dangerous to let
out into the world.

I told Quincy because I loved him. Because he
saw the scars on my soul and wanted to help me
heal.

I trusted him. I guess maybe I still do, because I
nod as his arms tighten around me. Then I take a
deep breath, close my eyes, and try to describe the
horror.

"He had me. He was dragging me back, and
Emma was gone. He—he killed her. And I was all
alone and I didn't know how to fight him, and—"

"Shhh." His lips brush my forehead, the touch
gentle and sweet and achingly familiar. "It's okay.
I'm here."

"Are you?" I know I shouldn't, but I tilt my
head up, wanting what I shouldn't want, craving
what I wish I didn't need. Quincy is the only man
who knows my secret past. The only one who has
ever been able to tame my demons, and oh, dear
Lord, I need him now. I want to slide under, to
surrender completely, and let him take me to all

those familiar places where I used to lose myself in his arms.

I want to bring the past back, and even if I can't have forever I want right now. And in this moment, I don't even hate myself for craving him so desperately.

His eyes meet mine, and I see the storm brewing. That familiar intensity, that controlled wildness, like a tempest in a bottle.

"Eliza," he says, though what I hear is, *no.*

"Just one kiss," I beg. "You owe me that much."

He doesn't answer, but my palm is pressed to his chest, and I feel the pounding of his heart. I feel his breath on my face and the heat of his skin against mine. I don't know what happened to us, and I have no illusions that anything will ever be like it was again. But right now, I need to bring the past back. I need to get lost in sweet memories, not in horrible, twisted ones.

I want Quincy, dammit, and I reach up, sliding my fingers through his coarse, dark hair. I'm never this bold, but I've spent more than four years craving something I couldn't have. I've been starving, and I didn't even know it.

He doesn't resist as I tug his head toward me, and I'm ridiculously grateful. I crave his lips, his touch. My desire for him is as strong as it was all those years ago in London, and I'm not sure my ego would survive if he didn't at least want me a little.

The air is charged between us, and I'm certain that I'm not imagining his desire. He wants this as much as I do, and that knowledge emboldens me. I brush my lips over his, a sweet, tentative touch. But I want so much more. I want what we had. His body pressed on top of me, his hands around my wrists, holding me still. The hard tension in his muscles as he takes what he wants, leaving me to surrender to the pure pleasure of being his.

I want that again. To be his. To belong. To *feel*.

I want it, yes, but right now, I will take whatever I can get, and if that is one single kiss then I'll hold it close and cherish it forever. *Just please, please, touch me now...!*

The words pound through my head as I tease his lips, willing him to open to me. I don't know what drew him away from me in London, and right now, I don't care. Those days don't exist. They don't matter. All I have is this moment and my nightmare and Quincy. I need him. I need him to erase the horror.

"Please," I whisper. "I'm begging you."

I don't know if it's my words or my touch, but the dam breaks. His fingers slide into my hair as he holds my head steady. His mouth devours mine, tongue and teeth clashing as he takes and takes, and in the process is giving me exactly what I've been begging for.

We've been sitting awkwardly on the bed, my

body twisted to face him. But now, he takes me by the shoulders, and I gasp as he pushes me back so that I'm lying on the bed. Before I can catch my breath, he's on top of me, one hand on my breast as he holds me steady and claims my mouth with his. I whimper, opening to him, my fingers clutching at his hair as I pull him closer, as if I can capture him in this moment and bring him back to me.

My heart pounds, my body fires, and a desperate heat settles between my thighs. "Please," I beg, and when I hear his soft murmur of, *Eliza*, I know he's back. Maybe not forever, but in this moment he's mine, and, I—

"*I'm sorry, El.*"

In the time it takes me to process his words, he's on the other side of the room. His eyes are wild, his breath coming hard. He looks like a man standing on a window ledge trying to convince himself not to jump.

I sit up, confused and embarrassed as I pull the sheet up over the thin tank top and panties that I'm wearing. "Quincy, what are you—"

"I can't." The words are heavy, and his expression impenetrably sad. "I'm sorry," he says. "I'm so goddamn sorry."

"But—"

He lifts a hand and shakes his head. "I'm sorry, Eliza," he says again, looking me square in the eye. "I do want you, but—"

I frown, and force myself not to press him. Clearly he *doesn't* want me. He hasn't wanted me for a long time.

"You should get dressed," he says. "We can get you a new phone on the way to the office."

I nod, too numb to talk, and he leaves the room, pulling the door closed behind him.

I pull my knees up to my chest, then hug them tight as I draw long, deep breaths. Light streams into the room, and as I sit there and force myself not to cry, I see the photos framed on the top of the dresser across the room. There's something familiar about them, and I frown, then crawl to the end of the bed for a better look.

I gasp, because these are photos of me. Standing beside the fountain near Buckingham Palace. Feeding the ducks beside the Serpentine. Sitting on the grass in Paris, the Eiffel Tower rising up in the distance. And one that a stranger took for us—me and Quincy holding hands in Montmartre, all of Paris spread out below us like a postcard.

He kept them.

I hug myself, hope rising. But the more I think about it, the more hope fades. Because even though it's clear that he still wants me, it's equally clear that he's determined to stay far, far away.

12

BLAM! Quince landed another punch to the center of the bag, then followed with a jab and a swift left hook. He hadn't bothered with tape or gloves, and he'd been going at it with his bare hands since he'd heard Eliza turn on the shower. Christ, but he wanted her, and he'd almost let himself believe he could have her. But no—dammit, *no*.

He should never have touched her. She'd been through so damn much, and she deserved so much more than a man who'd inevitably hurt her. It didn't matter how much he longed for her, he should have never opened that door.

But he had, and now the memories were pushing through. The dark humiliation, the searing pain. The terror. And the remorse.

Pow! Smack! Pow!

Again and again, over and over. As if he just needed to find the right combination of jabs and punches so that he could propel himself back into the past. Then maybe he'd have a chance to stop them. To start all over again.

Maybe she wouldn't be dead.

Maybe the bastards would never have—*No.*

He sucked in air, forcing his arms to keep moving. Faster and faster until his muscles ached and his knuckles bled. Harder and faster, as if he could force the memories out with the blood, and then, maybe, he'd be whole again.

A fantasy. A goddamn, fucking fantasy, and he was too old for fairy stories. He'd seen too much to believe that the good always won out in the end. He of all people knew better. The good were punished. The good lost everything.

And there wasn't a goddamn thing he could do about it.

Fuck.

One final punch, and he bent over, his hands on his knees as he sucked in air, exhausted. Physically and emotionally.

"Does it help?"

He froze, her soft voice seeming to lock him in to place. After a moment, he turned to see Eliza standing there. She was wearing the SSA track pants she'd borrowed last night, but the shirt was one of his. A threadbare Manchester United T-shirt he'd had for over a decade.

She tugged on the hem. "I slept in the tank top, so I borrowed this. It was sitting folded in a laundry basket, so I assumed it was clean. Do you mind?"

As far as he was concerned, the shirt had never looked better. "Yes. I mean, yes, it's clean. And no, I don't mind."

A hint of a smile touched her lips, and she nodded. He recalled how many times she'd helped herself to his T-shirts during their months together. Eliza was the kind of girl who would happily dress to the nines out in the world, but inside the house she was happiest in his old pajama bottoms and T-shirts. He'd happily shared his wardrobe, thinking she'd never looked sexier than when she wore his clothes. Except, perhaps, when she was out of them.

"Did it?"

He realized she'd asked him something. "I'm sorry, what?"

She nodded toward the bag as she headed into the kitchen. "I don't think you heard me the first time. I was asking again if it helps."

He studied her, wondering if she understood the full depth of the question. "Yes. And no." It was the simplest and truest answer. But he knew it wasn't nearly enough. Considering the way she studied him as she helped herself to a cup of coffee, she knew it, too, and he held his breath, waiting for her to ask him again about what happened in London. To press until he told her about the monster inside. The beast he had to constantly battle back down.

She didn't, though, and he told himself he was relieved.

But that was just one more of the lies he told himself.

————

"Okay," Denny said, as Quince and Eliza looked over her shoulder. "You should be all good to go." She passed the new iPhone to Eliza, who looked at it dubiously.

"I'm okay to use it? Even though they had it? My emails and everything?"

"We wiped your phone and logged you out of any apps that were already running. I just changed your ID, and I checked to make sure you're not logged on anywhere else. I put your apps back on, too. So, yeah, it should all be pretty seamless."

Eliza bit her lower lip and looked up at Quince. "It's really okay to use?"

Denny laughed. "Oh, yeah. I see how I rank. Trust the guy you used to sleep with instead."

Quince cringed as Eliza twisted her head to look between him and Denny, her mouth curving into a frown.

If Denny noticed, she didn't say anything. Just rattled on with, "I swear, you're good to go. But I have a filter set up. If your ID or email address end up logged in to any other device, I'll get pinged." She lifted a shoulder casually. "Just to be sure."

Eliza nodded. "Okay. That should work. I don't want to get a new cell number or new email address. Because what if Emma is trying to reach me?"

Quince caught her eye. "If she already emailed or messaged you and they deleted it, then emptied the trash, you're out of luck. But Denny just changed your passwords to your Apple and Gmail accounts. Anything new, they won't see."

She looked between the two of them. "Okay, then. I trust you."

It was a throwaway comment, but it settled in Quince's heart in a way that felt both nice and a little bit dangerous.

"What now?" she asked.

"Briefing in five," Denny said. She indicated the cavernous room now filled with over a dozen analysts manning their computer stations. "I'm waiting for a few reports, and then we're meeting in the conference room with Ryan and Liam."

"Anyone else assigned to the team?" Quince asked.

Denny shook her head. "Just us chickens. Trevor and Leah are in New York. And Winston's in Hong Kong." The organization was still new, and Ryan was very selective. Which meant that the SSA still boasted only a handful of active field agents. "If we need more manpower, you know Ryan will pull someone else over from the dark side for a temporary assignment."

"The dark side?" Eliza repeated. "What do you mean?"

"Denny used to work security at Stark International," Quince explained. "And Ryan used to be the head honcho over there. Still is, technically, though he's been kicked up the ladder. Day to day falls to someone else now, and Ryan oversees the daily grind here."

"But if we need manpower, it's a good picking ground," Denny added. She stood, her hands resting on the top of her monitor. "Anytime this year would be good, Mario. Just saying."

"Sending it now, boss," the skinny analyst on the far side of the room said.

"That should be the last of the reports," Denny said to him and Eliza. "And just in time."

Quincy turned in the direction she was looking, and saw Ryan enter the conference room. The three of them followed, and a moment later, Liam joined them, sliding into one of the padded chairs with a broad grin.

"Let me guess," Quincy said. "They put Pepsi back in the vending machine."

"Funny man," Liam said, then turned to Eliza with a conspiratorial gleam in his eye. "Sometimes it's best to just ignore him."

"Believe me, I know." She tossed a grin his way, and Quincy's chest tightened. For a moment, it felt like old times, the way it used to be so easy between the two of them.

"So what have you got?" Ryan asked.

"Just got off the phone with Enrique Castille," Liam said, referring to the head of the EU task force. "They're using the information you two retrieved to set up the sting to contact Corbu. It's going down tonight. With luck, he'll be in custody by tomorrow evening."

"Excellent," Quincy said.

"Good work, you two." Ryan nodded to Quince and Denny.

"I'll be more impressed with us once we find Emma and the princess," Quince said.

"I sent an email just now," Eliza said. "But I doubt she'll answer it even if she gets it. She's too careful. My whole life she's told me that in a pinch you can't communicate through regular channels."

"Pretty intense philosophy for a private investigator," Liam said, voicing what Quince was thinking.

"She's thorough." Eliza's eyes dipped to the tabletop, a reaction that probably slipped under everyone else's radar but caught Quince's attention. It was, after all, Eliza's most obvious tell, both at the poker table and in her daily life. Any fib, and she lowered her gaze.

Which made him wonder what secret she was keeping about Emma.

"We're getting ahead of ourselves," Ryan said, leaning back in his chair and looking at each of them in turn. "Right now, we're assuming that Emma has the princess with her. But we're basing that assumption on a mountain of circumstantial evidence. Are we getting any closer to finding actual proof? Figure out how those two got together —*if* they got together—and we may have a better chance of figuring out where they are."

Eliza leaned forward, looking around Quince so that she could focus on Denny. "Did those usernames I gave you last night help?"

Before they'd left, she and Denny had made a list of possible usernames that Emma might have utilized while navigating the dark web.

"Afraid not," Denny said. "But we knew it was a long shot."

"What was?" Liam asked.

"We were hoping that Emma had gone into the

dark web forums with a username that Eliza knows. That way we'd have a better chance of following her trail."

"I texted Lorenzo right after Denny fixed up my phone and told him to call me. But he hasn't yet. He might know the password, but I doubt it. That's not the kind of thing Emma would think about sharing."

"It's okay. I've got another lead," Denny said. "Since I couldn't get in as Emma, I made up my own username and went in. We know she was looking into sex trafficking, so I followed those kinds of rabbit trails."

Quince heard the enthusiasm in her voice and smiled. "And since you're telling us all this, I'm guessing one of those trails led somewhere?"

"The Perlmutter Hotel in Pasadena. And one guess who owns it."

"Scott Lassiter?" Eliza guessed.

Denny tapped her nose. "Got it in one. And it gets better. The chatter was about an auction for extremely high quality merchandise."

Eliza's eyes went wide, and Quince saw her shiver. He reached over and took her hand, then gave it a gentle squeeze. She and Emma hadn't been trafficked, but God knew they'd been abused. And none of this could be easy on her.

She squeezed back. And she didn't let go.

Across the table, Ryan pushed away from the

table and stood. "Obviously, we're all thinking that the princess was the merchandise in question. And I have to say, I think that's a solid bet."

Eliza frowned. "So that would mean that Emma learned the truth and got her out before the auction took place?" She tilted her head, her forehead furrowed in thought. "So she's poking around online, trying to get information on sex trafficking and stuff. And Mr. X sets her up. Tells her to meet him at Lassiter's party. Probably says he can be a source."

"Probably plans to kill her," Denny added, picking up the thread. "She's poking around where she doesn't belong."

"But then she learns about the auction," Eliza continues. "I have no idea how she gets the princess away, though."

"For now, we assume that she does," Quince put in. "Obviously, she has more important things on her mind than making the meeting with Mr. X."

"But since I don't know that, when I'm trying to find my sister and that's my only lead, I decide to go in her place."

Liam nodded thoughtfully. "And Mr. X is pretty damn surprised to see you there, but considers it a great opportunity to find out where the princess is, because—for some reason—he's convinced that you took her."

"But why would Emma be the only suspect?" Eliza asked.

Quince released her hand as he pushed back his chair, spurred to action by the force of his realization. "There's video," he said. "Somewhere, there's surveillance footage." He smiled at Eliza. "And that footage shows you taking the princess away."

13

"Me?" I gape at him, my jaw literally hanging open until I realize what I'm doing and give myself a solid mental shake. "Quincy, what the hell are you talking about? I didn't steal a princess? I can't even imagine the steps that would go into stealing a princess."

"Maybe not, but Emma could, couldn't she?"

I nod. "Well, yes. I mean, it's not out of the realm of possibility. That's sort of the assumption we've been going on. But you said *I'm* on the video."

"Let me put that another way. The video shows someone who looks like you. And Eliza, love, you two do look an awful lot alike."

"Not really. She's four inches taller than me and her hair is red. Plus, she's almost a D-cup, and

I'm really not," I add, glancing down at my chest to accentuate the point.

"I've seen the proof. Remember the photo of you two on the Santa Monica Pier. Black and white, and your hair looked almost the same color. She was taller for sure, but in those silly sweatshirts you were wearing, bra size was a mystery. And in a video, she would have been alone. No way to tell how tall she was without a point of comparison."

I continue to gape at him, trying to make sense of what he's saying. Denny seems to get it, though. She leans forward, her blond hair hanging like a curtain around her face. "You're saying Emma got away with the princess, and that somewhere there's surveillance footage which shows the whole thing?"

"That's what I'm saying," Quincy says, and as their words sink in, I realize I don't really have an argument.

"Too bad we can't ask Red if we're right," Denny adds. "But I should hear back about the fingerprints soon."

Both Quincy and I turn to look at her. "You didn't tell me you got fingerprints."

She grins. "I was right there checking his pulse and playing concerned citizen. It was the least I could do."

"You're really good," I say.

She wrinkles her nose with pleasure. "I know."

Quincy ignores our banter. Instead, he pushes

back from the table and starts to pace. "Assuming we're right, then that means that Emma figured out where they were holding the princess, managed to get there, get around security, and get the girl free. Again," he says with a sideways glance at me, "that's impressive for a PI."

I lift a shoulder. "We ran away when she was fifteen. You learn a lot of survival tricks being on your own that young."

"It's got to be the Perlmutter," Liam says, and we all look in his direction. "The odds are good that Emma was operating with much of the same information that we have. That would lead her to the Perlmutter. It's owned by Lassiter, who we already know is into some dicey shit."

"But he's never been on the radar for something as egregious as sex trafficking," Ryan adds.

"Maybe he got in over his head," Quincy says. "But Liam's correct. The Perlmutter is our best bet. Not only is it our only bloody lead, but it's also got a basement."

"Quince is right," Ryan says. "I remember Jackson talking about it once."

It takes me a second, but I remember that Jackson Steele, the architect famous for designing the Winn Building in Manhattan is also Damien Stark's brother. Not to mention the architect for The Domino.

"He said the Perlmutter was unusual for

Southern California because it has a basement and a sub-basement. It was a bank before it was a hotel, and apparently that's where the vaults were. He and Damien thought about buying the property at one time. Considering Lassiter signed on the dotted line, I guess they changed their minds."

"A sub-basement would make an interesting stage for the auction of extremely high-quality merchandise," Liam commented, using the language that Denny had run across in the forums.

"Yes," Ryan says, "it would."

"I'll get Mario on it," Denny says. "If he can't hack into the security feed, then it can't be done. But if it did show Emma stealing away with our girl, then I bet I'm going to find that large chunks of time are missing."

"Check traffic cams, ATMs, private security feeds," Quincy suggests. "We're just looking for confirmation at this point."

She nods.

"As for Lassiter, I think it's time we had a little chat."

"He may be a pawn in all this," Ryan says. "His parties at The Terrace are an open secret and technically legal. A bit risky to add sex slave auctions to his repertoire. Especially at this level. The kidnapping of a princess won't exactly fly under the radar."

"He hardly has clean hands," Denny notes.

"That disk we got is a blueprint to money laundering and blackmail. Enough to put him away for a good long time."

Quincy nods. "So we talk to him, find out what he knows about Emma or the princess, if anything, and then turn him over to the authorities. Ollie?"

My head is spinning watching them talk and plan a mile-a-minute. Granted, I've seen Emma in full-on investigative mode, but it's been a while. It's invigorating, but it's also exhausting.

I lean over and whisper to Quincy, "Who's Ollie?"

Apparently, I'm a louder whisperer than I realize, because Ryan explains that Orlando McKee is a good friend of Damien's wife, Nikki. A former lawyer, he's now with the FBI. "Should be a solid feather in his cap. And if we bring Lassiter in now, then there's less chance he'll discover the breach of his disk and report it back to Corbu."

"Liam and I will go talk to him," Quincy says. "And by talk, I mean bring him back here and into holding."

Liam grins. "Sounds about right. And then, my friend, I think you should be the one to do the talking."

Quincy shifts so that he's looking right at me. Heat spirals through me, so vibrant that for a moment I can't even breathe. Suddenly, it's as if no years have passed at all. I know exactly what he's thinking. I know that he's remembering the way Lassiter had his hands on me. The way he'd sidled up next to me, and tried to claim me.

"Oh, yes," Quincy says, leaning back in his chair. "I think we'll have a jolly good talk."

14

"MAKE A RIGHT HERE, and then a left at the light,"
I tell Denny. It's just past noon, and we're in Venice
Beach. I'd texted Lorenzo to tell him we were on
our way, and he'd responded immediately with a
Thank God, girlie. You've taken ten years off my life.

Considering he hadn't called, texted me, or
emailed me—at least not according to my shiny new
phone—I thought that was a tad melodramatic, but
I'd been so nervous about the party at The Terrace
that maybe I'd gotten my wires crossed. For all I
know, the standard protocol for an operative
walking into a sex party while pretending to be a
call girl is to contact her handler post haste, and
under no circumstances does said handler contact
the girl.

At any rate, I'd see him soon, and I was ridiculously happy about that.

"So how much does Lorenzo know about you and Quincy? I don't want to put my foot in it." She flashes me a grin. "I have a talent for doing that."

I frown as I consider the question and all of its implications. "Nothing, really. Just that we dated in London a while back. And he dumped me." Lorenzo is like a dad to me, but there are some things that parents don't need to know. "Um, how much do you know?"

She lifts a shoulder then lets it drop.

I'm not entirely sure how to interpret that, but my best guess would be *everything*. I frown. "Um, Quincy told me—I mean, are you two involved?" Quincy said they weren't, and I want to believe him. But I'm not entirely on board the Quincy-Trust Train.

Denny hits the brakes harder than necessary and I jerk forward at a red light. "Oh, crap, no. Never. And don't be mad. We've been working together for a while now, and we've gotten to be really good friends. He—well, he's been through a lot of shit, you know. So he gets my moods."

"Moods?"

She shoots me a sideways glance as she pulls into the intersection. "There's this situation with my husband," she says. "It's been a little rough."

"Oh. I'm sorry. Are you—I mean—" I shut up, because I assume that she's talking about a separation or a divorce, but I don't quite know how to phrase the question.

For a second, she looks confused. Then her eyes go wide. "Oh, no. No, no. I—we're happy. We're just apart. Really, really, really apart."

She sighs loudly, and I don't understand any more than I did a few moments before.

"He's a field agent. Off-the-books, high-level operative that I can't talk about because if I did, they'd hunt us down and kill us."

"Good plan." I clear my throat. "I guess he's away a lot."

"Going on three years now." She glances sideways at me. "It kind of sucks."

"But you can FaceTime and Skype and email and stuff, right?"

She shakes her head.

"Not a word? Not anything?"

For a moment, she says nothing. Then she lifts a shoulder as she veers right, following my gestured instructions, which are totally unnecessary since the GPS screen is showing every turn. "That pretty much sums it up."

"I'm so sorry."

"I'm not looking for pity, really. I'm just telling you that Q and I kind of bonded. Being so long away from the people we love."

I sit back, my chest so tight it's suddenly hard to breathe.

"It ripped him up, you know." Her voice is gentle, but I don't find it soothing.

"*Stop.*" The word is out before I can call it back. "Do you think you're helping? If it hurt him so much, he shouldn't have fucking left in the first place."

"Oh, God, I'm sorry. I—"

"Do you know?" I turn violently in the seat so that I'm facing her straight on. "Do you know where he was? What happened to him? Do you know if there is one shred of a reason that I can hold up against the wound he left in my heart to staunch the flow of blood? Because if you do, then tell me. Otherwise, please, just shut up, because it hurts too damn much."

Tears prick my eyes, and I scrunch them shut as I slam myself back against the seat and pull my knees up to my chest. *I will not cry. I will not cry.*

But I'm so afraid I'm going to lose that battle because between losing Emma and finding Quincy I am completely raw inside.

"I'm so sorry. And my timing sucks, too. But we're here," she says, at the same time that the GPS announces that we've arrived at our destination.

She passes me a tissue. "Do you want to wait a bit?"

I shake my head, hating that she has to tend to me. I need to be focusing on Emma, not on Quincy.

Do that, and maybe I can keep my shit together. I push the door open. "No. Let's go."

Once I'm out of the car, I can't get to the front door of Double-T Investigations fast enough. Tate and Tucker, for Lorenzo and Emma. Not the catchiest name, but they never seem to lack for business. Part of that is because Emma gets so many referrals from her friends in intelligence. Lorenzo just thinks it's because of their growing and stellar reputation.

The building itself is a plain office in a strip center located on a street that runs straight to the ocean. Not that you can see the Pacific where we are. On the roof, you can sometimes see a patch of blue if the sky isn't hazy, but that's about it. Not every corner of Venice Beach is as advertised. But it's home, and the office is owned outright by my sister, who made the first payment back when she was only sixteen years old. Life tried to squash her, but Emma kicked its ass. She's tough that way. And that's why I know she's got to be okay. Because after everything we've survived, I absolutely can't lose her now.

Denny and I have just about reached the door when it bursts open and Marissa races toward me. Just shy of twenty, Lorenzo's only niece started working for the firm about six months ago when her stepfather announced that she needed to understand the value of a dollar. Considering she's decked out entirely in designer clothes, I'm thinking the lesson is getting lost and her salary is going to Nordstrom.

"Eliza! Thank goodness, Uncle Lorenzo was so worried about you last night."

"Was not," the gruff voice says from the doorway. He winks at me. "I know she can handle herself." His bushy brows move as he squints at Denny. "And who the hell are you?"

"Denny," she says easily. "I'm going out on a limb and saying that you're Lorenzo."

"Smart girl," Lorenzo says to me. He cocks his head, ushering us inside. It's basically one giant room with four giant office-salvage desks for Lorenzo, Emma, Marissa, and anyone else who needs a workspace.

I hoist myself up onto the spare as Denny drops into one of the guest chairs. Marissa sits cross-legged on top of hers, and Lorenzo settles in behind his desk, his elbows propped on the laminate surface.

He points at me. "I know you didn't take your phone to The Terrace, but why the devil didn't you text me back this morning? Not that I was worried," he adds, shooting a narrowed-eye glance at Marissa. "I just wanted an update."

I meet Denny's eyes, and she fields that one. "Her phone was stolen. Sounds like they deleted anything that came in before we were able to wipe it."

"Great," I say, wondering what else I've missed ... and what personal info they now have on me.

"Stolen?"

"Out of Emma's apartment," I explain. And then, because it's all so complicated, I start at the beginning and give him a rundown of everything that's happened. Including Quincy.

"The lousy little prick?" Marissa asks, her eyes widening when Lorenzo zings a rubber band her way. "What? That's what Emma called him. He's the guy you dated in London, right? And he totally dumped you."

"Doesn't mean you say he's a prick out loud," Lorenzo says. "Didn't my sister teach you manners?"

"Sorry."

"'Course, you're right," Lorenzo says. "Anybody hurts one of my girls, they go on my shortlist. I don't care if this Quincy Radcliffe is the queen's right-hand man. He hurt my Eliza. That makes him a prick."

In the chair beside me, Denny shifts uncomfortably.

"He's helping me find Emma," I say. "So is Denny. They're friends."

"But for the record, you're right," Denny says. "And Quince would agree. He's beat himself up a lot for what happened in London. He didn't mean to hurt Eliza."

"Well, then he's a prick *and* an idiot. What did he expect? Congratulations and a parade?"

Denny grimaces. "Well, for the record, he's on-board now. Looking for Emma, I mean. And so am I."

"Why?" Lorenzo asks, shifting his attention from Denny to me.

I'm taken aback. "Why is he helping?" I don't know how to answer that. To make amends? Because he still cares about me? Because Emma's disappearance overlaps his own case?

I only know for certain that the last one is true, and that's the one I can't tell Lorenzo.

"Why is he involved at all?" Lorenzo asks. "The man's a banker. Or that's what Emma told me."

"You must have misunderstood," Denny says easily. "Quincy works in corporate private security. When he and Eliza met, that's what he was doing for an international investment firm."

"Right," I say, eagerly adopting the lie. "And it doesn't matter anyway, you guys. All that matters now is finding Emma."

I want to tell him about The Perlmutter Hotel and the princess, but everyone from Quincy to Ryan had drilled into me that I couldn't share. I'd gotten there on my own, of course. Basic rule of thumb: when an EU task force and missing royalty are part of the equation, you have to keep the details to yourself.

"Have you heard from her?" I'm sure the answer will be no, but instead, he breaks into a broad smile. "What?" I demand. "When? And why didn't you say earlier?"

"I'm saying now. Marissa got a text from her a little bit ago. At least, we assume it was her."

"We don't have a clue what it means," Marissa adds.

"Okay," I say. "Tell me."

Marissa holds out he phone, and I hop off the desk to go get it. I read the cryptic text, then look between him and Marissa. "What the hell?"

"I know," Lorenzo says. "Doesn't make a bit of goddamn sense."

I read the words once again, making sure to keep my expression blank. Because it makes perfect sense to me, and right now all I want is to get the hell out of here and go find my sister.

15

Tell my friend who talks to the animals not to drive angry, but to circle the wagons.

QUINCE SCOWLED at the screen as he read the text for the third time. No luck. It still didn't magically translate into something that made even the tiniest bit of sense. For a moment, he wished that Denny hadn't already headed back to HQ. She was always handy when faced with a puzzle.

Finally, he shook his head. "All right. I give up. Which one of you is going to interpret?"

"They don't get it, either," Eliza said, then pointed a finger at Marissa, a lanky college-aged girl with a habit of twirling her hair around her forefinger. "You should, though," Eliza said. "You've been there, after all. Twice."

"Dammit, where?" Lorenzo asked.

Quince had arrived fifteen minutes ago, after Denny had called and told him to get his butt to Venice Beach. Since things with Lassiter had gone far swifter than he'd anticipated, he'd been able to come right away.

For the first ten minutes after Quince arrived, Lorenzo had offered him a perpetual scowl. Now, at least, he seemed more wrapped up in the mystery and less in vetting Quince.

"The ranch," Eliza said, as if that should make sense to everybody. Though judging from the loud exhalations and chorus of, *oh, of course,* it finally did make sense to both Lorenzo and his niece.

"Explain, please," Quince said, a little frustrated at being the only one in the dark.

"My friend who talks to the animals..." She trailed off with an expectant glance toward Marissa.

"That's Eliza," Marissa said. "Emma's talking about Eliza."

Quince looked to Lorenzo and was happy to see the older man looked equally gormless.

Marissa rolled her eyes and sighed. "Talks to the animals, right? Dr. Doolittle. I mean, hello? The guy's even British. You should totally get it."

"Well, I'm not British and I still don't get it," Lorenzo growled.

"Dr. Dolittle. *Eliza* Doolittle. *My Fair Lady,* right? And her name is Eliza."

From where she perched on the desk, Eliza lifted her shoulders and nodded. "Yeah, that part refers to me."

"I'll take it on faith," Quince said. Maybe it was a sister thing. "What about driving angry?"

"Not sure about the angry part," Eliza said. "But drive means just what it sounds like. I'm thinking angry means driving fast. So she's saying that we don't have to hurry. Because clearly she's hidden away safe somewhere."

He nodded. "Go on."

"Circle the wagons means the station wagon," Marissa said. "Because that's how we'd get there. In that hideous old station wagon Emma had. And there's a circle of stones near the front of the house," she added as an afterthought. "We pretended it was a fort."

"See?" Eliza said, but to Marissa, not him. "It was easy. Why didn't you get it right away?"

Marissa's shoulders hunched. "Dunno."

Eliza turned to Quince. "Clear as mud?"

"It's about the most buggered up message I've ever run across. But, yes, it makes sense now that you've translated it. Assuming you know where this place is."

She laughed, and her whole face lit up. For the first time since he'd seen her at The Terrace, he saw no hint of worry when he looked at her. As far as she was concerned, her brilliant, self-reliant sister had made a clean break.

He wasn't as optimistic, but there was no way in hell he'd say something that would erase that expression of joy.

"Of course I do. It's our ranch house."

A chill shot up his spine. "*Our*. As in you and Emma own it?" That meant property records. And that meant they could be tracked. Odds were good Corbu's people were already there, coded message or not. "We need to get going."

"We do," she said. "But not because of what you're thinking. It's not in my name or Emma's. It's not even in our father's name."

"But it's yours? As in it belongs to you?"

She nodded.

"Then you can explain all that on the way."

"I've got a cooler in the back and some sodas and chips you can take," Lorenzo said. "Sleeping bags, too, in case you need them." He pointed to the women. "You two go pack up his car. I want to talk to the boy."

Eliza flashed an encouraging smile as Quincy stepped toward Eliza, feeling more like *a boy* than he could ever remember being. "Yes, sir?"

"I don't know what happened between you two

in London. And I don't know what's going on with you now. No," he held up a hand. "Not my business. I just want you to know that that girl and her sister are like daughters to me. You hurt her—you hurt either of them—and I will hunt you down like a rabid dog and kill you with my bare hands." He narrowed his eyes, his bushy brows coming to a point over his nose. "We understand each other?"

"Yes, sir," Quince said. "We understand each other just fine." He gave Lorenzo a nod, then stepped toward the door. He paused, then looked back. "For the record, sir. I think she's lucky to have you."

Then he stepped out the door without looking back.

In the small parking lot in front of the agency, Marissa was slamming the back hatch shut of his black Range Rover. "You're all set. Sweet car. Even if it is humongous."

By the passenger door, Eliza rolled her eyes. "Marissa's aiming for a Ferrari."

"I was supposed to get one for my twentieth birthday, but then Daddy Dearest went and got my mom all uptight about privilege and responsibility and stuff. I mean, come on. *He* has two Ferraris plus a Porsche."

"Yeah, you have it rough." Eliza gave the girl a hug, then climbed into the car.

"You'll keep us posted?" Marissa asked him as

she trotted back onto the sidewalk.

"Absolutely."

"Cool. Find Emma, okay. This whole situation blows."

He slid in the car, and repeated the assessment to Eliza.

"Well, she's not wrong," Eliza says. "It does blow. You want to get on the 10, by the way."

"Interesting kid," he commented as he pulled out into traffic.

"She's okay. A little confused about where she fits in the world." At his questioning glance, she continued. "Her mom is Lorenzo's sister. And they grew up in Inglewood, so not exactly rolling in money, you know? Single mom, got into acting. She ended up doing bit parts, then got a sitcom, then got a small movie role as a hooker who gets murdered after she has an affair with a cop."

"I think I saw that. Wasn't the cop that actor, what's his name? Huge star? John something?"

"That's him. They got married when Marissa was fifteen. So she goes from near poverty to having a stepfather who could probably buy Australia."

"And this is a problem?"

"I guess it is when mom and stepdad want to make sure she understands the value of a dollar."

"Ah. Frustrated youth."

"Like I said, she's a good kid. But according to Emma, she's been picking up more and more hours at the agency. I figure she's trying to prove she's responsible. Either that or earn enough to go shopping with her friends, who all have cash, of course." She shifted in the seat, tucking a leg up underneath her. "I guess she's like a cross between you and me. Started out as poor as dirt like me, but ended up pretty well off, like you."

"Except I had access to my money."

"True. Must be frustrating. Still, I've known her most of my life. She'll figure it out. Most people do."

He frowned. "Do what?"

"Figure it out," she said. "Life throws shit your way, you roll in it, get dirty and pissed off, but then you clean up and deal."

He shot her a sideways glance. "Is that what you do?"

"About most things, I think. But with you ... I don't think I ever managed to quite clean you off of me."

"I'm not sure I like the analogy."

She sat back, slipped off her shoes, and put her feet on his dashboard. "I'm not sure I meant you to."

He said nothing—honestly, he deserved that—and he didn't protest when she reached over and flipped on the radio. "You're going to take the 101 to the north," she said, leaning back and closing her eyes as classic rock poured out in stereo around them. "We're heading all the way up to San Luis Obispo."

For over three hours, The Doors, The Beatles, AC/DC, Aerosmith, and Queen blared out of the speakers, and Eliza managed to sleep through it all. Not that he was surprised. He remembered how she slept like the dead, wrapped naked in a sheet as he began his morning. For the first week, he'd tiptoed around the house. He was a naturally early riser and didn't want to disturb her, especially since he tended to keep her up so very late.

After a week of that, though, he learned not to bother. In fact, he soon fell into the habit of drinking coffee and listening to the news on the radio in bed, just for the pleasure of feeling her curled up beside him.

He missed that—hell, he missed her. But he knew damn well he couldn't have her. Not any more. Not after—

The sharp, musical chime of his phone yanked him from his increasingly maudlin thoughts, and he glanced automatically toward Eliza who, of course, wouldn't awaken unless hell was freezing over.

He punched the button to answer through the onboard system, and grinned as Liam's deep voice filled the car. The two of them had worked a lot of jobs together, and Quince was glad his friend had signed on with Stark. "Got your text. What's the story with this ranch?"

"Eliza tells me that it belonged to her grandfather—a hunting cabin. And he sold it to some land mogul who was buying up ranch land in the area and all around the cabin. He didn't want to sell, though, so the mogul made a side-deal with him. The family could have free access and use of the cabin for fifty years. But it's just a handshake deal with a signed agreement locked in the mogul's safe. Anyone checking the deed records would only see the rancher's name."

"In that case, it sounds like a safe enough place to hole up," Liam said.

"Sounds like. But you and I both know how often things that sound fine go south."

Liam chuckled, but not with humor. "You got that right."

"Speaking of going south, things didn't go too well for Lassiter today." The smarmy bastard had been easy pickings for Ryan and Liam, who'd delivered him back to Quince at HQ. "How's our houseguest feeling this afternoon?"

Quince had acquired many skills during his time with MI6, but the one that had proved to be the most useful was his interrogation repertoire. In fairness, MI6 had only introduced him to the art. Quince had honed his own techniques, refined his own tools, and mixed his own pharmaceutical aids.

When he'd first been trained, he'd found some of the methods distasteful and had been somewhat reluctant to put them to use. But he'd been green in those days. As soon as he crawled deep into the underbelly of the criminal world and saw the level of treachery and pure evil, his reservations had evaporated. And after he'd been tied to the victim's chair himself, he'd realized that he'd go to whatever lengths were necessary to put the scum away and protect the innocent.

"I've said it before and will say it again, you are one scary motherfucker in a room," Liam said. "Lassiter's just now realizing how much he told you, and he is beyond pissed at himself."

"The man wasn't even a fair test of my skill. He's a spineless little worm who doesn't give a damn about the consequences so long as it makes him a buck." It had been easy enough to wring information from Lassiter. He knew that his hotel was being used for a private sale, and though he hadn't been told outright, he suspected that a young girl named Ariana was on the block. After pushing the issue for a solid hour, Quince had been convinced that Lassiter didn't realize the girl was royalty. "At least we know the princess is really away."

She'd been put up in a room and assigned a

guard, and all Lassiter knew was that somehow she'd gotten out. Quince and the rest of the team assumed that it was Emma who had managed that feat, but as everyone knew the danger of making assumptions, they were still working to confirm that.

And since the process of extricating information about the girl had been so damn easy, Quince had taken the time to dig deep into the data buried in Lassiter's hard drive.

"Stark's brought his friend Ollie in for a conversation," Liam said. "Sounds like the FBI's going to take a nice long look at Scott Lassiter's books. Those feds are pretty damn touchy about things like blackmail and money laundering."

"That's what I hear," Quince said, biting back a grin.

They ended the call with Quince's promise to report in once they reached the ranch. Eliza was still asleep, but he needed coffee and the Range Rover needed gas, so he pulled into a petrol station and killed the engine, leaving her to her coma as he went in for sustenance.

"So you got Lassiter," she said, as soon as they were underway again.

He shot her a sideways glance. "You were awake for all that?"

She yawned and sat up straighter, then noticed

the coffee in her cup holder. "Tell me that's for me and I'll love you forever."

His mouth went dry as her eyes went wide.

"Sorry, I didn't mean—*Fuck*. I'm still half-asleep."

"Figure of speech. No worries. And yes, it's yours. I got some biscuits, too," he said, nodding at the box of shortbread cookies on the console between them.

She snatched the box and fumbled it open, but whether she really wanted the biscuits or was just covering her faux pas, he didn't know. "And, yeah," she said. "Sort of. It was like you were having a conversation in my dream. It was all very surreal. Did I hear that the princess escaped? With Emma?"

"Escaped, yes. With Emma? That's unconfirmed, but assumed."

"Well, that's our job, right?" Eliza said. "Yours and mine. To hit the cabin and confirm that my sister has her?"

"Denny's on it, too. She's searching for surveillance video that catches your sister on camera. We won't really need that if we find Emma herself, but—"

"We will," she said firmly, then leaned back and put her bare feet up on the dash again. Her toes, he noticed, were painted pink. They were damn cute toes.

After a moment, she turned to look at him, her head cocked and her mouth curved down into a frown.

He glanced her direction. "Problem?"

"Like I said—surreal."

He ran the conversation through his head, but it didn't translate any better the second time around. "Come again?"

"You. Me. Here on a road trip. I never expected to see you again, much less be together. Even if we are only together by virtue of proximity."

"Ah." He kept his eyes on the road and drew a breath. Then he turned enough to see her and addressed the very large pink elephant in the room. "I never told you I was sorry."

"No, you didn't. Are you sorry?"

"Of course I am."

"Hmm."

He frowned. "That's it? Just *hmmm*."

"I guess ... I don't know. You probably didn't apologize because it was pointless. You figured you'd never see me again, so why bother."

"That wasn't why," he said sharply. Her words were like a knife, and he regretted opening the damn door in the first place. Or had she opened it? He wasn't entirely sure.

He waited for her to ask what the real reason was, but she stayed silent, and her indifference, marked by the lingering silence, hurt more than he'd believed possible, especially after so much time.

The miles ticked by. Two. Four. After six, she spoke, her voice unbearably soft. "I called your office, you know. They told me you'd transferred to Taipei. Just had an urge to pull up stakes and settle in Asia, as one does."

"I shouldn't have—"

"I know you came back to London." The words were flat, no-nonsense, and entirely lacking emotion.

"What?" He'd heard her perfectly well.

"I saw you."

He sucked in air but had a hell of a time catching his breath. "I'm so sorry."

"Well, at least you can now say that you apologized."

"Eliza—"

"No. It's fine. It's more than fine. I mean, I survived, right? For awhile I didn't think I would. Honestly, Q, I was so in love with you it was overwhelming. Those three months? They felt like three lifetimes, and all I wanted was more. Then it was gone—*poof*—and I didn't understand. I was terrified something had happened to you. Then I was angry. Then I thought it was me. There was something wrong with me."

"No." He reached for her, but she flinched away.

"But it wasn't me. It was you." She drew a loud breath. "You're the one who fucked up, Quincy. We had something great, and you blew it. *You.*" For a moment, silence lingered. "I just wanted to make sure you knew that."

"Yes," he said. "I know it all too well."

16

"RIGHT THERE," I say, pointing to an overgrown dirt road off to the right.

"You're sure?"

I smack my foot against the dashboard in frustration because, no, I'm not sure. I haven't been here in ages. Probably not since Emma and I brought Marissa camping for her eleventh birthday.

"It's been almost a decade since I've been here," I snap. "And I was always a passenger, never a driver. So no, I'm not sure. Do *you* want to play navigator?"

He lifts his hands off the steering wheel as if in a gesture of surrender.

I deflate. "Sorry. I'm worried and I'm frustrated and—wait, that's not the turn after all. It's the next cut-off."

He glances at me, but says nothing. I see the question in his eyes, though. *Can I get us there?*

"Really," I assure him. "See the red X on the boulder? It's faded, but you can still make it out? Emma let me spray that. I was eight. Maybe nine. She did it to mark the turn. I'd totally forgotten."

Right then, I'm thankful for my sister's foresight. Because this ranch covers over six hundred acres, and the cabin is tucked in somewhere in the middle. Without landmarks, the odds of finding it are slim. And while that makes it an excellent hiding place, I'm fast-approaching my breaking point; I really, *really* need to find Emma and assure myself that she's okay.

"Still looking familiar?" Quincy asks after we've followed the winding road for what seems like forever.

I hesitate, not wanting to admit that nothing looks the same at all. Why would it? It's all mostly trees and shrubs and those things are constantly growing. Except—

Yes.

"We're almost there," I say, pointing to a dead tree split straight down the middle. A victim of lightning, and I guess the owners never thought it was worth ripping the tree's corpse out of the ground. "We'll crest a small hill, and then the cabin is in a little valley. There," I add gleefully, pointing to the dirt road that winds up a mound that barely qualifies as a hill but is sufficient to block the view of what lies beyond.

I practically vibrate in my seat as we climb the hill. I have fantasies that Emma will be out in front, her hand shading her eyes from the late afternoon sun.

That's not what I see.

Instead of joy, I'm rocked with fear. My stomach clenches, and I hear myself screaming for Quincy to stop the car, because I have to get out before I throw up from the horrible sight in front of me.

The cabin.

Except it's not. Not anymore. Now it's just the charred, still smoldering remains of a few support beams and pieces of the roof. Around it, the ground is also burned, the vegetation nothing more than ash.

I have a vague sense of throwing open the door. Of my feet pounding the ground. Of singeing my knees and hands as I fall to the ground, and then of Quincy's strong arms around me, pulling me back and holding me close as I sob against his chest.

"She got away," I whisper as Quincy folds me into his strong arms. "They must have gotten away."

Quincy says nothing, and after a moment I look up, then follow the direction of his gaze.

Her Jeep. Only now it's nothing more than a burned out shell.

My knees go out, and I fall to the ground, only Quincy's continuing grip keeping me from landing with a hard thud.

He crouches beside me, then pulls me close so that my face is buried in his chest and my tears are soaking his shirt. Gently, he strokes my hair, and I try to catch my breath. Try to *think.*

"We'll find her," he says, and I pull back, needing to see his face.

"You think they took them," I say, as tiny sprigs of hope poke up through the darkness that has filled me.

"Don't you?"

Slowly, I nod. Because of course they would take them. They want the princess—she's a commodity. And as for Emma ... well, she'd be worth a lot if they could manage to sell her. Which I'm quite certain they wouldn't. At the very least, they'd want to question her. To find out what she knows about the scope of their organization—and who she's told.

"Yes." I nod. "Yes, of course they'd want to take them both alive." I pull back, away from his embrace. It's too comforting, and I don't want to rely on what I can't have. Besides, it's hard to think straight in Quincy's arms.

I start to stand, then pause. "How did they find

them? Even if they intercepted that text, they couldn't possibly have decoded it. Could they?"

From his frown, I can tell that the question bothers him, too. "No, I can't imagine they could. It's possible they tracked her from the hotel. Or they embedded some sort of tracker in the princess. I don't know, but it's definitely disturbing. Right now, though, our problem is the opposite. If we want to recover your sister and the princess, we need to be the ones tracking them."

"Right," I say. "How?"

He gently kisses the top of my head, the touch simple and casual, and I'm far too aware of it. Then he stands and pulls out his phone. I close my eyes and try to think as I hear him say, "Ryan, it's me. What's the chance of calling in a few favors for satellite surveillance?"

As Quincy plays the role of super-spy, I start to walk the circumference of the burn zone. Something doesn't feel right, but then again, nothing about this situation feels right. Add to that the destruction of this one place from my childhood that actually has a few happy memories attached, and it's a wonder I can focus on anything at all.

Not that the cabin had been a happy retreat when our dad was alive. He'd lock us in the cellar while he went hunting, supposedly so we wouldn't go wandering around and accidentally get lost or shot, but Emma said it was because he was a controlling bastard who needed to always know just where to find us.

He made us sleep down there, too, but only when he wanted us *that* way. That's when Emma would get the bed and he'd tell me I had to sit on the wooden chair. I had to watch, he'd say. So that I'd know what to expect when it was my turn.

I tremble with the memory, grateful that the bastard is dead. Grateful that Emma got us the hell away from him.

And absolutely terrified that something horrible has happened to her. Something even more horrible than our father.

I jump as Quincy rests a hand on my shoulder, his touch yanking me back to the present. "Are you okay?"

"My father used to bring us here," I tell him.

He says nothing, just moves behind me, then wraps his arms around my waist. "And after that?"

"After?"

"You and Emma came by yourselves, didn't you? You toasted marshmallows under the stars. You walked to the stream. You used that old Canon of yours to take pictures of butterflies. And you brought Marissa here and made it a retreat for your real family. Not a cage built by a monster."

I close my eyes, both amazed and grateful that he gets it. "We never toasted marshmallows," I say, smiling a little. "Emma was afraid we'd burn the place down if we lit a campfire." I make an ironic noise in my throat. "Guess she saw that coming."

"But you're right," I add, as I turn in his arms, then lean back so that I can face him. "We did make it more of a home. Especially that vile cellar. We bought gallons and gallons of white paint, and we did all the walls. We even cleaned out the drainage tunnel so that we could get rid of the mildew smell before—*Oh.*"

I step back so quickly I almost fall.

"El?"

"The tunnel. Oh, holy crap, I forgot about the tunnel."

"What are you—"

But I'm off and running, Quincy right at my heels.

Emma called it a drainage tunnel because any water that collected in the cellar after a rain always dribbled off in that direction. But the truth was that we didn't know what the tunnel's real purpose was. From what we'd learned, the cabin wasn't the first structure on that site. We'd found what appeared to be a stone foundation a dozen or so yards away one time when we planted a vegetable garden, and Emma said it was probably a house, and that our tunnel may have been part of it.

We never tried to figure out the *why* of the tunnel, but we did follow it once. A horrible, claustrophobic experience that had me in tears by the end because the tunnel narrowed so much, it tore the sleeves of my shirt where my shoulders scraped the wall. I wanted to turn back, but I also didn't want to crawl backward, and Emma gently urged me on, telling me it would surely get better.

It did—because we finally came to the end. A small cave in a cliff-face overlooking a fast-moving stream.

That's my destination when I take off running, and when I reach the spot on the cliff above the cave, I lie on my belly and lean over. "Emma! Ariana! Are you there?"

Quincy catches up to me and pulls me to my feet. "What the hell?"

"The drainage tunnel." I point down. "That's where it lets out."

I can tell right away he gets it, and a few minutes later he's on his stomach, watching as I carefully follow the chiseled toeholds that Emma put in place over the course of years. I wiggle inside the small cave, then use my new phone as a flashlight.

"Anything?" he asks, as I sink to my knees in relief. Because there, on the stone wall is a message for me. All it says is *Alive*.

But that's enough.

17

It's late by the time we finally leave the ranch. We're both exhausted, emotionally and physically, and I'm really not looking forward to another long drive.

Even so, I'm surprised when Quincy pulls into a charming boutique hotel on Avila Beach, only about thirty minutes away from the cabin. I twist in my seat. "You're kidding, right?"

He draws a breath as he turns to look at me. "We're both exhausted and uncomfortable, Eliza," he says gently. "We need food and we need sleep. Tomorrow, we'll head back to LA."

I want to tell him that crashing here won't do a thing for my comfort level. Where Quincy is concerned, the only thing that will make me comfortable is curling up against him. Feeling his strong arm around my shoulders and letting his heartbeat fall into a pattern with mine. Because as much as I appreciate that he's helping me find my sister, being around him is hurting my heart.

Part of me wants to tell him so. To just say flat out that I want to keep driving so I can go home. But the truth is that here or there won't matter. Because even in LA, he'll insist on staying with me. I crashed Lassiter's party. Red died after a fight in my room. And I helped Denny and Quincy steal data. Emma may be my top priority—and the princess may be at the top of Quincy's list—but no matter what, he'll say that I'm in danger, too. And he'll stick to me like glue.

"We can stay," I say. "But I want to eat at the patio restaurant. Not room service." The weather is perfect, the ocean is beautiful. And the sunset is sure to be stunning. The only thing that would make it better would be if this were a date. But I figure three out of four is better than nothing.

Since we don't have luggage—something the barely pubescent desk clerk seems to find amusing —we head straight for the restaurant. And, because I need it, I order a bottle of wine. Red, because that's my favorite. Pinot Noir, because that's Quincy's.

"Are we going to find them?" I fire off the question as soon as the waiter pours our wine and drops off a basket of bread. I'm not in the mood for small talk or coddling, and I take a long swallow of the wine, enjoying the tingle on my throat and antici-pating the sweet lightheadedness that I know will follow. I've eaten nothing but shortbread cookies all day. I just want to eat my salad, drink my wine, fall asleep, and not dream a thing.

That, at least, is what I tell myself. Because what I *really* want to do isn't something I'm ever going to get to do again. And I want to do it with the man sitting across from me.

I draw a breath, gather myself, and study his face.

To his credit, he doesn't shy from my question or my steady gaze. "Yes," he says simply. "We'll find them."

"Good answer. Now explain to me why it's the truth and not bullshit."

"Because I'm not willing to accept failure, and because I don't bullshit."

I lean back in the seat and take a long sip of wine. "Clearly you're talking about work. Because as far as relationships are concerned, failure and bullshit are pretty much your stock in trade."

He pushes his chair back and stands. "I can only apologize so many times, Eliza, before it starts to sound redundant."

"You really think we've hit that point?" My heart is pounding. Part of me wants to call back the words. I just want to have dinner. I just want peace.

The other part wants to yell and scream and rant. I want to toss my wine in his face and smash the glass on the floor. I want to hear an explanation, not an apology. Because I don't give a crap that he's sorry. Everybody's sorry about something. I want to know *why*.

I want to know what the hell I did wrong.

I watch, baffled, as he seems to melt back into the chair, then reaches for my hand. "Oh, Eliza, love. You didn't do anything wrong. Not a single bloody thing."

Oh, hell. "I said that out loud?"

The corner of his mouth twitches. In London, I was always saying things I didn't mean to. Usually comments on how ridiculously hot he looked or how much I wanted to be having sex instead of doing whatever else we happened to be doing. I was always mortified. He thought it was adorable. So adorable that the sex part usually came true.

That's probably why I never tried too hard to control that little quirk...

Now, though, I really am embarrassed, and as my cheeks burn, his hand tightens around my fingers.

"Don't," I whisper.

"Don't what?"

Gently I pull my hand out of his. "Don't touch me. It—I'd just rather you didn't touch me."

We're not together. I know that. He doesn't

want to be together. I get it. But my body still reacts
to him, and just the simple brush of his fingers
against my palm sends shockwaves to my core.

I'm glad we have a suite—and I'm glad he's
giving me the bedroom—because I already know
that I'm going to fall asleep tonight with my hand
between my legs. Pathetic, perhaps, but at this
point, I really don't care. After London, I thought
I'd never see Quincy Radcliffe again. Under the
circumstances, I think I'm entitled to a little pathos
and a few self-induced orgasms.

He sucks in air and nods. "Of course. Whatever
you want."

"But that's not true either, is it?"

He doesn't answer, and I can't really blame
him. I'm pretty sure I've crossed the line from
wounded to bitchy. I take another sip of wine to
center myself. Then—what the hell—I finish the
glass and pour myself another. As I do, I notice that
he's finished as well, and I silently applaud. Misery
loves company, after all, and I refill his glass, too.

Our food arrives, and we eat in silence as the
sun sinks slowly toward the horizon. It is breathtak-
ingly beautiful, and my chest swells with awe. In
that moment, I feel the same sense of hope and
wonder and possibility as I used to feel with
Quincy. And the fact that I've lost that is so unbearably sad that I blurt out a question I swore I would
never, ever ask.

"Did you ever really love me at all?"

I see the pain slash across his face before he looks down at his empty plate. The echo of my question fades, and my heart twists with the knowledge that he's not even going to give me the satisfaction of answering.

Then he lifts his head, his eyes steady on mine. "How can you even ask that? Of course I loved you. I never stopped loving you."

My heart skips a beat, and I can't seem to catch my breath. I swallow, then blink as I look away, trying desperately not to cry. "Then why?"

"Please," he says. "Please don't ask me that."

I want to do just that, but the waiter arrives, and Quincy asks for the check. He signs it to the room, then stands, not asking if I'm ready. I'm not, of course, but I follow obediently, fully intending to get into this once we reach the room. *He loves me.* If he loves me, then we can make this work. And I don't understand why he doesn't see that.

"We need to talk about this," I say the moment the suite door closes behind us. But Quincy just shakes his head.

"We're both tired. I'm going to take a quick shower and then the bedroom's all yours."

"Quincy, please. We—"

"Tomorrow," he says. "I'll be a captive audience for more than three hours." He turns and heads for the bathroom, leaving me standing in the living area, wondering what the hell to do now.

I'm not ready to end this. I can't just leave it be until tomorrow when he's regrouped and pulled back even more. The man just told me he loves me. The same man who walked away from me without so much as a "see you later."

As far as I'm concerned, I don't owe him anything, and certainly not polite acquiescence to his request that I simply put this conversation on hold.

On the contrary, he played dirty in London. I can play dirty right now.

And even though I'm terrified that I might be crossing a line I can't come back from, I strip off my clothes as I walk toward the bathroom, then I turn the knob, push open the door, and step from the carpet onto the slick, cool tile.

The shower is huge and enclosed in glass. He's facing the back wall and the shower head, and doesn't see me, and for the moment I enjoy the view of his well-muscled back and his tight ass as he tilts his head back and lets the water pound his face.

He has a mole on his left side just above his hipbone and seeing it now, I can imagine the feel of it under my fingers. How many times have I touched his skin and lazily stroked that very spot as we lay together in bed after we made love?

I want that again. That intimacy. It's not even that I want sex, though I won't deny the way my body craves him now, or the building heat between my thighs. But that's not the core of it. I miss our closeness. The sweet touches. The long talks into the night. The way he always knew how to draw me close and make me feel safe.

I swallow, ridiculously sad, and for one tiny moment I almost back out of the room because I'm terrified that if I walk to him and he pushes me away again, that I really won't survive the loss.

But I'm not surviving now, am I?

I've been in limbo since London. Mourning the loss of him. Not moving on.

Maybe it's wrong to push him, but he was wrong to leave the way he did.

I need closure. I need to know if there's still the slightest chance for us.

I need to either take a step toward putting the pieces of our life back together, or I need him to finish the work he started and destroy me completely. One way or another, it's time for a new beginning, and the first step is to cross this bathroom.

Squaring my shoulders, I do just that. He still hasn't turned, which makes it easier, although I'm surprised he doesn't know I'm there. Quincy is always so aware of his surroundings.

I pause just outside the shower and take a

breath for courage. Then I reach for the handle on the glass door.

I see his body straighten as I tug it open. I freeze, then tell myself that I've already crossed the Rubicon. No point stopping now.

"I hoped you were going to change your mind," he says, with his back still to me. And I realize that, of course, he knew I was there all along.

"I almost did," I admit. "But I think we're worth taking the leap." I ease up behind him and slide my arms around his waist.

"I didn't want to have to push you away," he says.

"Well, you don't actually have to." I press my lips to his shoulder blade, my hands lightly stroking his lower abs. "Free will and all that. It's a thing."

I don't see him smile, and I don't hear him chuckle. But there is a slight quiver in his muscles that I think might be a laugh, and I silently rejoice.

"I wish you hadn't come in here."

I take a risk and slowly slide my hand down, then smile when I discover that he's hard. "Really? You don't seem displeased."

This time, I know I hear him chuckle. "I'm human, Eliza. I never said I don't want you. But I can't have you."

A wave of frustration washes over me, and I have to work to keep it out of my voice. "Yes, you can. I'm right here."

I ease around his body, needing to face him. "Talk to me, Quincy. Tell me what happened, and then maybe I can understand. But instead you just shut down on me. Like dropping one of those giant metal doors. *Boom*, and you were gone. Do you know how much that hurts?"

I'm looking at his face, and I see him wince. He gets it—I'm certain of it. He knows he's hurt me.

And he wants me.

But he's not giving an inch.

I just don't get it.

"Is it me?" This time, there's no keeping the frustration out of my voice. "Or have you just decided to be celibate?" He makes a sound that's almost like a laugh, and a hot blade of jealousy slices through me. "Oh, great. So you've slept with other women since you walked. I guess it really is just me." *Fucker*. It takes all my willpower not to say that last bit out loud.

"Slept with, no. Fucked, yes."

Stupid, stupid tears sting my eyes. "Why not me?"

His expression is so tender that the tears almost spill down my cheeks, and I'm grateful we're in the shower, where maybe he won't see.

Gently, he cups my face. "Because you matter."

I shake my head, not sure if I'm confused or angry or sad. All I know is that this isn't right. "You once told me you'd protect me. Do you remember?

You pointed out your mother's bedroom and you told me the story." I remember it all. How she'd shoved him under the bed. How he'd wanted to come out and fight for her but he was too scared. And how later he swore he'd never let that happen again.

"Didn't I live up to that promise?" His words are harsh, and I know I touched a nerve. "Didn't I get you out of The Terrace?"

"You did, yes. But that doesn't make it better. Because you're the one who hurt me, Quincy. You hurt me when you walked away."

I see the anger flare across his face, but it's banked quickly, fading into acceptance as he slowly nods. And then I see regret.

"Do you think I don't know that? Do you think I don't hate myself every single day?"

"Then why?" I shiver, but not from the water. It's still pounding hot, filling the room with steam. No, I'm shivering in fear, because I have no idea what his answer will be, but I'm certain I won't like it.

He starts to open his mouth and I think he's going to tell me. But then he lashes out, his fist landing so hard on the glass wall that I'm surprised it doesn't shatter.

I gape, not sure if I'm scared of his temper or pleased to have gotten a reaction. I don't have time to decide, though, because suddenly he has me by the shoulders. He pushes my back up against the wall and pins me there, his eyes wild as he looms over me. "Don't you get it? I can't be the man you need."

"I'm not asking for forever," I lie. "Just right now. Don't *you* get it?" Boldly, I cup his erection. "And right now, I think you're up to the task."

For a moment, we just stare at each other, both of us breathing hard. Then he swoops down, captures my mouth, and kisses me long and deep.

It's heaven and hell all at the same time. This is what I've wanted. What I've craved. And I fear that it's going to evaporate far too quickly. But, dammit, I'm going to take what I can now and screw the consequences.

With that as my mantra, I lock my arms around his neck, then practically climb him until my back is balanced against the wall but my legs are tight around his waist.

He turns the shower control, cutting off the water, then maneuvers us out of the bathroom and to the bed. We're both still wet, but I don't care. I'm not letting go of him for anything. Not until he drops me onto the bed, then closes his mouth over my breast.

I moan and arch up as he sucks hard, sending sparks of electricity shooting from my nipple down to my core. As if the thread is visible, he follows it down my body, tracing the path with his lips until he finally buries his face between my legs, his tongue working all sorts of magic as his fingers slide deep inside me, and I rock my hips, wanting so much more. Wanting everything.

When he starts to kiss his way back up my body, I know what's coming—what we both want— and I tremble in anticipation and desire. I reach up, stretching my arms above my head, waiting for him to grab my wrists. To hold me down and take me hard. Or to flip me over and spank me before sinking himself deep inside me.

And yet he does none of those things.

His mouth teases me and his hands stroke me, and it all feels delicious and wonderful. I'm not complaining, but at the same time, I want to fall back into the past. I want the Quincy who possessed me. Who forced me to surrender. Who let me slide down into my own desire and lose myself safely in those dark places. Because I need that right now. With Emma missing and fear nipping at me, I need him to push me to the edge. I need to know I can go there, that he will be with me, and that I can get back okay.

But he doesn't. He knows me so damn well— has always known exactly what I need—and yet he just doesn't go there.

Instead he keeps me on my back and he rides me hard, and yes, it feels amazing even if it is a little tame. I hook my legs around him and cup my hands on his ass, urging him deeper and harder. Until, finally, the friction of our bodies sends me spiraling over the edge and I explode, my body clenching tight around him until he follows me right over into the stratosphere.

It's incredible. Mind-blowing. And not nearly enough...

Stifling a sigh, I twine my fingers in his hair. He slides up my body, then pulls me close. I start to speak, though I'm not entirely sure what I intend to say. It doesn't matter, because he puts a finger over my lips, shushing me.

"You won the war, love. Give me this small victory. Just let me hold you. Just let me fall asleep with you in my arms."

Since that's hardly a difficult demand, I agree and snuggle close, feeling safe and loved for the first time in a long time.

I drift, half in and out of sleep, until I'm rocked into full wakefulness by the man tossing and turning beside me.

I shift, propping myself on an elbow, then gently lay a hand to his chest to coax him out of his dream.

But before I can even wrap my head around what's happening, he's grabbed my wrist and is hurling me out of bed. I hear my own scream echo in the room as he slams me against the wall, knocking the wind out of me.

I try to catch my breath, but now it's impossible, because his hand is at my throat, and I'm starting to feel dizzy and terrified and completely confused.

Frantic, I thrust my knee up and manage to catch him in the balls. He howls and opens his eyes, but it's clear that he's locked in a nightmare and doesn't see me. But at least his hand is no longer at my throat. And as he starts to reach for me again, I do the only thing I can think of. I scream, "Duck! Duckling! Duck!" at the top of my lungs, and hope to hell the old safe word gets through to him.

18

DUCK! Duckling! Duck!

The words burst into his head, past the red
haze of memory, and Quince stumbled backward,
horrified to realize that he was looming over Eliza,
who looked terrified.

This was it. This was why he'd left. Why he'd
been right to stay away. The Berlin mission had
destroyed him. He'd lost Shelley. He'd lost himself.

And even though they hadn't taken her from
him, he'd lost Eliza, too.

He sucked in air, his mind a mess of wild
thoughts and violent emotions. God, he should
have known better than to touch her. He'd been a
bloody fool to think it would be okay. To think he
could ever have any sort of chance again.

They'd broken him well and good, and he'd do
well to bloody remember it.

"Quincy?" She reached for him, her gesture tentative and her expression wary. Smart girl. "It's okay. You're awake now. Everything's fine."

He made a raw noise—everything was a long way from fine—then backed away from her, shaking his head. He opened his mouth, as if there were words he could say to explain, but of course there weren't. He was broken, and that was obvious enough just looking at him. What could he possibly add?

He lifted his hands, as if warding off her compassion. Blocking that confused, concerned expression, he turned, saw his jeans folded over the back of a chair, and tugged them on. He didn't bother with a shirt. Didn't bother with shoes. He just went out onto the back patio, opened the little metal gate, and followed the path down to the sea.

The sky was clear, the almost-full moon hanging low in the sky, its reflected light illuminating the froth on the tumbling waves. He stood at the edge, letting the frigid water of the Pacific slosh over his bare feet. For a moment, he allowed himself the fantasy that he could walk out into the waters. That he could swim toward the horizon until exhaustion pulled him under, and he would drop down, down, down, only to rise up again in triumph, cleansed of all the evil he'd witnessed. The horrors that clung to him like blood, staining and tainting him.

But he didn't have time for foolish fantasies, and he knew damn well that the blood on his hands could never be washed off. And so he clasped his arms around his bare chest to ward off the chill, and started walking along the shore, for no other reason than to clear his head and induce exhaustion. So that maybe, with luck, when he got back to the room he could creep in without waking Eliza, lie down on the couch, and sleep.

Of course it didn't work out that way. He should have known she wouldn't make it that easy. And there wasn't a damn thing he could do to avoid her, because she was sitting on a blanket on the sand right smack in the middle of the path he needed to walk to get back to their room.

"You should be asleep," he said, standing at the edge of her blanket.

She held his shirt up to him, and he took it gratefully. "So should you." She nodded at the space on the blanket next to her. "We should talk."

"I'm tired. I just want to go in."

"Sit," she said. "You owe me that."

"For attacking you." It wasn't a question.

She flinched. "No. Duh. For walking out on me. For leaving me in the dark for years. For not trusting me to help you the way you helped me." She crossed her arms over her chest. "Seriously? That's what you think of me? That I'd toss you aside because of a nightmare?"

He didn't answer. But he did sit down.

To her credit, she didn't push him. She didn't even look at him. She just sat with her knees pulled up to her chest and a second blanket around her shoulders. She reached out with her left hand and took his right, and though his first instinct was to pull away, he didn't. He wanted her touch, the comfort of knowing she was there with him. That she didn't hate him for what happened. And the reassurance that he hadn't scared her away.

He didn't want her to know what had happened in Berlin, but at the same time he wanted to tell her. He missed her so bloody much. Maybe if he'd never seen her again he could have lived with the hole in his gut. But he had. She'd stood there in The Terrace Hotel and he'd seen her and everything had changed.

Him, most of all.

"Quincy?" She started to twist at the waist, obviously intending to check on him.

"No," he said. "Stay the way you are. Give me a minute."

To her credit, she did as he asked. And though he never would have thought it possible, he heard himself start talking.

"You've probably figured out that I've never worked in high finance. And while I've been to Hong Kong, China, and Taipei many times, I didn't go that summer." He paused, but she didn't interrupt, and she didn't turn to look at him. He drew in a breath, grateful, and continued. "Instead, I was tasked with a quick and easy escort job. A favor for a key asset in Berlin. Nothing more. Very low risk. No espionage component. Just a trip like any other trip. At the time I was on the payroll of both MI6 and Deliverance, but I was on vacation from both, and enjoying myself very much."

She ducked her head, and he saw the hint of a smile. He hooked a finger under her chin and tilted her face up to look at him. "You were the best part of that down time."

She smiled, then started to turn away again.

"No. It's okay," he said, and closed his hand more tightly around hers. "At any rate, like I said, it was supposed to be a nothing gig. The girl had been traveling with friends, who turned out to be more into partying than she was. She called her father to come get her in London and take her back home, but he was in Hong Kong. So he called my boss and asked for a favor. All I needed to do was get her home to Berlin."

"I'm guessing it didn't go well."

"No. It really didn't." He drew in a breath, trying to think how to lay it all out quickly and simply. He wanted to tell her, but he didn't want to dwell on it. And once it was out and the air was clear, he wanted to go to bed and hope to hell he didn't dream.

"We were ambushed," he said quickly, just to get it out. "Grabbed and taken to an abandoned warehouse. Five men. I'd never seen any of them before. Or, at least, I didn't think that I had. Turns out I saw their ankles when I was seven years old."

He saw her throat move as she swallowed. "Your mother's murder?"

"I guess they weren't satisfied with killing her and my father. They wanted to take out the entire family. But more than that, they wanted to torture us, too." He stood up, because he couldn't sit still and tell the rest. "They started with Shelley," he said, his back to her, and his eyes on the ocean. "One simple job. Get the girl back home to Berlin." His voice hitched, tears clogging his throat. "I told her I'd keep her safe. They took me out with a tranq gun. I woke up tied to a wall, bare ass naked. And Shelley was in a chair in front of me. Arms tied. Ankles tied. Still dressed. They'd combed her hair. Said they wanted her to look pretty for me."

He turned his head, just enough to look over his shoulder to see her horrified expression. "They took pictures of her. Polaroids. Just let them fall there on the warehouse floor. Then they aimed a gun at her face and told her she was going to die. But if she begged me, maybe I'd save her."

"Oh, God." Her words were soft, barely audible, but they cut through his heart.

"She was only sixteen. And, yeah, she begged.

And every cry, every plea ate away at my soul. I swear to God, I died that day, too."

"They shot her."

He turned back to the ocean, dark and infinite. "Right between the eyes."

"They let you go?"

He made a scoffing noise. "They raped me." His voice was flat, emotionless. "Over and over."

When he looked at her again, he saw that she looked numb. Just like he felt.

"How did you get away?"

He twined his fingers behind his neck and closed his eyes, for just this once letting the memories flow. "Part of my training included drug resistance. Sometimes, they'd drug me and untie me. Guess they figured it made ripping into me that much more special. They dosed me, but they didn't want me completely unconscious because where was the fun in that. One time, they didn't use quite enough. On anybody else, it would have been plenty. But I had some resistance. They touched me, and I exploded. After that initial burst, I don't remember any of it. Just a red haze in my head, the smell of blood, and the sounds of their screams."

She had her knees up against her chest and she was hugging them tight, her eyes wide, her mouth open in horror.

"When I got my senses back, they were all dead, scattered and bloody across the floor. Five sprawled and bloody corpses. I left them there on the floor of that warehouse. I got out. Got to our Berlin safe house and radioed for assistance, then passed out. When I came to, I gave them the coordinates, but the bodies were gone. I was in the hospital for weeks. Then I went back to London for physical therapy. I think I'd been back about two weeks when you saw me, but I saw you before that."

Her head shot up, her brow furrowed. "What? Where?"

"You were with that friend of yours. The thin woman with the curly black hair. You introduced us once at the theater, and—"

"Right. Alicia. I went out to lunch with her a few times after you—well, we hung out a bit."

"I couldn't do it," he said simply. "You were laughing. You looked happy. And I was in a dark place, craving revenge. Not sleeping because of night terrors. And I couldn't—" He cut himself off with a shake of his head.

"What?"

"Sexually. Emotionally." He shook his head, rubbing his temples. "I wasn't in a good place. I'm still not."

He watched the play of emotions over her face and was certain she was trying to think of some argument. Some magic words to make it all better when there was no magic to be had.

"Sometimes I think I'm cursed," he said. "My mother. My father. Then me."

"No," she said simply, and he just scoffed, then held up his wrist, showing her the Patek Philippe.

"Did I ever tell you why I wear this? It's a compass," he continued when she shook her head.

"It's not just a watch?"

"I mean that it guides me. It was my father's, you know. They let me go through his things after they found his body. The watch was a gift to him from the royal family. He betrayed them. The country. So the watch became my compass. I wear it to remember that I have to keep a tight rein on myself. To always think before I act." He drew a breath. "I didn't do that tonight, and I'm sorry."

"You were trapped in a nightmare."

"I should never have taken you to bed in the first place."

She stood up, took a single step toward him. "You didn't hurt me. You snapped out of it."

Her words blossomed inside of him, like a tiny seed of hope. But he didn't trust it. Instead, he said, "I've missed you."

A small smile touched her lips. "I'm ridiculously glad it's not just me."

"I've missed you," he repeated. "And touching you felt so damn good. But I don't know how to make this work."

"Can we try?"

Inside him, the monster curled. Cold guilt and red rage. "I don't know."

"It wasn't your fault. You know that, right? Not what happened to Shelley. Not what happened to you."

"I know," he said simply. "But knowing really isn't enough."

19

"Is everything okay between you two?"

Startled, I look up from where I'm sitting with my feet in the shallow end of Damien Stark's pool. Denny is standing above me looking down, her green eyes reflecting the concern in her voice.

"What? Me and Quincy? Of course." I'm speaking forcefully, as if adding strength to my words will make them true. "What on earth makes you ask?"

Denny shakes her head. "Just a feeling." She kicks off her sandals then sits beside me, dangling her feet in the crystal clear water as well. "I've gotten to know him pretty well, and he just seems off today. You, too."

"You don't know me well enough to know if I'm off."

Denny points a finger at me. "True. We should get to know each other better."

I laugh. "Today may not be the best time for that. They'll all be back soon."

The entire team from Stark Security—including, by default, yours truly—has gathered at Mr. Stark's incredible house in Malibu for an impromptu welcome reception for Prince Michel of Eustancia, Princess Ariana's uncle and the National Security Director for the small country. He'd arrived in Malibu with a small cadre of bodyguards while his intelligence team remained in their suite of rooms at the Stark Century Hotel with Liam Foster there as the SSA liaison.

At the moment, the prince and most of the other guests are in Mr. Stark's massive, underground garage. Apparently Prince Michel is as much of a classic car aficionado as Damien Stark.

"For that matter," I continue, "I'm not sure today's the best day to talk about my relationship with Quincy at all. I mean, we really should be focusing on the princess."

Denny shakes her head. "A little free advice? I promise it's worth more than I'm charging you."

"Um, okay."

"You can't think like that. Not if you're going to survive in this business."

"I'm an actress. I'm not actually in this business."

Denny rolls her eyes and kicks, sending droplets of water flying. "Fine. I'll rephrase. If you're going to manage to have a life with someone in this business you need to learn that you can't wait for things to be calm. Because things will never be calm."

She blinks, and I realize that she's fighting tears. "Denny?"

"Sorry." She sniffles, then rubs her face with the palms of her hands. "Sorry, sometimes I'm perfectly fine and then, *poof*, I'm not. But that's kind of the point. I'd give anything to have Mason here. To talk about things we left unsaid. To just have a *life*. I took that for granted before—well, before his mission. And now there's been no word for so long, and I'm starting to wonder if I'll ever have the chance to say all the things we left unsaid."

I take her hand and squeeze it. "You will." It's a stupid thing to say, because I don't know that at all. But I want to believe it. And right then, I think it's what she needs to hear.

She pulls her feet up onto the deck. "Sorry about that. I didn't mean to get all maudlin."

I think about all the years without Quincy. "I get it. Really."

"Good. So talk to him. There's something real between you two. Don't let that get lost in all the noise." She exhales loudly. "God, I sound like someone's interfering grandmother. But I just—I guess I figure if I earn enough relationship Karma, then the universe has to send him back to me."

I have no idea what to say to that, so I just reach over, squeeze her hand, and say, "Thanks."

She lifts a shoulder. "If I'm meddling, just tell me to shut up. But Quince is like a brother to me, and I really like you. I just want to see you two crazy kids work it out."

I laugh. "I really like you, too," I say, which is a total understatement. I hesitate, biting my lower lip as I look at Denny. Then I decide I have nothing to lose and bite the bullet. "How much do you know? About Quincy's past, I mean."

"Ah, well, I could ask you the same thing."

I grin. "But I asked first."

"Fine. But this is just between us girls, right? If I accidentally tell you something you don't know, you didn't hear it from me. And you know that I'm only talking to you because it's for his own good. And because, well, wine and gossip."

"Scout's honor," I say, then cross myself.

"I think you got that part wrong, but whatever." She scrunches up her mouth as if considering her words, then says, "Do you know about his dad?"

"Yeah. And his mom. And that he still owns the house—or he did back when we were together in London."

"Then you know that eats at him. His dad. Not being able to save his mom."

Again, I nod.

"There's something else, too. Something big that messed him up back when he was still working with MI6 and Deliverance. You've met Dallas, right?" The latter seems like a non-sequitur, and it takes me a minute to remember that Dallas Sykes is Quincy's friend who founded Deliverance, which I've recently learned is now a defunct vigilante-paramilitary kind of organization that existed primarily to locate and rescue kidnapped children.

"Not yet," I say. "But I've seen pictures of him in the tabloids. Isn't he here?"

She nods. "He and Stark are friends, and I guess he also knows the Prince Regent—Ariana's dad. Dallas is like the playboy of the western world. Or he was until he got married. Anyway, not important. I was just saying that something happened back then. Something really bad, I think, but I don't know the details."

Since she doesn't know anything, I'm not sure why she's telling me this. My confusion must show, because she adds, "I asked him once if he wanted the name of my counselor—I see him sometimes when it gets too hard, dealing with Mason being away."

"Oh." I sit up, interested. "Did he?"

"No, and he didn't tell me why not. But I think

it was because he was living and breathing work, so he never cared enough about getting his personal shit together." She climbs to her feet, then lifts a shoulder as she looks down at me. "I think he might care enough now."

I grin, ridiculously warmed by her words.

"It's a party, and I'm having a drink," she tells me, in a tone that suggests it's time to leave serious topics behind. "Want one?"

"No thanks. Later." Right then I'm thinking about what she said. Or, rather, I'm thinking about Quincy and what happened to him. About what I know that Denise doesn't.

And about what Quincy and I didn't say this morning on the drive back to LA from San Luis Obispo.

He'd slept on the couch last night, which I suppose was to be expected, but I'd hoped that we would talk more on the drive. He clearly has demons to exorcise, and I wanted to help. But he'd been mostly silent, and when he did speak, it wasn't about last night's revelations—or his trip to the dark side—at all.

Instead, we'd talked about Emma and the princess and the details of the investigation. We'd both wondered how her pursuers had found the cabin. The place was completely off the grid, and yet the bad guys had made it there before us. And not by much, considering that the ground had still been smoldering when we arrived.

"Even if they somehow hacked her phone, there's no way they could have interpreted that message. I mean, even Marissa didn't get it, and she's been to the place."

"It's possible they have surveillance on her," Quincy had said. "If they worked fast after she took Ariana, they may have managed a tail."

"Then why not grab them sooner?"

"I don't know," he'd admitted, the truth of that statement frustrating us both.

I frowned, another question occurring to me. "Why ping Marissa?" I asked. "Why wouldn't Emma text me? Actually, never mind. She thinks I'm on that cruise."

"Even if she didn't, she might not text you. My guess is she wanted to keep her baby sister out of it."

I made a scoffing noise, but I knew he was right. "Did you ever hear back about the satellite?" He'd called somebody from the ranch, and I had a fantasy that even now NASA had a giant space laser pointed at the bad guys.

"Unfortunately, that's a dead end. There were no satellites tasked over that location, and no way to re-task one quickly enough to be any use to us. And as for traffic cameras, we have analysts reviewing feeds from the area, but this isn't Los Angeles, and there aren't as many cameras set up."

"Great." I'd slunk back in my seat, disappointed.

"At least we know about the truck."

I nod, because that's something. About half an hour before we arrived on site, the owners of the ranch house called the local police to report that their Ford F-150 pickup truck had been stolen right out of the driveway. "But Emma's too smart to keep it for long. Which means that unless a cop or a camera pick them up soon, that clue will be useless."

"True," he'd said. "But at least we know they got off the ranch."

I'd nodded, because that was something, and we'd spent the rest of the ride in silence with Quincy thinking God only knows what, and me having long conversations in my head about what happened to him and how to deal with it, and how if he'd just let me help him, we could get through it together.

In my head, it worked out great.

In the car, I said nothing as classic rock blared all the way back to Los Angeles.

We made a pit stop at Quincy's apartment to change clothes, then headed to Malibu, having gotten Ryan's message about Prince Michel while we were en route.

Since Emma's place had been ransacked, until all this was resolved, I was to be Quincy's permanent houseguest. I did tell him that I was sure I could bunk with Denise if he'd rather. Considering how much last night had freaked him out, I thought he might prefer me gone.

"No," he'd said, and that one simple word had elevated my mood for half the journey.

Now, I hear chatter from inside the house and realize that the group must be returning from the garage. I stand, wanting to get a drink before the whole crowd rushes the bar.

I ask for a martini, then watch as the college-aged bartender expertly mixes it. It occurs to me that he must have been vetted—he's at a billionaire's house serving drinks to royalty—and I wonder if he does this kind of thing a lot or if he's jumping up and down inside, desperate to get back to his friends and tell the story.

"You look amused," Nikki Stark says as I step away from the bar with my drink. "I hope that means you're having a good time."

Damien's wife is beautiful in a girl-next-door kind of way. I know there was a ton of gossip about her and her famous husband back in the day, but to be honest I didn't follow it at the time. Now, I don't really want to track it down. I like her too much, and I hate the thought that she'd been dragged through the tabloids, especially

since I've seen first-hand what a great couple
they are.

Another woman joins us, looping an arm
around Nikki's shoulder as she sticks her other
hand out to me. I take it, a little bit intimidated, not
just by her manner but by the fact that she is stunning. Like, leading lady stunning. And the more
that I think about it, the more I think I may have
seen her on television.

"I'm so sorry I'm late," she says. "I had to skip
out on work, but I couldn't miss this." She leans
forward conspiratorially. "I mean, *royalty*.
Honestly, Nicholas, you've come up in the world."
She hip-checks Nikki, who shakes her head, clearly
bemused. "*James*, I'd like you to meet Eliza Tucker.
Her sister—"

"—is the PI who rescued the princess from sex
traffickers. I swear I want the story. Can you
imagine what a coup it would be to do that interview and air it live?"

"Not the time, James," Nikki says.

"Sorry. It's not. I'm Jamie Archer by the way.
Well, Jamie Hunter, but I still use Archer profes-
sionally."

"*Oh*. Hi." It all falls into place now that I
realize she's Ryan's wife.

"Jamie and I have been friends since forever,"
Nikki explains. "Don't worry. She grows on you."

"Like mold," Jamie says dryly, and I laugh. I

like both of them a lot. "Oh, here come the menfolk."

Nikki shakes her head, looking like an exasperated mom, an expression I assume she has down since she and Damien have two little girls, both of whom are apparently staying with their aunt and uncle so as to be out of the way during the party.

As for menfolk, Jamie got that right. In addition to Quincy, I see Damien, Ryan, Prince Michel, two bodyguards, Dallas Sykes, and a man I was earlier introduced to as the FBI agent, Ollie McKee. He'd told Quincy and me that Lassiter was not only in custody, but that he was cooperating fully. It's amazing what the carrot of a minimum security Federal pen will do when the punishment someone is staring at is hard time with the likes of murderers and mafia types.

I assume that the guys are simply coming to join me, Nikki, and Jamie for casual conversation and refreshed drinks. So I'm unprepared when the prince pulls ahead of the pack, marches straight toward me, and says, "You. Tell me about this woman who has absconded with my niece."

"Absconded?" I repeat, looking from the prince to Quincy and then back to the prince. "Excuse me?"

Damien steps forward, then turns and makes the smallest of bows. "I'm sure Prince Michel misspoke. I imagine the word he was looking for was rescued."

The prince crosses his arms. I get the impression he's not corrected often.

He doesn't apologize, but focuses again on me. "She is your sister?"

I nod. "Yes."

"I understand there was a fire. That she kept my niece safe."

"Yes, sir."

"Why has she not made contact again?"

I glance to Quincy, but answer truthfully. "I don't know."

"Where would she go next?"

"I don't know that either."

"Why should I trust that this ... woman ... can keep my niece safe?"

I prickle at his tone and his implications. "I don't think you have much choice, *sir*, considering we don't know where they are."

His eyes narrow, and I'm sure I've angered him, but I can't say I care. I don't like him. And now I feel even sorrier for Ariana. I hope her father's a nicer guy.

The prince stares me down, and then surprises me by nodding his head, just slightly. "You will accept my apologies. I am concerned for my niece's welfare. We owe your sister a great debt, of course. I simply fear that the longer they stay on their own, the more likely whoever is pursuing them will catch up. I would appreciate, Miss Tucker, if you could reassure me as to your sister's ability to keep my niece safe."

"Oh." Okay, I like him better. "Emma's a survivor, sir. She pretty much raised me. She's taken every martial arts class imaginable, and she's absolutely brilliant. She's been working as a private investigator her entire adult life. And she's very good with kids. She'll take care of the princess, sir. And she'll also keep the poor girl from getting too scared."

I hope he doesn't ask more. I don't know why I didn't mention that Emma worked in intelligence for years. After all, *this* guy must be in intelligence if he's the director of security for his entire country. For that matter, he may already know about Emma. I consider that, fighting the urge to frown. Does he know I'm lying? Or if he does know Emma's secret, would he just assume that I'm in the dark?

I don't know. And all my meandering thoughts have done is reiterate that I am really not cut out for espionage. I can play a spy on television, but that's as far as I want to go with danger and intrigue.

I smile at the prince, hoping it looks natural, then focus on Quincy. Not because he can help me, but because it calms me just to know he's there.

Finally the prince gives another crisp nod.

"Thank you for your honesty. I am relieved to know my niece is in good hands."

Ryan had stepped back from the group to check a message on his phone. Now he steps to the front and addresses the prince. "Your highness, we've received word that Marius Corbu is in custody. With luck, we'll know by the end of the day which of his lieutenants kidnapped your niece."

20

"So GIVE," Dallas said as he followed Quince down the path toward Damien's private tennis court. "What's on your mind? By the way, I like Eliza. She's stunning, too. Just like you said, what, three, almost four years ago?"

"Closer to five," Quince said, then sat at the end of one of the lounge chairs set up along the perimeter of the court. Dallas pulled over a folding chair, straddled it like a teenager, and crossed his arms atop the backrest as he regarded Quince, those deep green eyes seeming to see all Quince's secrets.

He and Dallas had been best friends since they were kids at St. Anthony's, a prestigious boarding school just outside of London. Quince had gone there because his guardian found it easier to pack him up and ship him off. And Dallas had been sent all the way from the States because his father was convinced he needed to get his shit together.

They'd been at St. Anthony's, in fact, when Dallas and his sister, Jane, had been kidnapped. Quince had even witnessed the abduction and hadn't been able to do a goddamn thing to stop it.

As an adult, he realized that any attempt would have gotten him killed. As a kid, he'd felt the weight of guilt for years. And though Quince never learned all the gory details, his friend had confided in him enough that Quince knew that Dallas had been tortured. Brutally. Sexually. Emotionally. And that knowledge had only made Quince's guilt that much heavier to bear.

That was one of the reasons why, when Dallas used his inherited billions to found Deliverance, Quince had signed on without question, his only caveat being that he wouldn't betray MI6 by going behind its back. His father had been duplicitous, but Quince sure as hell wouldn't be.

Because of the possibility for additional intel, his handler had agreed, and a complex dual identity had been born, with Quince being one hundred percent loyal to two different entities. With the exception of national security, he fully shared intel. The only thing he didn't share with Dallas, in fact, was what happened during the Berlin mission. He'd told his friend only that it had gone south, he'd been injured, and that he needed to take some time off from Deliverance.

The truth was, he hadn't wanted to burden Dallas with his pain. His friend had already been through so damn much.

But now...

Well, now he looked at Dallas and saw a man who had his shit together with a beautiful wife and a baby on the way. And damned if Quince didn't want to understand how Dallas had pulled himself out of the dark.

"How's Jane?" Quince asked. "I'm sorry she couldn't make it. It's been too long."

Dallas practically lit up. "She's great. Frustrated as hell since the doctor has her on bed rest, but she's a trooper."

"Tell her I said hello."

Dallas shifted his arms so that he could rest his chin on his fist. "I will," he said slowly. "So what happened to you and retirement? For a while there, you were thinking of quitting this crazy lifestyle. Stark make you an offer you couldn't refuse?"

"Pretty much," Quince admitted. "And I did leave MI6. Easier not to have two masters. Mostly I realized I like what I do. And it needs to be done." He'd thought about Shelley. About all the victims he'd helped over the years. And he'd realized he didn't want to leave that behind. The job was hard, but it was also the light that battled the darkness in him. And that, when it got bad, helped to hold back the monster that lived inside him.

"Glad to hear it. You're too good at what you do to sit around doing jigsaw puzzles."

"Well, yes, that was my retirement plan."

Dallas cocked his head. "Are we done now?"

"Done?"

"With the bullshit small talk. Not that I mind catching up with you, but I don't really think chitchat was what you had in mind when you asked me to take a walk."

"No," Quince said. He stood, then shoved his hands in his pockets. "Honestly, I was wondering about Jane."

Dallas's brow furrowed. "Jane?"

"Did it help? Being with her, I mean. Did it help keep the memories away, or did it just make it that much worse."

For a full minute, Dallas said nothing. Then he simply said, "Berlin. Motherfucker, what did they do to you in Berlin?"

Quince sat, his head in his hands, then looked up at his friend. "Did she help?"

"You should have told me back then. Christ, man. Why go through that alone?"

Quince didn't answer. There wasn't a bloody thing he could say at that point. And after a moment, Dallas nodded and stood, taking a few steps and then returning, as if he had to move a bit or go crazy.

"It helped," he finally said, then made a scoffing sound. "Of course, getting together at all was the first hurdle. There are a few complications when you're in love with your sibling." He paused in front of Quince, his head tilted as he studied his friend. "But that was the key. We love each other. Do you love Eliza?"

"Yes," Quince said, realizing how pathetic it was that he was telling Dallas that fundamental truth before telling the woman herself.

"And her? She loves you back?"

"She does." He knew it. He'd always known it. And as far as he was concerned, the fact that she loved him was a minor miracle.

"Well, that's the key. But it's not a magic pill. You have to talk with her. You have to actually communicate. Scary stuff, right?"

Quince chuckled. "You could say that."

Dallas flashed his famous grin, the one that had been on the cover of dozens of magazines over the years. "Speak of the devil," he said, looking over Quince's shoulder.

Quince turned, saw her walking toward them, and felt the warm swell of pleasure curl through him. It was love, all right. For better or worse, Eliza was in his heart.

"Nikki said she saw you two head this direction."

"Do you need me?" He stood.

"Always," she quipped, then turned to look at Dallas, too. "Actually, I was hoping to talk to both of you."

"Fair enough," Dallas said, taking his perch on the chair again as Quince gestured for her to sit on the chaise.

"I, um, well, the truth is I wasn't entirely honest with the prince."

Quince met Dallas's eyes, and saw his own wariness reflected back at him. "Okay," he said slowly. "How so?"

"When he asked about Emma and why she's qualified to take care of Ariana, to keep the princess safe. Well, everything I told him was true. It just wasn't the whole truth." She grimaced. "I just— well, it wasn't my place to say, but there might be a problem." She looked between the two of them. "So I'm going to tell you."

Quince held out his hand, and she took it, flashing him a small, trusting smile as she did so.

"You can tell us anything," he said. "We'll keep your confidence, and we'll deal with it." He looked up at Dallas, who nodded consent. "So what's going on?"

She drew a breath, then said, "We ran away when Emma was fifteen. She—well, she pushed our father down the stairs. We honestly thought he was dead, and we ran. And then we lived on the street for years, bumming rooms in some really dicey neighborhoods, and Emma would do whatever she had to in order to provide for us. I was still pretty little."

Her shoulders rose and fell as she took a breath and looked between them again, as if to see if they were shocked. She must have been okay with what she saw in their faces, because she continued. "Like I said, she did whatever she needed to make sure we were safe, and when she was eighteen, she—well, she killed someone. It was justified, I swear. He would have killed both of us without even blinking. But the cops tagged her, and she had a pretty stuffed juvie record at that point and, I don't know, I guess they wanted to make an example." Her voice broke, and a tear trickled down her cheek.

She squeezed Quince's hand so hard he thought she'd crush his fingers. "They were going for the death penalty. And then, suddenly, all the charges went away. Her lawyer told me it was an evidentiary technicality, and I believed him. I was only eleven, and I was so happy that they weren't taking my sister. But it wasn't a technicality. She didn't have to tell me the truth—she wasn't supposed to tell me—but we've never kept secrets from each other. Not ever."

"They recruited her," Quince said, his voice little more than a whisper.

She nodded. "A black-ops group. Government, but buried deep. I think it's funded by NSC money, but I've never been clear. I just know that they trained her and they paid her well. We had a house. A real life. And she really liked the work, too. It was totally Emma, you know?"

"That's how she became a PI," Dallas guessed. "That was her cover?"

"Exactly. Anyway, she did it for years. Mostly jobs in the US, but some foreign work, too, though she turned those assignments down until I was old enough to take care of myself."

"You said she did it for years," Quince said. "So she quit?"

"A while back. She still does the odd freelance assignment, but she's legitimately a PI now."

"Why are you telling us this?" Dallas asked.

"Because I don't get it. She's on her own. She stumbled across a scheme to auction off a princess to a slavery ring. The bad guys got really close to her, and she's on the run. And the only one she contacts is Marissa?"

"Why didn't she reach out to some of her old contacts?" Quince said, following her train of thought.

"Exactly. Even if you were completely out of

the game, you'd still know how to reach people to help if you were in a jam, wouldn't you?"

He nodded. "No doubt."

"It's a good question," Dallas said slowly, clearly turning it over in his mind. "And I can only think of one reason that makes sense."

"Someone in the intelligence community is on the bad side of this thing," Quince said.

"Exactly." Eliza sat on the chaise, looking relieved to no longer be shouldering this burden alone. "I didn't want to tell the prince unless I was sure."

"Agreed," Dallas said.

Quince nodded. "I'll talk to Ryan and we'll see if we can narrow down a lead, then we can go to him with some solid information."

She sat beside him, then brushed a kiss over his cheek. "Thank you. Thank you both," she added to Dallas.

"No kiss for me?"

"Careful," Quince said as Dallas and Eliza both laughed. He shook his head, bemused. "Since we're discussing Emma's contacts, I'm not sure that she made the right choice reaching out to Marissa."

"Why not?"

"The timing, for one thing. Someone got to that cabin before we did, but the only one who had that message was Marissa."

"But she didn't translate it," Eliza said. "I did."

"And you were surprised she hadn't already managed that," Quince reminded her. "What if she had? What if she sent the location ahead well before we arrived? You said she's hard up for cash."

"No." Eliza shook her head. "No way. I've known that girl since she was tiny, and Lorenzo is like a father to me. There is no way she would sell us out because her stepfather's being stingy with her allowance."

"People have done even more for less," Dallas said.

"I know her," Eliza said. "You two don't."

"El, think about it."

"I am," she snapped. "Are you? Because not everyone betrays people who are important to them, Quincy. Not everyone is your father."

He flinched, but held his ground. "If it wasn't her, then how did they know about the cabin?"

"I don't know. Somehow."

He held her gaze, and she melted a bit. "I don't do this for a living. How does anyone in this business get information?"

"A bug," Dallas said, and Quincy nodded slowly.

"Possible. We talked. We loaded up the car. They would have only had a short lead, but that fits with the facts."

"See?"

He almost smiled. She looked so earnest.

Instead, he pulled out his phone and called the office. "Mario," he said when the young analyst answered. "I need you to get an electronics team to Emma's PI agency. Do a sweep for bugs and call me back."

He wrapped up the call and passed her the phone. "Let Lorenzo know they're coming. Tell him it's just routine."

"Thanks," she said, but to him it sounded like, "I love you."

And that felt pretty damn good.

21

QUINCY'S PHONE rings as we walk into his condo, and he answers it before the second ring, then gives me a quick nod to signal that it's the office. "Thanks, Mario. Right. That's brilliant. You'll handle it? What? Oh, well that's too bad, but I appreciate the heads-up."

I frown. The only reason Mario would be calling is to tell Quincy about the bug search at Lorenzo's. And from this side of the conversation it doesn't sound good. I still can't believe that Marissa is selling information about Emma to sex traffickers, though. That goes against everything I know about her, and I tell Quincy as much the moment he ends the call.

"What?" For a moment he looks confused. Then he grins, pulls me to him, and kisses my forehead. "You were right, love. The place was teeming with bugs. The sweepers left them in place and informed Lorenzo and Marissa. We'd rather the bad guys not know we're onto them yet."

"Oh, right. Good. But then what was too bad?"

"Red's fingerprints," he says. "Turns out there weren't any." He wiggles his own hand. "Acid."

I cringe.

"So that's a dead end, but at least we know there won't be any more leaks about Emma's location through her office."

"Which really isn't a problem," I say, "since we don't have any idea where she got off to."

"Hey." I'm still in his arms, and he tilts my chin up so that I'm looking right at him. "I'm proud of you, love. You pushed for what you believed in, and you're loyal to your friends. I should have listened to you."

"Thanks," I say, ridiculously pleased with his praise. "I appreciate that, but you were doing your job. And part of that job is to be suspicious. Besides, you did listen. That's how they found the bugs."

"Right you are," he says. "We make a great team."

He leads me to one of the bar stools then goes around and enters the kitchen. "Wine?"

"Yes, please." I feel the need to celebrate.

He pours for both of us, then passes me my glass as he leans on the counter across from me. "I listened to more than your suspicions about the bugs," he tells me. "I was listening last night, too."

My chest tightens with a hope I'm afraid to let blossom. "Last night?"

"When you asked if we could try. If we could try to deal with my rages or night terrors or whatever the hell you call the bloody things. If we could try to make it work between us."

I swallow, my fingers so tight on my wine glass I'm surprised I haven't snapped the stem. "You said you didn't know." My voice is little more than a whisper, and I'm afraid to let myself hope.

"I do know. We can try," he says, moving out of the kitchen and circling the bar. He stops in front of me, then twists my stool so I'm facing him. "And we can make it happen. Together."

I hear my pulse beat in my ear. "How?"

The corner of his mouth twitches. "Oh, you want to do the work? I think counseling's on the list. And communication." He brushes my cheek, and I realize that he's wiping away a tear. "Baby steps, okay?"

I nod, too happy to form words.

"I want to get past this," he says. "I want to get past this rage and this darkness so I can be with you. Really be with you. I love you, Eliza. I've loved you for a very long time."

"Quincy, oh God." My voice is thick with tears. "I like hearing that."

"Just hearing?" There's a tease in his voice as his hands slide down to my waist. "I can show you, too."

"Can you?" I hook my arms around his neck and my legs around his waist as he lifts me, cupping my bottom as he carries me to the bedroom. I laugh, then squeal as he tosses me onto the bed, then follows, caging me beneath him, his mouth attacking mine.

"Eliza," he murmurs, as his hands roam over me, and we tug and pull and twist until we're both naked and touching, with lips and hands and a wild passion that makes me laugh with joy and pull him close.

"You feel so good," I tell him. "Oh, God, *that* feels so good."

His hands are roaming all over me. Sliding over my breasts, slipping between my legs. I arch up into his touch, then cry out when his mouth closes over my breast and his teeth scrape my nipple as his fingers slide deep inside me.

I want to surrender completely to him. I crave the sensation of being completely overwhelmed, unable to do anything except fall deep into a sensual assault. But I bite my lip and say nothing. How can I when this feels so good and so right, and

I can't risk destroying this moment? Can't risk drawing out the darkness.

And what does it matter, anyway? Because I *am* surrendering. To his touch. To his kisses. To our own shared passion. Baby steps, right? And eventually we'll get there. Back where we were before. Until then, I let myself go, reveling in the knowledge that it's my time to take what I want. "Roll over," I whisper, pushing him as I speak as if in illustration.

His brow rises in amusement, and then with heat once he's on his back and I'm straddling him. I work kisses down his chest, then lower and lower until I take him in my mouth, enjoying the power I'm claiming. But I don't just want the taste of him. I want him inside me. I want the connection, the heat. I lean forward, losing myself in a long, slow kiss before rolling on a condom, then lowering my hips until I'm riding him, and the sensation of being filled by this man I love is almost too much to bear.

"Eliza."

My name sounds like a prayer, and I tremble, arching back as his hands cup my hips, then tighten at my waist as I rock against him. The sensation is so sweet, better still when he slips one of those hands between our bodies and uses his finger to tease my clit. I bite my lower lip, and I'm so close to exploding, and I know that he is, too. And I want it —that final thrust, that brilliant explosion—even while at the same time I never want this feeling to end.

"Eliza, love. Eliza, *fuck,* it's the office."

Only then do I hear the chirp of his phone. A unique ring tone that I understand is the SSA. "Bastards," I mutter, then slide up his body, curling against him as he answers. "Right," he says, sitting up and leaning against the headboard. "And we believe him? The Raven? You're serious? All right. Send them over."

He ends the call and slips the phone back onto the nightstand. "Sorry."

"No, it's okay. Disappointing, sure, but— anyway, was that Ryan? What did he say?"

"Corbu swears he had nothing to do with taking the princess. He says he wouldn't be that much of a damn fool, but he's certain he knows which of his lieutenants would be. He says the man's reckless, he put Corbu's enterprise in danger, and Corbu wants to take him down. He says he'll share information in exchange for clemency."

"Information?"

"His code name. His photo."

"Raven," I say, and he nods. "And the photo?"

"Apparently, it's coming," he says, right as his phone chirps again. I crawl over him to retrieve it, laughing as he smacks my ass lightly.

"Be good," I say.

"You're sure that's what you want?"

I scowl at him, but inside I'm cheering. This is sweet and easy and playful, and I think that maybe we're going to be able to conquer that damn, fucking beast that set up residency in the man I love.

His phone is locked, of course, so I pass it to him, then scoot beside him so we can both see the image. It's a bit blurry, but the guy in the picture is identifiable enough. He's standing in a doorway, his face almost full on to the camera. He has a strong jaw and chin, deep-set eyes, and thick dark eyebrows. He looks Italian. Frankly, he's damn good looking, which seems unfair to me considering we know he's evil.

"Right out of central casting as the sexy bad guy," I say, expecting Quincy's laughter. Instead, when I look at him, he's pale as a ghost. "Quincy? Quince, what is it?"

He doesn't answer. Instead he hurls his phone across the room, where it shatters against the wall.

I scramble off the bed, taking the top sheet with me without even consciously thinking about it. I just need to be covered. "What?" I say. "Talk to me."

I'm watching him, wary of the rage that over-took him at the beach. But there's no rage right now. All I see is cold calculation.

When he looks at me, his eyes are flat.

Emotionless. It's like he's crumbled into himself, and I have no idea what's going on.

"Who's in the picture?" I ask, my voice level and gentle and very afraid.

"A ghost," he says. "A ghost from Berlin. The ghost of a man I killed."

22

RAGE AND FEAR and pain and darkness. They burned inside him, eating him up from the inside out.

Right then, he wanted the monster to rise. Wanted it to consume him. To sniff out the Raven so that Quince could reach down his gullet and rip him apart.

But the monster didn't come.

Half blind, he got out of bed then pulled on his clothes. He didn't know where he was going, he just knew what he was going to do.

He was going to find the bloody prick and he was going to slit his throat.

"Quince. Quincy. Goddammit, Quincy, look at me."

He looked. Through the red haze of memory, he looked at her. And he shook his head. "No."

"The hell you say." She was standing as straight as a soldier, her naked body wrapped in a sheet. She was warm and beautiful and perfect, and in that moment he was certain that he should never have drawn her in again. Never let her get close. Because now they were going to be hurt all over again.

Hurt.

The Raven was going to hurt, too. Quincy would kill him—hell, yeah. But he'd make him suffer first. The monster that lived inside him? For the sake of the Raven, Quincy would happily free the beast.

Except it didn't come. He was too damn numb, and the beast was trapped behind a wall of shock.

"*Quincy.*"

He just shook his head. "I was a bloody fool, wasn't I? Thinking that it had all ended. That I could get past it and you and I could frolic through the world in search of a happy ending. Bollocks to that."

"What are you talking about?"

"I said we could try? How? This is my life. My legacy. And I'll be damned if I'm going to drag you into my torture chamber. I'm not that bloody selfish."

He was talking in circles and he knew it, but dammit he loved her. Couldn't she see that he was cursed? Tormented as a child. Tortured as an adult.

And now the ghost of bloody Christmas Past was back to haunt him all over again. It never stopped. He'd never be free of the monster, and she deserved a hell of a lot better than what he could give her. Because until the Raven was dead, he had nothing inside him to give. He had to strip down to the core. Rely on his training.

He had to become a hunter.

He had to finish what he thought he'd already accomplished. Because so long as the Raven was still alive, Quincy would always be a little bit dead inside.

He turned and looked at her again, knowing that he had to apologize, to explain. And damned if she didn't slap his face.

"*Stop it.* Just stop it."

The words burst out of her, harsh and angry. But she didn't cry. She stared him down, her face strong and fierce. "I know you're freaked. I know you're in shock. But you need to focus, Quincy. Because I'm not the problem. In fact, right now, I'm the solution to your problem."

He frowned at her, completely confused. "What are you talking about?"

"If this guy really is still alive—if he's the one who kidnapped the princess—then he's looking for Emma and Ariana right now. So are we. You want to destroy this guy, then we have to set a trap."

The churning in his gut started to calm, and he looked at her, deathly still. "Go on."

"We get them first. We get to Emma and the princess, and then we let him know we have them. A trap."

"He'll never fall for it. He'll know we don't have them, and—"

"No." She shook her head, cutting him off. "No, you're not listening. We get them. Really get them."

He started pacing, feeling more like himself as he worked this problem. "Eliza, you're missing the bigger picture. We don't have them. And we don't know how to get them."

"Yeah," she said with a very smug smile. "I do."

He gaped at her, certain he'd misunderstood. "What are you talking about, love? We've been looking for them for days. Now you know where they are?"

"No, but I know how to find out. It's so obvious I can't believe I didn't see it before."

As far as he was concerned, it wasn't obvious at all, and he told her so.

"It's in the first message she left us. Or that she left Marissa. Remember? *Tell my friend who talks to the animals not to drive angry, but to circle the wagons.* I assumed that the *angry* just meant that we didn't have to drive fast. That we weren't in a hurry."

"Go on."

"I was wrong. Angry Words."

He just shook his head.

"It's one of those phone games. It's a game you play on your phone against other people. It's like Scrabble, but you get extra points if you use curse words. So, you know, *angry* words."

"I know you're going somewhere with this, but I'm still not seeing it." He was, however, feeling more centered. Calmer. And even though he didn't see how it was going to play out, he could see the beginnings of a path. More than that, his promise to her was starting to seem less foolish. *We can try.* Maybe they could.

Maybe they'd even succeed.

She smiled at him, and that seed of optimism bloomed even more. "Come here," she said, pulling out her phone. "I'll show you."

He watched as she opened the app, then logged out. "I don't know Marissa's username, and in case he's got Emma's phone, I don't want to use my regular account. So I'm going to create a new name and then send her a friend request. Hopefully she'll realize it's me."

"What are you going to use?"

She grinned at him. "Mister Wellington."

It took him a second, but then he remembered the bear she'd had as a child. She created the profile, found Emma's username, and sent the request. They waited, but nothing happened.

"If she's not online, it could take a while." She frowned. "It's not that late, though. I can't imagine she's asleep. She never—"

Ping!

She met his eyes, and he felt his heart pound in his chest. On screen, there was a picture of linked hands and the words, "Friends Forever."

"Now I can message her."

"And he won't know?"

"He'd have to be logged in as her, have the app open, and be looking at notifications. Even so, I want to be vague."

She typed, *We've got an Angry Words club going. Better chance of winning when u play in a group. Join us? Just need ur location. Playing in person is more fun.*

She showed him the screen. "You think?"

"Give it a try."

He watched as she pressed her lips together, then pressed the button to send the message. They waited. And waited.

And waited.

"She thinks it's a trap," he said.

"Maybe. I need to send her something so that she—"

Ping!

They both stared down at the message: *RL. Have a glass on me.*

Frustration burned through him. "What? Is

that her way of telling us to fuck off?" But then he saw that Eliza was grinning.

"Come on," she said. "I know exactly where she is."

———

Exactly turned out to be not exactly true.

"She doesn't know the address," he told Ryan as they raced from Los Angeles to Redlands, a small town about an hour outside the city at the base of the San Bernardino Mountains. "But she's dead right about the plan." She was in the passenger seat, and he smiled at her, then reached over to squeeze her hand.

"I was only eight," she clarified. "We lived there for about two weeks when we were on the move. But it was an abandoned winery. And there aren't that many in Redlands. It's not really wine country."

"So Emma and the princess are holed up in this winery," Ryan clarified. "We're going to locate and extricate, get them safely back to HQ, and set a trap for the Raven."

"That about sums it up," Quincy said.

"We're doing research now, trying to locate abandoned vineyards. Each team will take a different location. Denise and Liam, Prince Michel and his team. I'll come out to be on site and I'll arrange for extra manpower from the Stark International security force. Keep communications open. And if you see any sign of the Raven or anything suspicious, radio in."

"Roger that."

He ended the call then turned to Eliza. "Anything?"

She was on her phone, poking around on a tourist site. "There's a pretty famous abandoned vineyard, but Emma wouldn't go there. It would be off the grid. Probably not even on the web, or very difficult to find if it is."

"And you don't have a clue."

"Even if I did, the town's changed. More houses, fewer orange groves. Nothing stays the same except—*oh*. There was a graveyard. I played in it. Graveyards stay. And if you walked in through the gate, you were facing the mountains. Which doesn't narrow it down a lot, but—"

"—every little bit helps. See what you can find."

She poked around on her phone some more, then squealed in victory. "Take the next exit, like you're going to Lake Arrowhead. Then you're going to turn left after a few blocks."

While he followed her directions, she called it in, giving Ryan the location of the vineyard they'd be checking so that the other teams wouldn't overlap.

It took another ten minutes of cruising residential streets and weaving down a few dirt roads, but they finally found the graveyard. The vineyard itself had been developed, turned into small, box-like houses. But the sales office still stood, broken and dilapidated, on a large plot of undeveloped land.

The property was gated, but someone had cut through the chain. Emma, most likely, and they pushed open the gate, then drove through slowly.

"Familiar?" He turned to look at Eliza, who was gazing out the window as if she were lost in time.

"Yeah." He could hear the awe in her voice. "It's all coming back. There are huge wine cellars under the house. Like a rabbit warren. I used to explore, and Emma would get so nervous because she couldn't find me. I got locked in one of the cellars once. They have these iron doors—I guess so that the owners could store the high end wines there—and I pulled it shut. It locked automatically. Emma never did find a key."

"How'd you get out?"

"Turns out you could get out, but not in. There was a hidden latch camouflaged in the stone. I found it accidentally. That was the only time Emma ever spanked me. She was so furious."

"More like frantic, I bet."

"True."

After a few more minutes, they found the stone

patio that marked where the cellars used to be. "There was a building here before," she said, toeing the ground as they walked around. "It looks like it burned."

"Here's the entrance." He'd found a set of stairs that seemingly led straight into the earth. That, however, was an optical illusion, and once they actually started down, the path turned into a concrete tunnel that led the way into a series of concrete and stone storage rooms. A rabbit warren, just as she'd described.

"She must be down here," Eliza said, her mouth curving into a frown. "Should we split up?"

"Absolutely not." He was already worried about having dragged her into the crossfire, but under the circumstances he hadn't had much choice. But if anything happened to her...

She paused, reaching out to grab his arm. "Did you hear that?"

He cocked his head. "What?"

"Behind us. I thought I heard—"

But he didn't hear what she thought, because instead he heard a throaty female voice saying, "Eliza?"

"Emma!" She ran forward, Quincy at her heels, then launched herself into one of the small cellars. He was a few steps behind, saw her disappear from his sight, and felt his heart skip a beat.

He caught up to her, then relaxed. She was safe

in the cave-like room, her arms wrapped around a woman who looked like a slightly older version of Eliza with red hair instead of Eliza's muted chestnut.

They were clutching each other as a petite blonde teenager sat on a wine barrel, her eyes wide and a small smile on her pretty face. A few other barrels were scattered throughout the room, along with a pile of empty wine bottles on the far side of the cellar.

After a moment, Eliza turned to him, her face streaked with tears. "We found them," she said, and he couldn't help but laugh. "Yes," he said, "we did."

"I'm Emma," the redhead said, extending her hand.

"I figured. I'm Quince." She had a firm handshake and a bright smile.

"Yeah, I figured that out, too." Her clothes were dusty and lived in, her face drawn with exhaustion. Even so, she was lovely. And her bright smile erased some of his worries.

She crossed to the girl and took her hand. "This is Princess Ariana."

Quince bowed. "It is a pleasure, your majesty."

The girl smiled brightly, then looked to Eliza, who curtsied. "You're a difficult young woman to find."

"Your sister has been taking good care of me." She spoke with heavily accented English and great composure. "But I would like to see my father now."

"Do you know who did this to you?"

She started to answer, then sat up straight, her eyes going wide.

Quincy turned to see Prince Michel hurrying into the room. "Ariana! Thank God you are safe. Dear girl, your father and I have been so worried."

He took a step into the room, and as he did, the little girl opened her mouth and screamed.

But Quince didn't know if she was afraid of her uncle or the man behind him.

The all-too-familiar man who'd just fired the Glock, straight into the back of the Eustancian prince's head.

23

I HEAR someone screaming and realize it's me.

The world is exploding around me, nothing making sense at all. Except it is. It's like one of those moments in the movies where everything slows down and you can catch all the details. Or like the way survivors describe car wrecks. Everything's crystal clear, but you're not able to stop any of it.

This is exactly like a car wreck. And as it all happens, every tiny detail makes sense. A horrible, awful kind of sense that, maybe, we should have seen coming.

The guy with the gun now pointed at Quincy is the Raven—that's easy enough to figure out since I'd been looking at his picture only hours ago.

And the Raven is one of the men who tortured

Quincy. A man Quincy thought he'd killed but who had, somehow, survived.

"I suggest you remove your weapon, Mr. Radcliffe. Because if you don't, I'll put a bullet through your pretty little girlfriend's brain."

My mouth goes dry; I'm certain he means it. And while I wish I was brave enough to tell Quincy not to comply, I'm not. I stay silent. I don't want to die. Not right then; not like that.

Quincy's wearing a plain white T-shirt and it's obvious he has no shoulder harness. But he does have a small gun in a holster inside the waistband of his jeans. Slowly, he takes it out, then squats to put it on the ground.

"Kick it over here."

He kicks it, but the gun slides right past the Raven, coming to a stop only when it hits the far wall.

"Overshot," Quincy says. "Sorry about that."

The Raven takes a menacing step toward him, and Quincy glances down at the prince's body. "Why?"

The Raven shrugs. "He was losing his nerve." His words are slow and thick in my head, as if they were carved in syrup. "His own idea to punish his bastard of a brother, and he starts to get sloppy. He would have given himself away eventually. I did him a favor."

He's looking at Ariana as he speaks, and I think

that I may be the only one in the room who sees Quincy leap. I want to scream at him to stop, because the Raven still has a gun, but the words stick in my throat. I'm too afraid that the Raven will react to my scream, and if he fires it will be because of my warning.

And then Quincy tackles him, and the gun goes flying.

Immediately, Emma bursts into action. She grabs Ariana's wrist and yanks her off the barrel, then sprints for the door. The Raven manages to get free of Quincy and dives for the gun, and I realize that it's right by my foot. I kick it, hard, and it slides across the floor.

For a moment, I cheer my victory. But that's premature, because the Raven launched himself at it, and just as Emma reaches the door, he reaches the gun. He fires, and Emma goes down, and I scream.

It's her thigh, and I see the pain on her face as she hobbles toward the door, she and Ariana locked together as they try to move toward freedom.

The Raven lifts the gun to fire again, but Quincy lands a solid kick, knocking the gun out of his hand and sending it sliding across the floor and into a drain, dropping so far down it seems to take forever to hit the ground.

Quincy attacks, but the Raven counters and

they both tumble, giving Emma and Ariana time to get out of the room.

"Go!" Quincy calls. "Shut the door!"

Emma stumbles, sickeningly pale. But her gaze finds me. The Raven is on top of Quincy, pushing himself up to his knees. There's clearly no way I can beat the Raven to the door, and so I tell her to shut the door and call for help. She stumbles again, and Ariana grabs her, then kicks the door firmly closed.

The bottom of the door is solid, and that means I can no longer see them. All I can do is pray that Ariana gets Emma outside and that there's a medic to treat her.

In the meantime, I have to fight.

For a moment, everything seems to freeze. Then the world snaps back into real time and I go from feeling like an observer to being very much in the middle of all of this. And completely terrified.

Except it turns out that my terror isn't complete after all. Because there's still room for more, something I find out when Quincy catches my eye. He starts to stand and the Raven lashes out with a hard, fast kick, connecting with Quincy's head and sending him tumbling back to the ground. I wait for him to get up, but he doesn't move.

That's it. He's unconscious—and, honestly, I'm terrified that he's dead, but I can't dwell on that question because the Raven is now coming toward me. Walking slowly and with menace. I've worked on plenty of action movies and this isn't the way it's supposed to happen. Trained spies who are the good guys don't get taken out with one blow. Evil bad guys do not get to win.

But apparently life doesn't imitate art, and I'm left to wonder how—if the Raven managed to knock out Quincy—I'm going to have any chance at all.

I've got only one option—get the hell out. And if I'm going to get to the hidden latch, I have to cross almost the entire cellar without the Raven grabbing me. Even then it's not ideal, because either the Raven will manage to escape with me, or else I'll end up locking him in with Quincy. But if I'm free I can help. Inside, I'm just a victim that Quincy will try to protect. Assuming he ever wakes up.

Please, please wake up.

I glance around, plotting the best course. I decide to race to the side and grab a wine bottle to use as a weapon, then make a run for the hidden latch. He'll know where it is, of course, but I don't see a way around that. And I need to get out. I need to check on Emma. I need to get help for Quincy. And if I stay in here, I know damn well I'll end up dead. Or worse.

Before I can talk myself out of it, I bolt toward the cluster of wine bottles. I smash one, turning the raw end into a weapon. I don't know why I expected that to slow him down. He charges me anyway, and I hurl my broken bottle, hitting him but not slowing him at all.

I reach for more, practically losing my mind as I throw bottle after bottle at him. He dodges them, and they shatter on the floor. He barely slows, and when I finally have had enough and make a break for the door, he dives for me, grabs me around the waist, and sends us both tumbling to the ground.

I thrust my hands out automatically to break my fall, and then scream in pain as I land on dozens of shards of glass that cut deep welts into my hands.

"Bitch," he says, and before I can even react, his arm is around my neck and I'm struggling to breath as he drags me across the room. I kick, but each kick is weaker than the next one, and soon the world turns grayer and grayer until it's nothing more than a deep curtain of black, and my last, lingering thought is that I haven't said goodbye to Emma or Quince.

24

QUINCE FELL in and out of consciousness as the
world shifted and moved, and his battered body
screamed in protest. His mind was fuzzy, but he
realized that he was being dragged across the floor,
the broken glass beneath him tearing into his skin.
His wrists were bound behind his back, and as he
tested the bonds and felt the sharp edge of hard
plastic, he realized that he'd been bound with cable
ties. He struggled, but it was no use. The ties held
fast.

The Raven grunted, hunched over with his
hands under Quince's arms as he pulled him,
leaving Quince's useless hands to drag. Or maybe
not so useless.

He clutched at the debris on the ground as it
slipped by, taking care not to show his pleasure
when his fingers caught a shard of glass.

He hoped it would be enough.

He hoped the Raven wouldn't notice it.

When they reached the far side of the cellar, the Raven dumped him, then stood up and stretched. Quince groaned, intentionally loud, and he pressed the shard into the indention where the floor met the wall.

In front of him, the Raven crouched. "You should have killed me right the first time. Because now it's not only you I'm going to fuck with, it's your girlfriend. Pretty thing. But I don't think she's going to look quite so pretty when she's dead."

"You even think about touching her, and I'll kill you," Quince promised.

The Raven pressed his fingers to his mouth. "Oh! Too late! That's all I'm thinking about. How I'm going to do it. How I'm going to make it hurt. I'll probably fuck her, too. Just because I can. But don't worry—I'll let you watch."

Quince hauled back and spit in his face.

The Raven wiped it away impassively. "Not very nice. I'll remember that when your turn comes. And it will come. I won't kill you fast. Not even close."

"They'll find us here," Eliza said, her voice groggy, but at least Quince knew that she'd come to. "You won't get away with it."

"Don't be stupid," he said. "I'm part of the team, remember? And this vineyard is off the grid.

Going to take them a while to find it. Plenty of time for your sister to bleed out. For you two to die. And for me to be the last victim of his highness. Pity he snapped like that. Jealous of his brother. Decided to sell his niece. Then had to take us all out to cover his crimes. I only barely survived."

He pressed a hand to his ear. "What's that? You say that Ariana knows the truth? She does. She saw me kill her uncle, the man who arranged for her sale. Lots of witnesses to back that up. And then she saw me defend myself. Of course she was scared, poor little thing. But I wasn't going to hurt her. I was trying to rescue her."

"Bullshit," Eliza said, and Quince felt a surge of pride. She was a fighter, that's for damn sure.

"That's not very nice." He stood and walked to her, scooping up a piece of glass along the way. "I think you need a lesson in manners."

Quince saw the fear in her eyes and struggled to rise, but his legs were tied together as well. He could only watch, helpless, as the Raven cut off her shirt and then, very slowly, started to make shallow cuts along her belly.

He heard her whimper, and the sound almost killed him, but he stayed silent, watching as she squeezed her eyes shut, his fingers grappling for his own piece of glass. Twisting it in his grip. Then scraping it like a saw over the ties that bound his wrists.

There was no way to accomplish the feat without slicing his own skin, and he bit the inside of his cheek in defense against the rising, raw pain. He worked as fast as he could, but carefully, too. It was one thing to draw blood, but if he accidentally cut his wrist too deep, he'd be no help to anyone, much less Eliza.

Again and again he sawed at the zip-tie. And again and again the Raven taunted Eliza.

Almost there, love. He wanted to scream the words. Wanted to tell her that he would never even think about leaving her again. That he was wrong to think he had to do this first. Fight this battle. Wage war against the pain he'd suffered and the dark inside him.

On the contrary, she was what gave him the strength to get through it. Now, in the horror of this prison. And every day, when the memories rose.

His only regret was realizing that truth now, when he might never get the chance to tell her. Show her.

No.

He'd get free. He'd kill the Raven. And they'd walk out of this room together.

He just had to keep going.

"So pretty," the Raven said, stepping back from Eliza's body so that Quince could see the red lines that crisscrossed her abdomen. Her eyes were on his, and he could see the pain. But also strength. *Good girl*, he thought. *Just hold on a little longer*.

"Should I fuck her now?" the Raven asked. "Or should I carve my name on her face? Hard decisions, but I think I'll fuck her. And I think you need to watch."

On the wall, Eliza struggled. Quince did the same, the reaction instinctive. But as he fisted his hands and lashed out, he felt the snap as the ties he'd been sawing broke from the force of his violent response.

He allowed himself a second to rejoice before returning to reality. Because his legs were still bound and he couldn't cut those ties without giving himself away. Which left him at a decided disadvantage.

Unless...

He started to scoot along the wall, trying to remember where the gun had landed. Across the room, Eliza had her eyes screwed shut as the Raven dragged a shard of glass down to her sex. *Christ, was he going to mutilate her?*

"I'll fucking kill you," he said, just to get the tosser's attention.

It worked. The prick turned, glowered at him, then opened his eyes in surprise. Quince still had his hands behind him, but he'd inched down the wall. And the Raven had to know his destination.

"Not too bright are you? Grab a gun with your

hands tied like that and you'll probably shoot your own ass off. Not to worry. I'll save you from temptation."

He stepped away from Eliza—thank God—and started toward Quince. "Naughty, naughty."

Quincy waited. He was weak and sore and battered, and that meant he couldn't be sure of his aim. He needed to be dead-on. Which meant he had to risk waiting.

One step toward him, then another. The Raven flashed that vile smile. Silently promising Quince unendurable pain.

"I'll just get that gun out of your way. Don't want you playing with naughty toys, do we?"

He bent over as he came closer, and as he did, Quince thrust out his arm, his fingers closing over the handle of his small Ruger. He twisted, aimed, and got off three to the chest.

If the whole situation wasn't so horrible, the expression on the Raven's face as he fell forward would have been comical. Blood pumped out of him as his heart pounded out its last few beats. Then the Raven stilled, his blood spreading.

The bloody bastard was dead.

As fast as he could, Quince used his shard of glass to cut through the ties around his ankles, calling out to Eliza as he did, telling her he'd be right there.

He pulled his phone free and saw that there

was no signal, which meant the team couldn't track them. Hopefully Emma was okay. With luck, she'd gotten clear of the cellar and even now Ryan and the others were arriving with a full medical team.

But he couldn't worry about that now. Right then all he wanted was to get Eliza free. And he stumbled to where the Raven had bound her to a built-in wine rack, then gently cut the zip-ties to release her. Her wounds weren't deep, and he rejoiced in that one small blessing as he peeled off his shirt and then carefully covered her.

"I love you," she said, her voice slurred with exhaustion but her words filling his heart to bursting. "I'm so damn tired."

"Shock," he told her. "It's okay. I've got you. And Eliza, love, I promise, I'm never letting you go again."

EPILOGUE

Quince woke to sound of children laughing and the feel of a naked woman in his arms. Slowly, he slid his hand over her waist and hip, careful not to touch her injured belly.

Eliza sighed and wriggled against him. "Nice way to wake up," she murmured. "Will be even nicer when I can move without pain."

"You'll get there," he said. "We both will."

He sat up, intending to go relax by the pool with some coffee. Stark and Nikki had insisted that Emma, Ariana, Eliza, and Quince stay on the property overnight, along with the doctor he'd brought in to treat them. Emma and Ariana had stayed in the actual house, while Quince and Eliza had been given the guest house.

Now, they both dressed quickly and headed to the pool where Ariana was in the water with the

Starks' daughters, Lara and Anne. Emma was by the pool, her thigh thoroughly bandaged and a promise from the doctor that she would make a full recovery.

Ryan had ordered a full briefing that morning, and Denny was already present. Liam was probably inside, as he was perpetually prompt.

"I'm going to go get a coffee," Eliza said. "Bring you one?"

"I'll get it for you," he said.

"Nope. I can manage. It's the least I can do for my hero." She bent over and kissed him, long and slow, then pulled back with a grin. "Once I'm healed I can do more than that, too."

He laughed. "Fair enough. For now, it's coffee and kisses."

While she went inside, he sat down by Denny, who shot him a bright smile.

"I'm so glad you two are together," she said. "You were meant to be, you know."

"I do," he said. "And I'm determined not to blow it. We're even doing counseling. First session next Thursday."

"Good for you. I'm really happy for you."

He believed her, but he couldn't ignore her melancholy tone. He pressed his hand over hers. "Are you okay?"

She blinked quickly, then nodded. "Just melancholy. I love you, and you're one of my best friends, so don't take this the wrong way, but I miss Mason so much, and right now I'm so goddamn jealous I can't see straight."

"I'm sorry, Denny. I wish I could give him back to you."

She nodded. "I know." She twisted around and pointed toward the door where Eliza was emerging with a tray. "Looks like she brought coffee for everyone. You should give her a hand."

He recognized it as a dismissal, and did as she suggested.

"Is Denny okay?" Eliza asked as he took the tray.

"Lonely," he said, and saw the compassion on her face.

She smiled up at him. "Just goes to show you. We can never take anything for granted."

"Never," he said. "That's a promise."

She followed him as he took the tray to the table beside Emma, then they settled in two of the empty chairs beside her in the shade of the patio umbrella.

"When do you leave?" he asked. Despite her injury, Emma had insisted on escorting Ariana home that afternoon, on temporary assignment to the SSA.

"Not for a few more hours. It's nice to just chill after yesterday."

"That it is. Still, if you feel the need for a little more excitement in your life..."

He let it hang out there; he knew that Ryan had already talked to Emma about recruiting her.

She laughed. "You people are relentless."

"Maybe we just know talent when we see it. You'd make a great team member."

"I'm not really a team player." She shot a glance toward her sister. "But if I were, this would be a pretty good place."

Behind them, he heard Denny's phone ring, and she stood up, then crossed to the far side of the patio to take the call.

A few moments later, she returned, looking more than a little shell-shocked.

Eliza stood, going immediately to her side. "Denny? What's wrong?"

"That was Colonel Seagrave," she said, her voice thin. Shocked. "Mason's boss."

She lifted her face, her eyes not quite focused as she looked around the group. "Mason's back," she said. "And he doesn't have a clue who he is."

The End

Want to find out what happens to Denny and

Mason? Be sure to preorder your copy of Broken With You!

Charismatic. Dangerous. Sexy as hell.
Meet the men of Stark Security.

Shattered With You
Broken With You
Ruined With You

RELEASE ME

CHAPTER ONE EXCERPT

From the author - Release Me introduced millions of readers to the world of Damien Stark. If you haven't read Nikki & Damien's story, I hope you enjoy this peek into their world!

A cool ocean breeze caresses my bare shoulders, and I shiver, wishing I'd taken my roommate's advice and brought a shawl with me tonight. I arrived in Los Angeles only four days ago, and I haven't yet adjusted to the concept of summer temperatures changing with the setting of the sun. In Dallas, June is hot, July is hotter, and August is hell.

Not so in California, at least not by the beach. LA Lesson Number One: Always carry a sweater if you'll be out after dark.

Of course, I could leave the balcony and go back inside to the party. Mingle with the millionaires. Chat up the celebrities. Gaze dutifully at the paintings. It is a gala art opening, after all, and my boss brought me here to meet and greet and charm and chat. Not to lust over the panorama that is coming alive in front of me. Bloodred clouds bursting against the pale orange sky. Blue-gray waves shimmering with dappled gold.

I press my hands against the balcony rail and lean forward, drawn to the intense, unreachable beauty of the setting sun. I regret that I didn't bring the battered Nikon I've had since high school. Not that it would have fit in my itty-bitty beaded purse. And a bulky camera bag paired with a little black dress is a big, fat fashion no-no.

But this is my very first Pacific Ocean sunset, and I'm determined to document the moment. I pull out my iPhone and snap a picture.

"Almost makes the paintings inside seem redundant, doesn't it?" I recognize the throaty, feminine voice and turn to face Evelyn Dodge, retired actress turned agent turned patron of the arts—and my hostess for the evening.

"I'm so sorry. I know I must look like a giddy tourist, but we don't have sunsets like this in Dallas."

"Don't apologize," she says. "I pay for that view every month when I write the mortgage check. It damn well better be spectacular."

I laugh, immediately more at ease.

"Hiding out?"

"Excuse me?"

"You're Carl's new assistant, right?" she asks, referring to my boss of three days.

"Nikki Fairchild."

"I remember now. Nikki from Texas." She looks me up and down, and I wonder if she's disappointed that I don't have big hair and cowboy boots. "So who does he want you to charm?"

"Charm?" I repeat, as if I don't know exactly what she means.

She cocks a single brow. "Honey, the man would rather walk on burning coals than come to an art show. He's fishing for investors and you're the bait." She makes a rough noise in the back of her throat. "Don't worry. I won't press you to tell me who. And I don't blame you for hiding out. Carl's brilliant, but he's a bit of a prick."

"It's the brilliant part I signed on for," I say, and she barks out a laugh.

The truth is that she's right about me being the bait. "Wear a cocktail dress," Carl had said. "Something flirty."

Seriously? I mean, *Seriously?*

I should have told him to wear his own damn cocktail dress. But I didn't. Because I want this job. I fought to get this job. Carl's company, C-

Squared Technologies, successfully launched three web-based products in the last eighteen months. That track record had caught the industry's eye, and Carl had been hailed as a man to watch.

More important from my perspective, that meant he was a man to learn from, and I'd prepared for the job interview with an intensity bordering on obsession. Landing the position had been a huge coup for me. So what if he wanted me to wear something flirty? It was a small price to pay.

Shit.

"I need to get back to being the bait," I say.

"Oh, hell. Now I've gone and made you feel either guilty or self-conscious. Don't be. Let them get liquored up in there first. You catch more flies with alcohol anyway. Trust me. I know."

She's holding a pack of cigarettes, and now she taps one out, then extends the pack to me. I shake my head. I love the smell of tobacco—it reminds me of my grandfather—but actually inhaling the smoke does nothing for me.

"I'm too old and set in my ways to quit," she says. "But God forbid I smoke in my own damn house. I swear, the mob would burn me in effigy. You're not going to start lecturing me on the dangers of secondhand smoke, are you?"

"No," I promise.

"Then how about a light?"

I hold up the itty-bitty purse. "One lipstick, a credit card, my driver's license, and my phone."

"No condom?"

"I didn't think it was that kind of party," I say dryly.

"I knew I liked you." She glances around the balcony. "What the hell kind of party am I throwing if I don't even have one goddamn candle on one goddamn table? Well, fuck it." She puts the unlit cigarette to her mouth and inhales, her eyes closed and her expression rapturous. I can't help but like her. She wears hardly any makeup, in stark contrast to all the other women here tonight, myself included, and her dress is more of a caftan, the batik pattern as interesting as the woman herself.

She's what my mother would call a brassy broad—loud, large, opinionated, and self-confident. My mother would hate her. I think she's awesome.

She drops the unlit cigarette onto the tile and grinds it with the toe of her shoe. Then she signals to one of the catering staff, a girl dressed all in black and carrying a tray of champagne glasses.

The girl fumbles for a minute with the sliding door that opens onto the balcony, and I imagine those flutes tumbling off, breaking against the hard tile, the scattered shards glittering like a wash of diamonds.

I picture myself bending to snatch up a broken stem. I see the raw edge cutting into the soft flesh at the base of my thumb as I squeeze. I watch myself clutching it tighter, drawing strength from the pain, the way some people might try to extract luck from a rabbit's foot.

The fantasy blurs with memory, jarring me with its potency. It's fast and powerful, and a little disturbing because I haven't needed the pain in a long time, and I don't understand why I'm thinking about it now, when I feel steady and in control.

I am fine, I think. *I am fine, I am fine, I am fine.*

"Take one, honey," Evelyn says easily, holding a flute out to me.

I hesitate, searching her face for signs that my mask has slipped and she's caught a glimpse of my rawness. But her face is clear and genial.

"No, don't you argue," she adds, misinterpreting my hesitation. "I bought a dozen cases and I hate to see good alcohol go to waste. Hell no," she adds when the girl tries to hand her a flute. "I hate the stuff. Get me a vodka. Straight up. Chilled. Four olives. Hurry up, now. Do you want me to dry up like a leaf and float away?"

The girl shakes her head, looking a bit like a twitchy, frightened rabbit. Possibly one that had sacrificed his foot for someone else's good luck.

Evelyn's attention returns to me. "So how do you like LA? What have you seen? Where have you been? Have you bought a map of the stars yet?

Dear God, tell me you're not getting sucked into all that tourist bullshit."

"Mostly I've seen miles of freeway and the inside of my apartment."

"Well, that's just sad. Makes me even more glad that Carl dragged your skinny ass all the way out here tonight."

I've put on fifteen welcome pounds since the years when my mother monitored every tiny thing that went in my mouth, and while I'm perfectly happy with my size-eight ass, I wouldn't describe it as skinny. I know Evelyn means it as a compliment, though, and so I smile. "I'm glad he brought me, too. The paintings really are amazing."

"Now don't do that—don't you go sliding into the polite-conversation routine. No, no," she says before I can protest. "I'm sure you mean it. Hell, the paintings are wonderful. But you're getting the flat-eyed look of a girl on her best behavior, and we can't have that. Not when I was getting to know the real you."

"Sorry," I say. "I swear I'm not fading away on you."

Because I genuinely like her, I don't tell her that she's wrong—she hasn't met the real Nikki Fairchild. She's met Social Nikki who, much like Malibu Barbie, comes with a complete set of accessories. In my case, it's not a bikini and a convertible.

Instead, I have the *Elizabeth Fairchild Guide for Social Gatherings*.

My mother's big on rules. She claims it's her Southern upbringing. In my weaker moments, I agree. Mostly, I just think she's a controlling bitch. Since the first time she took me for tea at the Mansion at Turtle Creek in Dallas at age three, I have had the rules drilled into my head. How to walk, how to talk, how to dress. What to eat, how much to drink, what kinds of jokes to tell.

I have it all down, every trick, every nuance, and I wear my practiced pageant smile like armor against the world. The result being that I don't think I could truly be myself at a party even if my life depended on it.

This, however, is not something Evelyn needs to know.

"Where exactly are you living?" she asks.

"Studio City. I'm sharing a condo with my best friend from high school."

"Straight down the 101 for work and then back home again. No wonder you've only seen concrete. Didn't anyone tell you that you should have taken an apartment on the Westside?"

"Too pricey to go it alone," I admit, and I can tell that my admission surprises her. When I make the effort—like when I'm Social Nikki—I can't help but look like I come from money. Probably because

I do. Come from it, that is. But that doesn't mean I brought it with me.

"How old are you?"

"Twenty-four."

Evelyn nods sagely, as if my age reveals some secret about me. "You'll be wanting a place of your own soon enough. You call me when you do and we'll find you someplace with a view. Not as good as this one, of course, but we can manage something better than a freeway on-ramp."

"It's not that bad, I promise."

"Of course it's not," she says in a tone that says the exact opposite. "As for views," she continues, gesturing toward the now-dark ocean and the sky that's starting to bloom with stars, "you're welcome to come back anytime and share mine."

"I might take you up on that," I admit. "I'd love to bring a decent camera back here and take a shot or two."

"It's an open invitation. I'll provide the wine and you can provide the entertainment. A young woman loose in the city. Will it be a drama? A rom-com? Not a tragedy, I hope. I love a good cry as much as the next woman, but I like you. You need a happy ending."

I tense, but Evelyn doesn't know she's hit a nerve. That's why I moved to LA, after all. New life. New story. New Nikki.

I ramp up the Social Nikki smile and lift my

champagne flute. "To happy endings. And to this amazing party. I think I've kept you from it long enough."

"Bullshit," she says. "I'm the one monopolizing you, and we both know it."

We slip back inside, the buzz of alcohol-fueled conversation replacing the soft calm of the ocean.

"The truth is, I'm a terrible hostess. I do what I want, talk to whoever I want, and if my guests feel slighted they can damn well deal with it."

I gape. I can almost hear my mother's cries of horror all the way from Dallas.

"Besides," she continues, "this party isn't supposed to be about me. I put together this little shindig to introduce Blaine and his art to the community. He's the one who should be doing the mingling, not me. I may be fucking him, but I'm not going to baby him."

Evelyn has completely destroyed my image of how a hostess for the not-to-be-missed social event of the weekend is supposed to behave, and I think I'm a little in love with her for that.

"I haven't met Blaine yet. That's him, right?" I point to a tall reed of a man. He is bald, but sports a red goatee. I'm pretty sure it's not his natural color. A small crowd hums around him, like bees drawing nectar from a flower. His outfit is certainly as bright as one.

"That's my little center of attention, all right,"

Evelyn says. "The man of the hour. Talented, isn't he?" Her hand sweeps out to indicate her massive living room. Every wall is covered with paintings. Except for a few benches, whatever furniture was once in the room has been removed and replaced with easels on which more paintings stand.

I suppose technically they are portraits. The models are nudes, but these aren't like anything you would see in a classical art book. There's something edgy about them. Something provocative and raw. I can tell that they are expertly conceived and carried out, and yet they disturb me, as if they reveal more about the person viewing the portrait than about the painter or the model.

As far as I can tell, I'm the only one with that reaction. Certainly the crowd around Blaine is glowing. I can hear the gushing praise from here.

"I picked a winner with that one," Evelyn says. "But let's see. Who do you want to meet? Rip Carrington and Lyle Tarpin? Those two are guaranteed drama, that's for damn sure, and your roommate will be jealous as hell if you chat them up."

"She will?"

Evelyn's brows arch up. "Rip and Lyle? They've been feuding for weeks." She narrows her eyes at me. "The fiasco about the new season of their sitcom? It's all over the Internet? You really don't know them?"

"Sorry," I say, feeling the need to apologize.

"My school schedule was pretty intense. And I'm sure you can imagine what working for Carl is like."

Speaking of ...

I glance around, but I don't see my boss anywhere.

"That is one serious gap in your education," Evelyn says. "Culture—and yes, pop culture counts—is just as important as—what did you say you studied?"

"I don't think I mentioned it. But I have a double major in electrical engineering and computer science."

"So you've got brains and beauty. See? That's something else we have in common. Gotta say, though, with an education like that, I don't see why you signed up to be Carl's secretary."

I laugh. "I'm not, I swear. Carl was looking for someone with tech experience to work with him on the business side of things, and I was looking for a job where I could learn the business side. Get my feet wet. I think he was a little hesitant to hire me at first—my skills definitely lean toward tech—but I convinced him I'm a fast learner."

She peers at me. "I smell ambition."

I lift a shoulder in a casual shrug. "It's Los Angeles. Isn't that what this town is all about?"

"Ha! Carl's lucky he's got you. It'll be inter-

esting to see how long he keeps you. But let's
see ... who here would intrigue you ...?"

She casts about the room, finally pointing to a
fifty-something man holding court in a corner.
"That's Charles Maynard," she says. "I've known
Charlie for years. Intimidating as hell until you get
to know him. But it's worth it. His clients are either
celebrities with name recognition or power brokers
with more money than God. Either way, he's got all
the best stories."

"He's a lawyer?"

"With Bender, Twain & McGuire. Very prestigious firm."

"I know," I say, happy to show that I'm not
entirely ignorant, despite not knowing Rip or Lyle.
"One of my closest friends works for the firm. He
started here but he's in their New York office now."

"Well, come on, then, Texas. I'll introduce
you." We take one step in that direction, but then
Evelyn stops me. Maynard has pulled out his
phone, and is shouting instructions at someone. I
catch a few well-placed curses and eye Evelyn sideways. She looks unconcerned "He's a pussycat at
heart. Trust me, I've worked with him before. Back
in my agenting days, we put together more
celebrity biopic deals for our clients than I can
count. And we fought to keep a few tell-alls off the
screen, too." She shakes her head, as if reliving
those glory days, then pats my arm. "Still, we'll wait

'til he calms down a bit. In the meantime, though ..."

She trails off, and the corners of her mouth turn down in a frown as she scans the room again. "I don't think he's here yet, but—oh! Yes! Now *there's* someone you should meet. And if you want to talk views, the house he's building has one that makes my view look like, well, like yours." She points toward the entrance hall, but all I see are bobbing heads and haute couture. "He hardly ever accepts invitations, but we go way back," she says.

I still can't see who she's talking about, but then the crowd parts and I see the man in profile. Goose bumps rise on my arms, but I'm not cold. In fact, I'm suddenly very, very warm.

He's tall and so handsome that the word is almost an insult. But it's more than that. It's not his looks, it's his *presence.* He commands the room simply by being in it, and I realize that Evelyn and I aren't the only ones looking at him. The entire crowd has noticed his arrival. He must feel the weight of all those eyes, and yet the attention doesn't faze him at all. He smiles at the girl with the champagne, takes a glass, and begins to chat casually with a woman who approaches him, a simpering smile stretched across her face.

"Damn that girl," Evelyn says. "She never did bring me my vodka."

But I barely hear her. "Damien Stark," I say. My voice surprises me. It's little more than breath.

Evelyn's brows rise so high I notice the movement in my peripheral vision. "Well, how about that?" she says knowingly. "Looks like I guessed right."

"You did," I

Wicked Dirty
Excerpt

Don't miss *Wicked Dirty* — part of a scorching series of fast-paced, provocative novels centering around the ambitious, wealthy, and powerful men who work in and around the glamorous and exciting world of the Stark International conglomerate ... and the sexy and passionate women who bring them to their knees.

It seemed like the perfect plan. Let a guy into my bed. Let him touch me. Let him fuck me.

Why not?

I was desperate, after all. And you know what they say about desperate times.

Besides, it's not as if I was going to fall for one of my clients. I'm not one of those prissy girls who loses her heart at a kind word or a soft touch.

I'm not a woman who falls at all. Not for a man. Not for anybody.

I've been screwed far too many times. And if I'm going to get screwed anyway, I might as well get something out of it.

That was what I thought, anyway.

Then he walked in, with his beautiful face and his haunted eyes. Eyes that hinted at secrets at least as painful as my own.

He touched me—and despite all my defenses, I fell.

And now ...

Well, now I can only hope that when I hit the ground, I won't shatter into a million pieces. And that maybe—just maybe—he'll be there to catch me.

Chapter One

The setting sun cast a warm glow over the Hollywood Hills as nearly naked waitresses glided through the crowd with a rainbow-like array of test tube shots. Or, for the more traditional guests, highball glasses of premium vodka and bourbon.

The liquor flowed, the guests laughed and gossiped, the hottest new band in Los Angeles shook the roof, and entertainment reporters took photographs and videos, all of which they shared on social media.

In other words, the lavish party at Reach, the hip, new rooftop hotspot, was a dead-on perfect publicity event.

The purpose, of course, was to officially announce that Lyle Tarpin, one of Hollywood's fastest rising stars, had joined the cast of *M. Steri-*

ous, next year's installment in the wildly popular Blue Zenith movie franchise.

The script was solid, the action pulse-pounding, and Lyle still couldn't believe that he'd been cast, much less that he was set to play the eponymous M, an emotionally wounded antihero.

It was a role that could catapult him from the A-list to over-the-moon, transforming him into a Hollywood megastar with his choice of meaty roles and the kind of multimillion dollar paydays that had only been a glimmer of a dream when he'd started this Hollywood journey.

In other words, this was an opportunity he didn't intend to fuck up.

Which was why he forced himself not to wince and turn away when Frannie caught his eye and smiled. She tossed her head, making her auburn locks bounce as she walked toward him, her sequined cocktail dress revealing a mile of toned legs ending in a pair of strappy sandals that showed off a perfect pedicure.

One of Hollywood's most bankable stars, Francesca Muratti was set to play Lyle's love interest—the Blue Zenith agent who turns M from his dark ways and recruits him to the side of justice —both saving him and, hopefully, adding another long-running hero to the franchise.

"Hello, lover," she said, sliding her arms around his neck and pressing her body against his. Frannie had a reputation for being a wild child who made it a point to sleep with almost every one of her male co-stars, and she'd made no secret that she wanted Lyle to join that little fraternity.

Honestly, Lyle didn't know if she was insecure, overly horny, or simply into method acting. All he knew was that he wasn't interested. Which, considering the damage a pissed-off Francesca could do to his career, was ten kinds of inconvenient.

"Kiss me like you mean it," she murmured, then leaned in, preparing to make the demand a reality, but he angled back, taking her chin in his hand and holding her steady as her eyes flashed with irritation.

"Anticipation, Frannie." He bent close so that she shivered from the feel of his breath on her ear. "If we give them what they want now, why would they come to the movie?"

"Fuck the fans," she whispered back, her hand sliding down to grab his crotch. "This is what I want."

And goddamn him all to hell, he felt himself start to grow hard. Not from desire for her, but in response to a familiar, baser need. A dark room. A willing woman. Just once—hard enough and hot enough that it wore him out. Soothed his guilt and his pain. Quieted the ghosts of his past, the horror of his mistakes.

Enough to tide him over until the next time. The next woman.

And to maybe, if he was lucky, chip away at the wall he'd built around his heart.

His thoughts churned wildly, and he imagined the feel of a woman's soft skin under his fingers. A woman who wouldn't look at him with Jennifer's eyes. Who wouldn't remind him of where he'd run from or what he'd done. A woman who'd give herself to him. Who wouldn't care about his flaws as he let himself just go, hard and hot and desperate, into the wild, dark bliss of anonymity.

"Mmm, I don't know, Lyle," Frannie murmured, her hand pressed firmly against his now rock-hard erection. "Here's evidence that suggests our onscreen chemistry is real. Give me a chance and I bet we can really raise that flag."

"I like you fine, Frannie," he said, taking a step back and cursing himself for giving into fantasy. "But I'm not fucking you."

From the glint in her eye, he was certain her famous temper was about to flare, but an editor he recognized from *Variety* walked up, and Frannie downshifted to charming.

Lyle hung around long enough to greet the guy and answer a few questions about the role, then made his escape when the conversation shifted to Frannie's new endorsement deal.

He grabbed a bourbon from a passing waiter

and sipped it as he crossed to the edge of the roof. He didn't like heights, which was why he sought them out. Hell, it was why his apartment was on the thirtieth floor of a Century City high rise, and the reason he'd spent countless hours getting his pilot's license. When something bothered him, he conquered it; he didn't succumb to it.

And that's part of why this bullshit with Frannie irritated him so much.

"You never struck me as the stupid type."

Lyle recognized the throaty, feminine voice and turned to face his agent, Evelyn Dodge. An attractive woman in her mid-fifties, Evelyn had been in the industry for ages, knew everyone worth knowing, and was as tough as nails. She also never took shit from anybody.

Lyle studied her face, trying to get a bead on what she was thinking. No luck. His agent was a blank slate. Good when negotiating deals. Not so good when he was trying to gauge a reaction.

"That girl's got more power than you think," she continued when he stayed silent. "You want the quick and dirty route to Career-in-the-Toilet Town? Because that path runs straight through your pretty co-star. You piss Frannie off and suddenly Garreth Todd will be playing M and you'll be lucky if you can get a walk-on in a local commercial for a used car lot."

"Thanks for giving it to me straight," he said

dryly.

"You think I'm exaggerating? I thought you knew your ass from a hole in the wall. Or have I been misreading you all this time?"

"Christ, Evelyn. I'm not naive. But I'm not sleeping with Frannie just to make things nice on the set. Are you honestly saying I should?"

"Hell no, Iowa," she said, using his home state as a nickname. "I'm telling you that you need to be smart. As long as you're single, she's not going to let it drop." She sighed. "You've worked damn hard to get where you are, and you're flying high. But let me remind you in case you think that makes you invincible — the higher you are, the more painful it is when you crash back down to earth."

"I'm not going to screw anything up, Evelyn."

"You don't know Frannie the way I do. She's destroyed careers more established than yours—and that was before she had a hefty gold statue on her mantle."

Fuck. He ran his fingers through his hair.

"How long have we worked together?" she asked, obviously not expecting an answer. "Two, three years? And never during all that time have I seen you date. A few women on your arm at a party, but you go stag more often than you go with a woman."

"What the hell, Evelyn?" He knew he sounded defensive, but she was coming dangerously close to pushing buttons he didn't want pushed, and to peering into dark corners that were better left in the shadows.

"You told me once you weren't gay, and that's fine. Thousands of teenage girls across the country sleep easier knowing you're on the market."

"Is there a point to this?" He tried—and failed —to keep the irritation out of his voice.

She cast a sharp glance at his face. "I'm just saying that if you have a girlfriend tucked away in an attic somewhere, now's the time to pull her out and dust her off. Because our girl Frannie is like a dog with a bone. A very pampered, well-groomed dog, who has one hell of a bite when she doesn't get her own way. But she doesn't mess with married men."

"So, what? I'm supposed to trot off to Vegas and make a showgirl my bride?"

"Just be smart. And if you do have a girlfriend hidden away, then bring her to a party or two. And if you don't, then get one."

"It's bullshit," he said mildly. "But I'll take it under advisement."

"Good. Now let's go mingle."

With a sigh, he glanced around the set-up. At the free-flowing alcohol and never-ending stream of finger foods offered by waitresses in outfits that were just a little too skimpy to be decent, but which covered a little too much to be obscene. At the napkins and stemware that displayed the series' logo, and at the band in the corner that was playing a never-ending stream of music from the franchise, while on the opposite side of the roof, clips from the previous movies played in a continuous loop on a giant screen.

It was opulent, ridiculous, and completely over the top.

Jennifer would have loved it.

She would have swept into Hollywood and conquered it, making Francesca Muratti look like an amateur in the process.

Go big or go home. Wasn't that what she'd always told him? Jennifer? With her innocent eyes and her not-so-innocent mouth?

But she'd never gotten the chance.

And now here he was, thirteen years to the day since that goddamned hellish night. And Jenny was dead, and he was standing in a spotlight wearing Armani and living her dream.

How fucked up was that?

"I lost you somewhere," Evelyn said. "Let's head to the bar. I think you could use another drink."

Damn right he could, but he shook his head. "I was just thinking." He gestured with his hand, indicating the whole area, including the city beyond the rooftop. "This really is where dreams come true."

But only an unlucky few—like Lyle—knew how many nightmares hid inside those bright, shiny dreams.

He forced a smile for Evelyn's sake. "It's past seven. I've been here for almost two hours. I've been effusive and charming and a team player. I've done everything they've asked. Officially, anyway," he added, thinking of Frannie's overtures. "That should at least earn me a cookie, don't you think?"

She crossed her arms, shifting her weight as she looked at him. "Depends on what kind of cookie you're looking for."

"I'm leaving—"

"Dammit, Lyle."

"Do I ever cause you problems? Do you have to run interference for me? Do I not live up to my damned golden boy reputation?"

She said nothing.

"Make an excuse for me. Anything. I don't care." For just a moment, he let his mask down. The innocent Iowa boy who'd been discovered at seventeen, plucked out of obscurity to ride to fame on his Midwestern good looks and piercing blue eyes. He'd thrown himself into the work, scrambling up through television and indie films to where he was today. A genuinely nice guy, untarnished by Hollywood's bullshit.

Except that was all just a part, too. And for a flicker of a moment, he let Evelyn see the pain underneath. The loss. The darkness. And all the goddamn guilt.

Then he was the movie star again, and she was looking at him, her brows knit with an almost maternal concern.

"Please," he added, his voice low and a little hoarse. "It's not a good day. I need—"

What? A drink? A fuck? Magic powers so he could change the past?

"—to go. I just need to go."

"Do you want company?"

Hell, yes.

He shook his head. "No. I'm fine. But thanks."

But he did want company. Just not the kind that Evelyn was offering. He wanted the kind of company that was raw. That was dirty and fast and anonymous. With complete discretion. And absolutely no fucking strings.

Wanted? No, he didn't want it. Not really.

But he damn sure needed it.

Needed to open the valve and release the pressure. To erase the guilt, even if only for a few glorious minutes. To escape the ghosts and the memories and all the shit that he tried so hard to keep buried. That he never let anyone see.

That's what he needed, because without that release, his mask really would start to crack, and the whole world would learn that the clean-cut Lyle Tarpin was nothing more than a goddamn fraud.

ABOUT THE AUTHOR

J. Kenner (aka Julie Kenner) is the *New York Times,
USA Today, Publishers Weekly, Wall Street Journal*
and #1 International bestselling author of over one
hundred novels, novellas and short stories in a
variety of genres.

 JK has been praised by
Publishers Weekly as an author
with a "flair for dialogue and
eccentric characterizations" and
by *RT Bookclub* for having "cor-
nered the market on sinfully
attractive, dominant antiheroes
and the women who swoon for them." A five-time
finalist for Romance Writers of America's prestigious RITA award, JK took home the first RITA
trophy awarded in the category of erotic romance
in 2014 for her novel, *Claim Me* (book 2 of her
Stark Trilogy) and the RITA trophy for *Wicked
Dirty* in the same category in 2017.

In her previous career as an attorney, JK
worked as a lawyer in Southern California and
Texas. She currently lives in Central Texas, with

her husband, two daughters, and two rather spastic cats.

Visit her website at www.juliekenner.com to learn more and to connect with JK through social media!

f 𝕏 ◎ a BB g

Made in the USA
Coppell, TX
25 March 2020

17668531R00193